I0544671

Evernight Teen ®

www.evernightteen.com

Copyright© 2025

Jase Peeples

ISBN: 978-0-3695-1175-1

Cover Artist: Jay Aheer

Editor: CA Clauson

JASE PEEPLES

Jase Peeples

Copyright © 2025

Chapter One

Danny

"Are you tired? Some of you already look tired. Keep the energy up. Perform through to the very end," our winter guard instructor, Nikki, yells from the top of the concrete steps outside the gym. We've been running the same thirty-two counts—our ending ensemble flag feature—for the past twenty minutes. She's on a mission to get it "sparkling clean."

We really should be inside. After all, this is *winter* guard season, but here we are in the chilly quad, making the most of the space available while we wait for the basketball team to get out. They're over time, again. Because of course they are. They're the big sports team, and we're just that group of people who spin flags, rifles and sabers—the color guard. So, even though we win way more than they do, basketball still gets priority on

5

the gym schedule while we remain the best kept secret at East Valley High.

"Okay, reset. We're going to do it once more with music." Nikki presses play on the portable sound system at her feet, yelling over the blaring beats as she continues. "This time I want you to really go for it. Check those hand positions in the middle and watch one another for timing on the toss. This flag feature is the final impression you'll leave the judges with. So, come on, show me how you're gonna serve it on Saturday!"

Her reminder that our first competition of the season is this weekend lights a fire in me, burning away any thoughts of cold weather, tired muscles, or the sweaty t-shirt under my hoodie clinging to my back.

The musical cue hits and we attack the downbeat, leaping into what is some of the most challenging flag work we've ever done—up, down, up, blind pass behind the back and turn. Halfway through, I can't hold back the big smile that stretches across my face, because moments like this are why I love this sport—when I can hear the sound of fabric spinning in sync all around me and I can feel our entire team is absolutely killing the choreography—it's like the closest thing on Earth to living inside music.

Then we toss our flags high in the air, pull our arms down to our sides as the poles complete two and a half rotations before landing back in our hands with the kind of satisfying *smack* only a clean catch can make.

Nikki shuts off the sound system. "Yes, East Valley Winter Guard! That. Is. How. It's. Done!" she says, punctuating each word with an enthusiastic clap. "You perform like that this weekend and they'll have no choice but to give you a high score right out of the gate." She glances at her watch. "All right, everyone take five and grab some water. I'm going to see if the basketball team is finishing up so we can move in."

We break and I trade high fives with my boys, Sanjay and Conner, as we chill with the rest of the guard on the steps.

"That ending feature slaps so hard," Sanjay says after taking a sip of water from his pink sports bottle. "People in the audience are going to lose their shit when they see it."

"For real though," Conner adds. "They're gonna be like, *Damn, East Valley, we weren't ready for all that.*"

I nod. "Yeah, we—" A direct message notification sets off my phone, which is both unexpected and embarrassing. Unexpected in the sense that I thought my phone was on silent, and embarrassing because it couldn't have happened at a worse time.

I sit very still, hoping maybe if I ignore the notification everyone else will too, or at least they won't realize that distinctive loud-ass sound came from my pho—

Brrrap.

Shit.

"Oh, my God, that's totally that gay hookup app, isn't it?" our teammate, Catalina says, way too excited and way too loud. She's always got to say something.

"*Oh*, scandalous," Sanjay teases.

"No," I blurt, feeling the heat of everyone's eyes on me as I frantically dig my phone out of my pocket. I glare at Catalina. "And for the record, QTIE isn't just a *gay* thing. "I'm—"

Brrrap.

Jesus. I flip the ringer switch to vibrate so hard the plastic creaks.

"*So* popular," Sanjay says, ribbing me with an elbow.

Luckily, most of our teammates seem to be losing interest already. (It takes a bigger show than this to hold their attention.) I can feel their stares slipping away as they return to their own conversations, except for Catalina, who can't take a hint and is smiling at me like she's living her best life. "You were saying? Before we were interrupted by your boy-booty call?" she says.

"It's not a booty call, it's…" I hesitate because, well, technically it could be someone fishing for a hookup, but I'm hoping at least one of those alerts is what I've been waiting for all day—a reply from Ethan Decker.

He's a senior on the Landon High School Winter Guard, which is only the best Winter Guard on the planet, literally. They've won Winter Guard International World Championships six times in a row now. I've had a thing for Ethan ever since I saw Landon High perform at a competition a couple of years ago, but I've never worked up the nerve to talk to him.

I mean, Ethan is basically the winter guard equivalent of a rock star. People in the crowd even scream his name at competitions. I personally haven't done this (not out loud, anyway), but I totally know how they feel.

When Ethan is performing, you can't take your eyes off him. He can spin every piece of equipment—flag, rifle, saber. And damn, can that boy dance. Then there's his floppy red hair, light green eyes, and I'm not even going to pretend I haven't saved a few of the shirtless TikToks he's posted. Hey, if he's going to post thirst trap videos like that, he can't blame me for looking at them.

Ethan is so freakin' hot, which is why I haven't been able to say a word to him. That is, not until a couple of days ago when I saw him pop up on QTIE and nearly fell out of my chair.

I have no idea what came over me, but I just went for it, shot him a quick "hi," and he actually replied. Before that, I'm pretty sure he wasn't even aware that I existed and I guess there's really no reason he would have either.

While we've technically competed against each other for years, let's be real. Landon High School is light years ahead of my winter guard. They always perform way later than we do every time we're at a show together, which is good. I mean, nobody wants to have to follow the world champions at a competition, right?

So, I'm betting Ethan has never seen the East Valley Winter Guard perform live or has any idea who we are. I'm sure to him, I was just another nameless face in the crowd of people who rushed to pack the back stands when Landon would take the floor.

But with any luck, that's about to change because we've been chatting online a bit and—I still can't believe I did this—but earlier today, I asked him if he'd be cool with us exchanging numbers so we could text instead of DMing through the app. The waiting is torture—even worse than having to deal with Catalina's drama right now.

"It's … ugh, it's none of your business," I say, narrowing my eyes at her. "And, again, QTIE isn't just a gay thing." I point to myself. "Bi guy here, remember?"

Catalina rolls her eyes. "Whatever, Danny."

My jaw tightens. I don't get why some people can't figure it out. Being bisexual doesn't mean being half in the closet. If this was a year ago, I probably wouldn't say anything. But dismissive shit like that right there really gets under my skin lately.

"No, not *whatever*. We exist too, you know," I say.

9

Conner bounces over to my side, probably recognizing the sharpness in my voice.

"Come on now, Cat." He places his hands on his hips and starts doing that thing where he rocks back and forth on his heels, the way little kids do when they get all excited because they know they're about to say something they think is really smart.

"Sexuality is a spectrum, not a binary construct. Those who identify as bisexual have the capacity to be attracted to people of more than one sex and/or gender, though not necessarily at the same time, in the same way, or to the same degree." He says all this as if it were one complete sentence, speeding through without taking a breath.

"All right, geez. Sorry," Catalina says, hands up like she's pressing against an invisible wall.

"Thanks, dude," I say.

Conner play-punches me in the shoulder and grins. "No sweat, bro. I got your back"

"Oh, bitch, that was deep," Sanjay says. "Did you memorize the GLAAD website again or something?"

Conner bites his lower lip, laughs, and jumps straight up. "Damn. Busted," he says to himself before turning to Sanjay. "You got me. But, yo, dude, come on, I should totally get extra points for that, yeah?" He looks at me for approval.

And this is reason number 732 why I freakin' love Conner Li. He does things like this that let me know he's in my corner while simultaneously reminding me not to take myself too seriously.

It's like, when I came out to him the summer after our sophomore year, all he said was, "Really? Cool," and then asked me where I wanted to go for lunch. Nothing changed. He was so chill and I never told him this, but that was exactly what I needed from him that day, because my dads were making such a big deal about it, just like I knew they would. That's part of why they were the hardest to tell.

And, yeah, I'm aware that sounds completely nuts, that a bisexual kid would have a tough time telling his gay dads that he's queer too, but I did, and not for the reasons you might think. Don't get me wrong, my dads were everything great parents should be in that situation—they listened, told me how much they loved me, called me brave, all that stuff. But that's exactly what made it suck.

See, I'd been a total dick to them for a while, said some really fucked-up shit too. All because I couldn't face the truth about myself. God, I mean, what is it about junior high that turns us into the absolute worst for a while?

Anyway, my dads being so awesome just reminded me what a hypocrite I was. Fortunately, they realized pretty quickly that I wasn't in a space to have a deep talk about my feelings and they just let me be. It took a little time, but I eventually came around and we're good now ... really good, actually. Those first couple of weeks though, man, they were all kinds of awkward. But it's never been like that with Conner. We've been like brothers since the day we met playing dodgeball in second grade.

"One point, dude. You get one point for effort," I tell Conner, playing along.

"And I'll give you one more for your delivery," Sanjay says. He purses his lips and adds, "But you get a fat *zero* for originality."

"So, two points? Hey, that's cool. I only need fifty more to unlock my next super-ally achievement anyway," Conner says and we all laugh, except for Catalina who's standing there, arms folded, full stink-face on, shaking her head.

"You guys are such dorks," she says, making a point to only gesture to me and Conner, not Sanjay, then she gives me a pinched look. "And I still say," she jabs a judgmental finger at my phone, "*booty call*."

I let that one go, because, whatever. Sanjay says he thinks she gets like this because she still has a thing for me and it's easier for her to just be a bitch. I don't know. Maybe. I guess that's why she's always trying to insinuate she thinks I'm gay instead of bi—then she can hang our breakup on my being into guys instead of not being into her anymore. That's so not it, though. I mean, yeah, I'm attracted to some guys, but girls like Cat—a little curvy, big eyes, full lips—that's totally my type too. But her constant unnecessary drama? Hell to the no.

Catalina turns to leave, snapping her head around so fast her ponytail whips the air behind her as she walks—excuse me— *prances* away, butting into another conversation. (See what I mean?)

"Eww, don't let her slut shame you. She's just jealous," Sanjay whispers to me.

My phone buzzes in my hand. Another direct message.

"That's right, get you some," Conner says, all proud-big-brother-like.

"I'm not *getting* anything, guys. Just chatting is all," I say, unlocking my phone.

Sanjay slithers up next to me, a mischievous grin on his face. "Any J.T.s?

I hide my phone screen against my chest. "Nosey much?" I say with mock indignation.

"Bitch, please," Sanjay says flatly and we exchange knowing smiles.

It's kind of funny. Sanjay's personality is on the complete opposite end of Conner's. Two years ago, I never would've imagined the three of us becoming as tight as we have, but now I can't picture going through our senior year any other way.

I give my new message inbox a quick scan and don't recognize any of the senders' names. Disappointing, but I smile wider anyway. "Okay, fine. Lightning round?" I ask, holding my phone out just far enough so only we can see it.

Sanjay gives me an affirmative eyebrow waggle, his full attention already on my screen, while Conner says, "Hell, yeah," leaning in for a better look.

This is a game the three of us play. J.T. Roulette. It's like a harmless version of Russian Roulette where we open unread DMs, checking for unsolicited dick pics from trolls. First person to overreact, gets dinged. Three dings, you're out—unless it's a lightning round. Then one-and-done rules are in effect.

I don't remember how we got started on this game exactly, but Conner began calling it J.T.—short for "Jelly Troll"—Roulette after we opened a pic some rando sent of himself from the neck down, violating a jar of grape jelly. That one had us cracking up for days and the name has stuck ever since. It's stupid, I know, but it works. I mean, we still haven't come across a photo as whacked as that one, so I guess you can say Jelly Troll sort of set a standard—not that a few others haven't come close. Apparently, freaky food fetishes are a real thing and there are a lot of weirdos online.

I open the first unread message and it's just a simple "Hi."

"*Boring*," Sanjay says.

I swipe up to give his profile a quick check and he's not bad. A white, skinny, emo-looking dude with bright blue eyes and a nose ring. But then I see at the bottom of his stats he has "*No Asians*" written in all caps.

13

"And racist, gross," Sanjay sneers.

"Ouch," Conner says, chuckling, as he feigns a pain in his chest.

If it were just me, I'd probably take a few seconds to fuck with this douchebag. Like yesterday, when some asshole sent me a DM that straight-up said, "Hey Papi. I'd love to see your hot brown ass." So, I replied with a GIF of a braying donkey. I'm funny like that. But I'm not even going to waste our time right now. My finger heads straight for the block button.

I open the next DM and—*score*. The three of us bust out laughing.

"Dude, that thing is HUGE! What the—" Conner pauses, realizing he's drawing unwanted attention our way. He lowers his voice to an intense whisper and continues. "What do you even do with all that?"

"Oh, I can think of a few things," Sanjay purrs. "And you just lost again."

Conner throws up his hands in defeat, but he's still laughing. Not in that nervous, *I'm really uncomfortable* kind of way, but for real.

I should probably point this out. You know how I know Conner is 100% straight? He can play a game like J.T. Roulette with us and have fun. Trust me, if you've got a guy friend who freaks out over a little dude-on-dude stuff or gets all weird when he sees a picture of a penis, then yeah, he's probably, definitely, thought about it.

"All right then, new challenge," Conner says, reaching into his equipment bag and pulling out his rifle. "Cold seven?"

"Bring it," Sanjay says, snagging his saber.

They jog a few steps back into the quad where several of our teammates are already spinning, working on various pieces of choreography from our show.

"Come on, Danny, you too," Conner says.

Being on the East Valley High Winter Guard is legit awesome and I can hold my own in a toss challenge with just about anyone else. I mean, we didn't take 7th place at WGI World Championships last year because our team sucked. But this right here isn't even going to be a competition. Sanjay is the best saber on our team and Conner can make the most insane rifle trick look easy. But I grab my rifle and join them in the quad anyway, because it's like our instructor Nikki says, you don't back down from a challenge. You gotta step up and meet it, before you can beat it.

"All right. Let's go," I say.

Sanjay counts us off with a loud, "Five, six, seven…" We all hit the dip position with our equipment on "eight," then push to release high above our heads on the next downbeat.

The second my rifle leaves my hand I can tell something's off. It still goes up and completes seven full rotations, but I have to step to my left to stay under it and my catch is so not good. Unlike Sanjay and Conner, who—spoiler alert—crack the shit out of theirs.

I can throw rock-solid tosses once I've warmed up on that specific piece of equipment, but that's the point of a cold seven challenge—you gotta throw it cold.

"Damn," I grumble at the same time Sanjay says, "Motherfucker!" I'm surprised to see he's a fraction of a fraction off center. My eyes go immediately to Conner who's holding his annoyingly perfect catch position.

"Boom, bitches," Conner says. He sticks his tongue firmly between his teeth, giving us that damn *I'm hot shit and I know it* look of his.

Sanjay exhales dramatically. "Ugh, I hate you so much right now."

"Don't shoot, man! Don't shoot!" someone behind us says.

15

We all turn to see the basketball team filing out of the gym. One of them, Devan Washburn, is holding his hands up like he's surrendering. A few of the guys behind him laugh as they run past us. You'd think by now they'd be tired of making that same joke, but nope. It doesn't even make any sense. It's not like we're spinning real swords and guns. I mean, okay, the sabers are real metal, but no one would look at this wooden rifle in my hands— all wrapped in white electrical tape like a mummy with a shiny gold bolt in the middle—and think, *Oh, shit, that's totally a real firearm.*

"Okay, everyone, let's go," our instructor Nikki announces, poking her head outside the door. "Set up quickly and quietly, please. We've got a lot of work to do tonight if we want to be ready for Saturday."

I gather my things and I'm two steps inside the gym when I feel my phone buzz again.

Damn, Sanjay was right. I guess I have been kind of popular on this app since I turned 18 last month.

I pull my phone from my pocket, watch the Face ID unlock the screen, and swipe up. My heart punches me from inside.

1 New Message from: **GuardGuy18.**

He replied! He finally replied!

I bullet over to the bleachers, drop my equipment bag and take a seat, guarding my phone so no one else can see my screen. Sharing random dick pics is one thing, but a message from Ethan Decker is for my eyes only.

Another message from Ethan sets off my phone, making my bones vibrate.

"Please be his phone number. Please be his phone number. Please be his phone number," I mumble to myself, trying to manifest my wish, will it into existence. I want this more than anything, just a chance to get to know him on a more personal level—and for him to know me too.

My hand shakes a little as I swipe a finger across my screen.

GuardGuy18: **Sure.**

GuardGuy18: **925-224-6003**

Holy shit. *Holy shit.* Holy shit!

Ethan Decker just sent me his phone number.

Chapter Two

Ethan

This has been our thing forever—Navi, Micaela, and me—grabbing a bite at Sandy's Kitchen on Wednesday nights after rehearsal. It's a 1950s-style diner near school. We love it here because the "kitschy-fabulous décor" (Micaela's words) makes us feel like we're hanging out in a theme park—classic black and white checkered floor tiles, pink vinyl upholstered booths with aqua strips down the middle, and tons of vintage record albums hanging on the walls.

They also have the best burgers in the Bay Area and fries with this special seasoning that are to-die-for, which is the perfect comfort food after a long practice.

We're sitting at our usual booth in the back and we've barely finished placing our order when Navi says, "Aw, you guys, it's our last Wednesday hangout before a first competition."

These two girls are the best of my best, but this new thing Navi has started doing—pointing out every experience of our senior year as the "last"—is totally annoying.

"The winter guard season is just getting started. We literally have months," I say, wrinkling my nose. I pull out my phone, open Instagram, and start scrolling, because I can't with her right now.

"Seriously, you've got to cut that shit out," Micaela says. "Just because *someone* found out she got accepted to NYU already doesn't mean she can act like she's got one foot out the door." She waves an invisible wand through the air like she's casting a spell. "As headmistress of House Bitchindor, I decree we're going out with a freakin' bang."

"Yeah, we're making history here, people," I say with a thick Southern accent, doing my best imitation of our instructor, Andrew, which always gets a laugh. Andrew has said that exact phrase to motivate us so many times, it's become an inside joke of ours. Except when we say it, we're being ironic. Driving to school? *We're making history here, people.* Just woke up from a nap? An historic accomplishment! Bingeing a new Netflix series? You guessed it.

The thing is, Andrew's right. The Landon High School Winter Guard has made history since he took over. I mean, our team was already undefeated for three years before any of us here were even old enough to join (a fact my older sister never lets me forget). But the stakes are higher now. If we can pull it off, this will be the seventh time in a row LHS will win the Winter Guard International World Championships. So, yeah, just a little pressure there, but we all want it so badly, me most of all.

You see, I've got a list of "need to have" and "nice to have" goals for my senior year, and winning WGI again definitely falls into the "need" category. I mean, how many people can say they're a four-time world champion at something when they graduate from high school? I'll give you a hint—very few—and my sister isn't one of them.

"Well, duh, of course our last season together is going to be kickass. I just want to make sure we're enjoying every moment of it, that's all," Navi says in her usual upbeat, bubbly tone. Then she frowns and sticks out her lower lip as a thought occurs to her. "Just promise me, no matter how far apart we end up, we're still getting together for summer trips to Wizarding World, right?"

Navi and Micaela are the only people I know whose knowledge of all things Harry Potter rivals mine.

Every summer since the sixth grade, we take a trip to Universal Studios and spend the whole day at The Wizarding World of Harry Potter, one of the coolest places on the planet. (Shut up, yes, it is, and no, we're not eight.)

Two years ago, we even went to the one in Orlando, Florida, and got to do the Sorting Hat Ceremony. We all self-identified as House Gryffindor until that moment, but that damn hat put Navi in Hufflepuff, Micaela in Ravenclaw, and me in Slytherin, which ... eww. That's when Micaela decided we should just make up our own and, *poof,* House Bitchindor was born, which is a way better fit.

"Um, duh," Micaela says.

"Duh," I echo, adding, "And since I'll be at UCLA, Universal Studios Hollywood will basically be in my back yard. So, yeah, that's happening."

Okay, technically, I haven't been accepted to UCLA yet, but I will. Along with winning WGI, that's right at the top of my "need" list.

I stop scrolling through my Instagram feed, do a search for Danny Wheeler-Hall, and open his account. I started following him on IG this morning and oh, my God, I'm so glad I did. The pics he posts here are way better than the ones he has on QTIE.

"By the way, what do you think?" I show Micaela my screen and watch her amber eyes go wide.

"Hello, hottie," she says.

"I know, right?" I say, handing her my phone.

"Are you stalking straight boys on Instagram again?" Navi asks, putting her long brown ponytail up in a sloppy bun.

I scoff at this. "He's not straight. His name is Danny and we've been chatting for a minute."

Micaela shows Navi his picture.

"Oh, wow. Look at those dimples. And that smile. He's adorable," Navi says.

"Totally," Micaela agrees, swiping through more of Danny's photos. "But it looks like he's in color guard too, so, minus one point there."

"He's in guard? Which one?" Navi asks.

"He told me, but I don't remember. Not one we know, I think," I say quickly before turning to judge Micaela. "And, um, hypocrite, your boyfriend is literally on our team."

Micaela smirks. "Liam doesn't count. He's an exception."

He's an exception because he's basically a Disney Prince come to life. Liam is super smart, loves animals so much he wants to be a veterinarian, and looks like Tom Holland if you squint just right. His only downfall is that he has the personality of a doorknob. Seriously, he's so boring.

Micaela's got a one-performer-per-relationship rule, but between those two, the spotlight is always firmly on her. Liam practically worships her, and, I get it. If I were into girls, I'd probably be all about Micaela too. She's got the body of a ballerina, flawless brown skin, is an amazing makeup artist, and already has a successful career going as a YouTube influencer. The last time I checked, she had over 240,000 followers. Plus, did I mention she has great taste in friends?

"And for the record," I announce to the table, "I'm not stalking him. I'm, maybe, sort of, considering which pic to use for his contact photo."

"What? Ethan, you asked for his number?" Navi squeals.

"I didn't have to. He gave it to me when he asked for mine," I shrug, pretending to be smug as I snatch my phone back from Micaela.

"And?" Micaela probes. "Did you?"

I can feel myself blushing and an unexpected giggle bursts out of me, answering her question.

"Look at you, putting yourself back out there. Good for you," Micaela says and playfully slaps my thigh.

"See, Ethan, we told you you'd be over Jimmy in no time," Navi says, straightening the gold Chai charm neckless I gave her for her for Christmakkah last year.

Ugh, Jimmy Richards. Just hearing his name is enough to send my eyes rolling skyward so hard. He's this closet case on our school's water polo team whom I pretend-dated for about two and a half weeks. I say "pretend" because messing around in his bedroom a few times and then him ghosting me after I suggested we go somewhere in the real world together is not actual dating. Not that I've ever been on an actual *date* date, but that's beside the point.

Anyway, the whole thing with Jimmy really sucked because he seemed so into me and would say all the right things and, as much as I hate to admit it, he's a really good kisser. Then suddenly, he just quit responding to my texts and blocked me on every social media account known to man. When I tried to ask what was up in-person at school, he got all nervous and said he didn't know what I was talking about. Un-freaking-believable.

I'm still mad at myself for crying about that in fourth period, but I'd thought I was actually starting to feel something for him—that we were starting to feel something for each other—and the thing I've been daydreaming about for years was finally going to happen.

Okay, so I know this might sound lame and, yes, I've heard all those affirming phrases people love to turn into memes and share, like "being single is about appreciating the space you're in" and "you don't need

23

someone to be someone" and blah, blah, blah. However, I am so tired of being single.

I mean, is that really such a bad thing, to want to be with somebody? And not just *be with them*. In the gay world, if sex is all you want, a hookup is never more than a few swipes away on your phone. It didn't take long for me to learn that after signing up for a few apps. That's not me, though.

What I want is the real thing. The long talks and walks holding hands, the nights where we actually Netflix and chill. And if I'm totally being honest here, yeah, okay, I also want the flowers and sunsets and texts where we use cute nicknames and way too many heart emojis. You know, romance.

That's why, even though I know it technically belongs in the "nice to have" category, finding a boyfriend feels like a "need." But I'm beginning to think other gay guys don't want that—at least, not any of the ones I meet.

Still, there's something about this Danny guy that feels ... I don't know ... different. The entire time we've been messaging, he hasn't made a single comment about sex or asked me to send him nudes or anything like that. Not that I wouldn't. I'm not exactly an angel here. It's just been a nice change from the typical stuff. You know—having someone actually seeming like they're interested in you and how you're doing, not just asking how big your dick is.

I look at Danny's photo again, the one that's quickly becoming my favorite, and a warm tingly sensation spreads over my skin. It's a simple selfie, nothing crazy, but his dark hair is styled just right—short on the sides, a little longer on top—and the crisp white shirt he's wearing contrasts against his light brown skin so nicely. Not to mention that the way it hugs his chest totally makes me want to rip it off his body and touch him everywhere. But I also wonder how it would feel to have his arm wrapped around my shoulders and if he could get lost in my green eyes the same way I totally would in his coffee-colored ones.

"Ethan," Navi says. Her insistent tone makes it clear she's said my name more than once.

I look up at her. "Hmm?"

"Oh, my God." Navi turns to Micaela, grinning. "He's doing it again."

"What? No," I say quickly.

"Please. You practically have little hearts where your eyes should be," Navi says.

"I do not," I protest, feeling my face turning the same bright pink as the vinyl upholstery in our booth.

Micaela giggles. "Uh, yeah, you're totally making that *and they lived happily ever after*

face."

"In a super cute apartment in West Hollywood with two cats," Navi adds, teasing me.

"You're so wrong," I say, and I don't even try to hold in the big smile that bursts out of me. I can't hide anything from these girls. "It wasn't two cats. They were dogs. Specifically, Corgis."

"Aw, I love Corgis," Micaela says and inhales sharply. "Oh, my gosh. Did you guys see? Liam posted the cutest TikTok yesterday of him and a Corgi doing this cute little butt-wiggle dance."

She says this like Liam hasn't uploaded hundreds of similar videos. Since he got that receptionist job at the Curtner Pet Clinic, aside from TikToks of him and Micaela being sickeningly sweet together and stupid challenge vids, that's all he posts. I don't have the heart to tell her the reason they get so many views is because the animals are the real stars. And, okay, fine. I guess

Liam isn't exactly hard to look at either. Whatever.

"Yes, your two single besties totally want to watch a video of your hot boyfriend again," I deadpan.

"Ethan, you really don't look good in bitter," Micaela teases as she pulls out her phone and unlocks the screen.

"Um, hello, I'm clearly wearing *only mostly envious*," I say and we all laugh, fully aware that under all the joking, there's the teensiest bit of truth there.

Micaela plays Liam's latest video for us and fifteen seconds later, I flatly say, "Adorbs. Now, can we get back to focusing on me and the potentially soon-to-be-changing landscape of my love life?"

"I do love a good post-apocalyptic story," Navi says.

"You're so funny," I say in a high-pitched, mocking voice before returning to my normal tenor. "But seriously, I'm really hoping he asks me out."

Navi smiles and shrugs. "Ethan, this guy is obviously interested. If you like him, don't wait for him to make the next move. Just ask him yourself."

"Right, because that worked out so well with Jimmy Richards," I say.

Micaela rolls her eyes. "Jimmy has issues, and I told you it wasn't a bright idea to get involved with a boy who isn't out yet."

"Thanks, Princess Prophecy," I say sarcastically.

"Look, Ethan, I love you to death, but if you really want a boyfriend, you can't just sit around waiting for some Prince Charming to sweep you off your feet," Navi says. "You're lucky. You're gay. Gay guys don't have to worry about overcoming stupid rules made up by the patriarchy about who can ask who out."

I sigh, playing with the buttons on the miniature jukebox at the end of our table. "That's the problem, though. There aren't any rules, and guys can get so weird about the D word." I realize what I've said a second later and everyone cracks up like we're thirteen again. "The *other* D word, I mean."

"Ethan, you perform in front of thousands of people at nationals every year, and you're going to let some guy make you nervous? Come on," Navi says. "It's just a date, you're not asking him to marry you. And if he gets all weird about that, then you know he's not worth your time."

"Right," Micaela says. "And as someone in a relationship, can I offer you some extra advice?"

Navi and I both groan at this, but I gesture for Micaela to continue and say, "Thrill me."

"Boys are dumb—no offense," Micaela says.

"Mmm hmm. It's a scientific fact. Boy brains take longer to develop than girl brains," Navi quickly adds.

"Exactly," Micaela says, "And as such, sometimes they need a little guidance to help them figure shit out."

"Okay," I say slowly.

"Trust me. If you know a guy is into you, you've already got the upper hand. Be confident, lead them down the path you want—in a cool, casual way—and they'll follow you like an eager puppy," Micaela says. "Of course, they're also easily distracted like a puppy, which is why you've got to start their training right away."

I give her my *bitch, are you for real* look.

"She's saying, what you need to do is take charge," Navi says.

Micaela smiles. "Yeah, be a top."

"Shut up." I pull a sugar packet from its glass holder on the table and throw it at her. The packet bounces off her chest.

"Yeah, you're a good performer, Ethan. You

should be able to pull that off for a little while at least," Navi says, laughing.

I grab two more sugar packets, fire them her way, and we all laugh.

"Fine, I'll think about it," I say.

"No, you're going to do something about it right now," Micaela says. She grabs my phone from me.

"Hey! Don't—" I begin to protest, but Micaela holds up a hand to cut me off.

"Chill out. I'm not going to send anything. Trust me. Now, what's his full name?"

I squint at her with suspicious eyes.

"Top, remember?" Navi says.

"Fine," I sigh. "It's Danny Wheeler-Hall."

Micaela smiles. "Mm, a hyphenated last name. Love that. Makes him sound like he could be a future famous actor or something." She finds Danny in my contacts and starts typing a text to him. "Here." She hands my phone back without hitting send and I read the message she's constructed: *What are you up to Saturday night?*

"But, we have the competition Saturday night," I say.

"So," Micaela shrugs. "Ethan, we'll be wrapped up by 8:00. You can meet him after. You're making excuses."

"I'm not making excuses, it's just—" I see the frown that quickly forms on her face and I stop. "Okay, okay." I add to the text, doing my best to type something that channels that "cool and casual" vibe, then read the message out loud. "How's this? *What are you up to Saturday night? I have a show but should finish around 8.*"

"Excellent. It says, *I know what I want and I'm interested, but I've got my own shit going on too.* Now, hit send," Micaela says, and I do. "There, was that so hard?"

"You know, I don't remember all this confidence when you and Liam started hav—" Three floating dots appear under my last text, sending a bolt through me. "Oh, my God. You guys, he's replying."

I stare at the screen, trying to mind-command the three dots to hurry up and turn into a text already. An eternity later it does and something between a bark and a laugh slips out of me when I read it.

"Well?" Navi asks.

"Yeah, don't keep us on the edge here," Micaela says.

I shake my head in disbelief and hold out my phone, so they can read the message for themselves.

Danny: **We have a show that night too, so later Saturday is perfect.**

Danny: **I know a cool spot if you'd be down for dinner.**

Chapter Three

Danny

You know that feeling you get when you wake up on Christmas Eve and you know the thing you want most is wrapped under the tree with your name on it? That's how I feel when I open my eyes before my alarm goes off and remember the almost unbelievable thing that happened last night.

The memory makes me jolt upright in bed. I grab my phone off my nightstand and unlock it, needing to make sure the whole thing wasn't just a dream … and, nope. There it is on my screen in alternating gray and blue boxes. A legit text thread between me and Ethan Decker. I read every bit of it again. When I finish his last line, there's this electric kind of feeling buzzing through me, like my veins have turned into neon lights.

Ethan: See U Saturday!

A date. I have a date with Ethan Decker—*the* Ethan Decker.

I can feel the lit-up smile on my face, all warm and glowy, and then suddenly, the floor falls out of my stomach and my insides go dark. Because, *shit*, I told him I knew a cool spot for dinner, like I'm some suave dude who does this sort of thing all the time. We can't just go for pizza. I have no freakin' clue where to take someone on a real date. I'm an idiot. What was I thinking?

I grab my laptop, wake it from sleep mode, and double curse myself when I see I forgot to close the browser after my last search. So stupid. That's some straight-up amateur shit right there. Three tabs. I left three whole freaking tabs open, each one a different kind of search for the same name. Ana Ramos—my

31

birthmother. The woman who both gave me life and gave me up, so I could have a better life. A woman I know almost nothing else about—which is still more than I know about my biological father (absolutely nothing), but that's another story.

In addition to my birthmother's name and what she looked like eighteen years ago, thanks to the one and only photo my dads have of her, here's everything I know about Ana Ramos. She was very pretty—I've got her same big smile, rounded nose, and thick dark hair. She was about the same age I am now when she got pregnant with me. She was the daughter of Mexican immigrants. She lived in Salinas, California, and stayed in touch with my dads until I was about five years old. That's when she moved out of the area and seemingly fell off the face of the Earth.

God, I used to ask so many questions about her when I was little, and I've got to give my dads credit— they always answered them as honestly as they could. I mean, sure, there was a little bit of a sugar-coating over the complicated stuff when I was really young, but I never felt like they were talking down to me, you know?

Like, when I was around six, I asked my dad, Glenn, why people give babies up for adoption if they really love them. I'll never forget the tiny sad smile that flashed across his face, like his heart kind of broke a little for me. Then he and my other dad, my pop, Clayton, had a quick conversation with their eyes before he came over and joined us on the couch.

They explained that sometimes people realize they aren't ready to be good parents when they find out a baby is on the way, but that doesn't mean they don't love their child. Pop said I should always remember that my mom loved me so much that she set out to find a couple who would love me more than anything else in the whole world, and that was them. My two dads.

"And our family is one of the luckiest. Do you know why?" Pop asked me as he gave Dad a wink. "Because we got the best son and you got double dads, which means you got double papa love, which means you get *double the tickles*." Then they attacked me with tickles from all sides and I laughed and laughed until I turned red.

I know it's corny as shit, but that memory is one of my favorites—from a simpler time, when all that really mattered was knowing how much they cared for me and feeling like there was no question they couldn't answer. That was before the things I asked got way more complicated and those silent conversations between my dads would get longer before they responded.

Years later, when I asked them if they thought I'd ever be able to meet my mom, I remember the awkward way Pop stumbled over his words and Dad had to jump in and explain they didn't know where she was or how to get in contact with her anymore. Dad is way better with that kind of stuff than Pop, but when it comes to hiding how he really feels, not so much. I could tell by the way he deflated a little that my question made him super uncomfortable, even as he tried to assure me that I had two parents who would give me the moon if they could.

I left it alone for a while after that, but I never stopped thinking about her.

Then there was the time in eighth grade that Dad had to leave work and pick me up from school because I'd gotten a three-day suspension for fighting. Now, to be fair, Mikey Climber had it coming. He constantly picked on me, and that day, he took it too far, shoving me really hard and calling me a fag butthole baby. So, yeah, I introduced his mouth to my fist—twice. No regrets.

Still, getting all violent usually isn't my way. I

mean, it wasn't the first time someone had made fun of me for having gay parents. Far from it. But that kind of stuff seemed to get so much worse in middle school. Then *I* got worse. I was angry all the time and so embarrassed of my family—especially my dad, Glenn, who, let's just say, doesn't have a butch bone in his body.

So, when he picked me up and started lecturing me, saying he understood how I felt but that I couldn't just go around punching people, I exploded. "Why do you say that? You always say that. You have no idea how I feel! You don't know what it's like to be a brown boy with two *white gay dudes* for dads and no mom! I wish she was here instead of you!"

Yeah, total dick move. I fully deserved every word they yelled at me when we got home. The worst part was seeing Pop fight back tears while he did it. Family means everything to him, and I know all the shit he went through with his own parents.

I feel horrible that I put them through stuff like that, a lot, but what I don't think I could've explained before is that part of what I said that day was true. I wasn't just being dramatic. They *didn't* understand what I was going through, or what I felt. I mean, how could they, right? Hell, I didn't understand myself. All I knew was that there was a lot about me that was different from everything else in my world, and I hated it.

Funny how so much of that began to change once I came out. Well, okay, it didn't happen overnight. It took a little time and a lot of therapy. But today, I can honestly say I'm proud to be a bisexual Latino with parents who are pretty awesome—most of the time.

As much as I love my family, though, knowing there's a woman out there I've never met, who shares fifty percent of my DNA, well, it's kind of weird, like an itch I can't scratch. And I really want to. I want to meet my mom, now more than ever. Not because I feel like I'm missing a mother in my life … not anymore anyway, but because I feel like I need to connect with that part of myself. I can't explain why exactly, I just do.

There's a knock on my door. I slam the laptop closed and answer with a panicky, "What?" like I'm watching porn or something. Ugh.

"Nothing, just, I made breakfast if you're hungry. That's all," Dad says, and I can tell from his suspicious tone he probably thinks he's caught me in the act.

"Sure. I'll be there in a minute," I say, trying to switch up my voice, so I don't sound like I'm jerking off.

"Okay, don't take too long. It'll get cold," Dad says, practically smirking through the door.

I don't respond. Let him think whatever. Honestly, I'd rather be caught masturbating than have him know I've started searching for Ana on my own. Not that I like hiding this sort of thing from them, but I've used it to hurt them way too many times in the past, and I'm not that guy anymore. Besides, there's nothing for them to know, yet. The only thing I've found is that there are a lot of ladies named Ana Ramos on the internet—and none of them seem to be my mom.

I give it about thirty seconds, throw on a t-shirt and my favorite lounge pants, then head into the kitchen. I find Dad there pulling something out of the oven, and the most amazing eggy-breakfasty aroma fills the room.

"Good morning," Dad sings, as I take a seat at the table.

"It smells like an episode of *Top Chef* in here. What did you make?" I ask, all dreamily, inhaling deeply. My mouth is totally watering right now.

"Oh, just a little something I whipped up," he says as he sets the glass Pyrex dish on the table, then presents it with a flourish. "Voilà! Baked frittata."

I glance down at the steaming rectangle with this incredible texture that reminds me of rock formations we're studying in geology. It's basically a golden-brown slab of marble with red and green striations running through it.

Mind. Blown.

"A baked fri-what-a?" I ask.

"Frittata." Dad laughs and begins speaking in what he calls his "old Hollywood accent," which is this light and airy, almost royal sounding way ladies used to speak in old black and white movies. "It's an Italian breakfast dish, dear. Sort of like an omelet, you know, with organic eggs, baby spinach, sliced cherry tomatoes, sautéed onions, bits of maple bacon, and goat cheese, all baked to a fluffy cloud of perfection."

"Well, it looks amaze—" I stop, searching for a better word, something grander like Dad would use. Because this isn't just amazing, it's... "positively scrumptious," I finish, trying my best impersonation of his fake accent.

"Ah. Wonderful!" Dad exclaims. He's wearing his favorite black and pink polka-dot cooking apron with matching oven mitts. So, when he poses RuPaul style, with one hand on his hip and the other lifted in the air above his head, the picture is so extra, I laugh. Then he does too.

See, this sort of moment right here—the fancy breakfast and Dad being all, well, Dad—would've made me cringe a few years ago. When you've grown up with so many people making fun of you for something, the last thing you want to see is your parent being more of that. I'd think, *Jesus, why can't he be more normal like Pop? Why can't he just act like a man?*

Of course, that was before I understood concepts like "toxic masculinity" and realized the reason I was uncomfortable with my dad being effeminate was because I wasn't secure in my own masculinity.

I'm not going to pretend that little voice of doubt doesn't still whisper stupid shit in my ear sometimes. Only now, I know how to tell it to shut the hell up.

Dad once told me something that really stuck with me. He said, "Masculinity isn't some superpower. It doesn't make you better or stronger. However, it can leave you in a fragile state if you're always obsessed with projecting it. Being less than one hundred percent of who you are can never make you something more, it can only make you smaller."

I wasn't sure what he meant by that at the time, but I get it now. Authenticity, that's where real strength comes from—and Dad is definitely one of the strongest people I know.

He cuts into the frittata, scoops out a square-shaped serving and places it on my plate. I immediately dig in, take a bite, and, "Oh, wow," I say around a warm mouthful. The salty-sweet, creamy rich, fluffiness of it all is… "Wow," I repeat, smiling as I chew.

"A *triumph*! Just the sort of high praise I was hoping for," Dad says, clasping his hands together. He takes off his oven mitts and asks our Alexa device to start his "club classics" playlist. I'm guessing this will likely be some of his favorites from the '90s and, sure enough, within seconds, "Finally" by CeCe Peniston is being pumped through the kitchen speakers.

Even if this weren't a track that pops up every time we play Song Quiz, I've been to enough Pride celebrations over the years that every word is burned into my brain.

When the chorus hits, Dad starts mouthing the lyrics into a spatula as if it were a microphone. I quickly join in—a love of performing is the number-one thing

Dad and I have in common—and within seconds we're having a full on lip-sync battle. Just then, Pop walks in with a confused grin on his face, and Dad and I crack up.

"Hey, nobody told me we were getting breakfast and a show this morning," Pop says, straightening his tie. "No fair. Now I'm even more bummed I gotta run."

"Clayton," Dad says, in that parental *you need to eat something first* tone.

"Sorry, babe. Minor dental emergency. Patient lost an old crown this morning and 8:45 was the only time I could fit them in for the next couple of days." Pop shrugs. "So, duty calls."

Dad purses his lips and says, "Okay, Dr. Wheeler-Hall. But I'm fixing you a to-go plate so you can eat on the way. You won't be saving very many smiles if you're starving all day."

"I don't know. Is that even edible?" Pop asks with a sly smile as he winks at me. He makes this kind of joke every time he's around good food. We could even be at the fanciest restaurant, enjoying a meal so fantastic, he'll have practically licked his plate clean, and when the server comes by to ask how everything was, Pop will say something like, "Wretched. I couldn't eat a bite," and then laugh at his own joke. Seriously.

Dad and I usually just roll our eyes, but this morning, I shovel a big bite of frittata into my mouth and say, "It's terrible," only it sounds more like, "Eh-ta-wa-bow."

Pop chuckles.

"What have I told you about encouraging him?" Dad asks me, shaking his head. He scoops a serving into a Tupperware container and gives it to Pop. "Now, don't make me poison your food, you two."

Pop makes sincere eye contact with Dad and says, "I'm sure it's delicious. Thank you."

"You're welcome," Dad says, softer, and then they give each other a lingering kiss that makes me turn away and fish my phone out of my lounge pants' pocket. Who wants to watch their parents making out?

"Come on, guys. I'm eating here," I groan, burying my face in my Instagram feed. "Gross."

I'm only half-serious. Anyone who spends more than a few minutes with my dads can tell they are in capital L-O-V-E. After twenty-four years together, you'd think their feelings might've dulled a little, but no. They're always holding hands, kissing hello and goodbye, doing all kinds of sweet, thoughtful little things for each other. I tease them about it, but honestly, their relationship gives me hope that I might find an endless love of my own someday.

They ignore my comment and tell each other to have a good day. Pop checks his watch and rushes to the coat rack by the door.

"Danny, it's still my turn to pick out the film for Sunday movie night, right?" Pop asks as he throws his messenger bag over his shoulder.

"It is," I say enthusiastically. He picks the best movies—usually the so-bad-it's-good kind. "And Conner and Sanjay are both coming, so make it an extra cheesy one."

"Can do," Pop says, adding, "Okay, love you guys. See you tonight," over his shoulder as he hurries out the door.

"Bye, Pop," I say at the same time my phone buzzes with a text. My pulse trips over the possibility it could be from Ethan, but when I see it's a random meme from Conner, I must look pretty disappointed because Dad asks, "Something wrong?"

"No," I say, waiving off his concern. "It's nothing." Then a thought occurs to me. "Hey, Dad? Do you remember your first date with Pop?"

"Our first official date?" Dad wrinkles his forehead, thinking as he fixes a plate for himself and joins me at the table. "Oh, yes." He smiles at the memory. "I was so impressed with what a gentleman he was. He made reservations for us at this restaurant in Sea Cliff with an incredible ocean view. He insisted on picking me up and even brought me flowers. I couldn't believe it. I'd never had a man make such a fuss over me before. I thought it was all very sweet and romantic." Dad sighs, taking a second to glance over at his favorite framed photo of the two of them hanging on the wall, from a time long before me when Dad still had a full head of hair and there wasn't a hint of gray near Pop's temples. "Why do you ask?"

"Well, because ... I sort of have a date on Saturday ... with a guy," I feel myself blush and look down at the table.

"Danny, that's fabulous! Who's the lucky fella?"

"You know the red-haired boy on the Landon High School Winter Guard, Ethan Decker?"

"Is he the one who always steals the show?" Dad asks.

"Yeah, that's him," I say, laughing to myself. "Anyway, I really want to make a good impression, and I've never been on a date with a guy before. So, I'm just trying to think of some good ideas."

"Son, boy or girl, makes no difference—and it's not about where you go as much as who you're with. Don't put so much pressure on yourself. You two are both in color guard, so I'm sure you already have a lot in common. Whatever you do, just be yourself and have fun. The rest will fall into place."

Sometimes, I swear, Dad totally channels Oprah. I love him for his encouragement right now. I reply with an affirmative nod, smiling as I take another big bite of breakfast and let his words sink in while I think about Saturday.

The first competition of the season and a date with Ethan Decker. This is going to be epic—or rather, it will be. Just as soon as I figure out where we're going.

JASE PEEPLES

Chapter Four

Ethan

Okay, I can't stand when people post shit like this, but I am totally feeling *#blessed* right now. I know, don't judge me, and I hate to sound like I'm bragging. It's just, I can't think of a better way to describe how fucking excited I am. This season is starting off even better than I'd hoped.

We're at Homestead High School, the host of tonight's competition, and our guard just finished a warm-up that was absolute fire. No lie. I'm talking about the kind of warm-up where catches are so solid, flag phrases are so tight, that other guards stop and stare at us with eyes that say, "Holy shitballs, they're amazing." And it's only the first competition of the year.

"All right, everyone. Circle up," Andrew says, directing us to prepare for our pre-competition ritual outside the gym. The muffled music of the guard currently performing inside seeps through the closed doors, reminding me that we're only seconds away from showtime and less than two hours away from my date, a *real date* with the most gorgeous boy who has the sweetest smile and—no. Bad Ethan. Stop. First, get in there and perform the house down. Then, you can think about what comes next.

Butterflies are fluttering in my stomach, but they begin to settle down when Micaela and Navi appear at my sides. Having them nearby always makes me feel more chill. They each grab one of my hands. I give them both an enthusiastic squeeze and they give me one back while the rest of our guard finishes forming our circle around Andrew.

Standing shoulder to shoulder now, I can feel our body heat beginning to change the temperature inside the cocoon we've created—our final stage of transformation from people to performers.

"Focus all of your energy here in this circle. Combine it, feel it, let it flow through you as we breathe together. In through your nose," Andrew says, scooping both hands into the air dramatically, like he's about to command lightning down from above, "and let me hear it on the way out."

Everyone exhales together with a controlled "*shh*" sound, matching the speed of Andrew's hands as they slowly descend from high to low. He leads us through a second breath, a third, increasing in intensity each time. Then on our fourth and final breath, he says, "Now let me hear *fierce* on the way out."

We push air through our teeth with a guttural growl as Andrew launches us into the call-and-response chant we recite before every performance.

"Can you see it in your mind?" he asks.

Our collective answer is immediate. "We can."

"Do you believe it in your heart?"

"We do."

"Will you achieve it with your hands?"

"We will." The space between us and Andrew practically shimmers as we finish our mantra together. "We can! We do! We will!" Our three quick unison hand claps that follow crack like thunder, then we each punch a fist skyward and shout our school name. "*Landon*!"

I am so ready to perform the shit out of this show.

The gym doors open and warm air from the packed room inside rushes past us. I can hear the audience cheering for the other guard that just finished their performance as we gather our equipment and line up.

Andrew says, "Okay, y'all have a good show and remember, nothin' hits the ground."

"Hell, yeah, let's do this, Landon!" Micaela exclaims and we all respond with random hollers and woo-hoos. The minute we pass through the doors, though, we're all business. Chins up. Chests out. Game. Faces. On.

Navi and I push the wheeled handcart with our floor tarp to the edge of the court and immediately get to work setting the stage. The audience oohs and ahhs as our guard unrolls our tarp, unveiling its design.

I love how something as simple as this can get a crowd reaction, not that I blame them. Creative sets like ours are part of why I prefer winter guard season over the fall season with the marching band. Outside on a football field, you just don't get this level of detail—one of the many reasons winter guard is also called "the sport of the arts," I guess.

I mean, what other activity can you find where each team has their own vinyl tarp with a unique look, sort of like a giant painting, that covers the entire basketball court and *that's* what they perform on? If that's not next-level art, I don't know what is.

This year, our floor is basically a gigantic star chart with countless constellations that swirl and stretch from end to end—a navy blue snapshot of the night sky that looks so amazing with the powder blue shade of our new uniforms.

Once the tarp is in place, we quickly set the rest of our equipment around the floor and take our starting positions.

"Please welcome our next group in competition," the announcer's voice booms. "Performing their program *Across the Stars*, from Landon, California, the six-time WGI World Champions, the Landon High School Winter

Guard."

A wave of cheering washes over me, filling me with a mixture of adrenaline and anticipation that makes my skin tingle.

Finally, "Concerto for Violin and Orchestra" by Philip Glass swells through the gym speakers and the crowd goes silent. I slide into our opening choreography, an extended dance feature that ends with a barrel turn and jump, rolling onto the ground to grab our sabers.

Saber is my favorite piece of color guard equipment. The rounded hilt and gleaming metal of the blade just look so cool, and spinning it has always seemed to come more naturally to me than anything else.

I feel the corners of my mouth curl upward while I whirl the saber around my body, carving it through the space above, below, and left to right. Then I take a deep breath, flip the blade over with both hands and lock it into position for our first big trick—a six-turnaround toss.

Push. Release. Then a blur of motion as I turn in place. I know I've got this before the saber even reaches its peak in the air.

Crack.

Applause erupts from the audience and I'm a giant sparkler inside—a billion bits of light and energy exploding all at once. Because no matter how many times it happens, pulling off a catch that perfect during a live show always feels like magic.

Rocket fuel is pumping through my veins now, powering my performance through the remaining saber work, into my entrance on rifle.

We are definitely making history here, people, I think, practically feeling that fourth gold medal around my neck already. We're on fire. So, I'm not sure how it's even possible when I reach out to catch a simple rifle toss seconds later and grab nothing but air.

My rifle lands with a thud on the ground, sliding several feet across the floor. The entire gym makes this horrible groaning-gasp noise and it's like someone dumped ice water directly into my stomach. This isn't just a drop, it's a disaster.

Everything goes slow motion and I stand there, frozen in place with a sea of shocked faces staring at me until my brain screams, *what are you doing? Recover! Recover!*

Time speeds back up. I move, rushing for my rifle, and almost collide with two team members on flag, causing one of them to stop and break for several counts. After what feels like an eternity, I finally get my hands on my equipment again and speed back to my spot.

"You got this, Ethan!" a voice in the crowd says, but I don't. I fumble a backhand spin, nearly losing my grip, and fall so far behind tempo, I don't even throw the next toss.

I'm on autopilot now, not performing so much as just trying to get through the choreography. Relief floods my chest when I manage a decent catch on the next sequential seven. Then I hear a dreaded sound, like bombs going off all around me, as one, two, *three* other rifles hit the ground.

Can the big one just hit California right now and bring this whole building down around our heads, please?

Somehow, none of us die of embarrassment before we all switch to silver flags for our final big feature, but I wish I had when I miss a grab somewhere and completely screw up our ending. The final note of our music fades. I've never been so happy for a show to be over.

"Let's hear it for the Landon High School Winter Guard," the announcer says.

The crowd cheers and though they're not as

enthusiastic as they were before we started, it's still more than we deserve. It honestly feels like pity applause, which causes the little fires in my cheeks to burn brighter. I can't even look at anyone in the audience right now. I keep my eyes mostly on the ground as we rush to clear the stage.

A few guard members collect our equipment while the rest of us roll up our floor tarp like a giant burrito and snake it out of the gym. No one says a word while we walk to the tennis courts where we finally drop everything and Andrew gathers us together again. Only this time, there's no excitement, no enthusiastic hand squeezes. Just tension and a general FML feeling in the air.

"What the hell was that?" Andrew asks. I can almost see the steam coming out of his ears. Just half of the lights around the tennis courts are on, casting long shadows across his face, making him appear more threatening than usual.

Someone sniffs and then there's nothing but crickets for a stretch of time.

"Well, someone better start talking, because that was..." he makes a growling noise and sucks his teeth like he's pulling back the words he really wants to say. There's another long silence and then he comes at us again. "Well, come on. Micaela? Ethan?"

God, really Andrew? Individual drop-shaming. Awesome. Guess how totally not awkward this is right now.

I make eye contact with my friend and she instantly bursts into tears, making me want to hug her so badly. I had no idea she had a horrible performance too. Then Liam is there, wrapping his arm around her. She buries her face in her boyfriend's chest, and now I feel shitty for so many reasons.

"I don't know," I finally manage, and it's true. I have no idea why things suddenly went sideways. "It kind of surprised me. I thought it was there in my hands and then it—"

"I'm not talking about just the drops," Andrew interrupts. "It's early. Mistakes are bound to happen at this point of the season, but y'all were a bunch of deer in headlights out there." His eyes lock on me. My shoulders tense. "Ethan, you looked like you didn't even know where you were for half the show. Considering where you come from, I expect a hell of a lot more."

Okay, as an instructor, Andrew can be super inspiring. He can also be such a dick when he's mad. Everyone has a bad show from time to time. It's called being human, and we're doing some hard shit this year. *Considering where you come from.* I hate when he makes comments like that.

Yes, both my parents were WGI champions in the '90s. Yes, my sister is a three-time gold medalist and was captain of the Landon guard her senior year. No, despite what some members of our team think, I've never believed that makes me something special. I'm my own person, thank you very much, and I work my ass off too. So, after a shitty performance, the last thing I want to be reminded of—by our instructor in front of everyone—is how great my whole freakin' family is at guard. And what a letdown I am.

I open my mouth to say something, then close it again. I mean, I don't even know how to respond to that right now.

Andrew wags a finger at the group. "And the rest of you, panicking after that. Mistake after mistake and not a single good recovery. Ridiculous. This guard is better than that. You're all better than that," he says, letting out an exasperated sigh. "We're aiming to make history here, people. That means you carry yourselves like the champions you already are every time you get on that floor, regardless of what happens."

Great. Now I'm wondering if this is sort of my fault. Could my fuck-up have set that chain of craptastic events in motion? A lump starts forming in my throat, and I swallow hard to fight it back.

Several guard members nod, as if in agreement with Andrew, and then our captain, Heather Yun, raises her hand like she's in class. (She's such a kiss ass.) Andrew gestures at her and she says, "I think it's an overconfidence thing. Like, I know I personally had a good run, but I also put in a lot of extra practice this week." She turns and addresses the group. "We can't just assume we've got this in the bag because of who we are or how many years we've been in guard. We all need to work hard too."

Oh no, she did *not*. I am literally biting my tongue right now.

You know, when Andrew picked Heather for guard captain over me last summer, I was like, fine, at least I won't have to listen to her talk shit about how I only got it because of special treatment. Because she would if I had, just like in our freshman year when I made the saber line and she didn't or when I got a big solo in our sophomore field show, or the million other times she said it. But I thought we had agreed we were going to be cool this season, not take cheap shots like the one she just fired at me. Sorry, but no. I can't just let that go.

"Everyone works really hard here, Heather," I say sharply.

"But maybe we could all use a little more rehearsal time, yeah, guys?" Navi suggests, butting in, cheerleader voice in full effect. Thank God for her.

Seriously. "I mean, it couldn't hurt. Right? And we're not going to let one bad show keep us down, are we?"

Most of the group agrees and there's an instant improvement in everyone's mood. You can't help it. Navi's positivity is so contagious, she could even make Grumpy Cat purr.

"Heather, Navi, good points," Andrew says. "I want everyone at rehearsal 30 minutes early on Monday. We'll have a longer equipment sectional before we get into the show and I expect that if you dropped a toss tonight, you'll have taken it at least 100 times on your own beforehand. Got it?"

We answer with a collective, "Yes," then Heather adds, "That means be there at 5:15, not 5:30. If you're early, you're on time. If you're on time, you're late."

I'm glad it's kind of dark out here, so no one can really see how hard I'm rolling my eyes.

Andrew dismisses us and we're all pretty quiet while we gather our things, fold our floor tarp, and pack up the equipment truck. On our way back to the gym for the awards ceremony, Navi comes up beside me and gives me a long side hug as we walk.

"How we feeling?" she asks.

"Like I just bombed the first show of our senior year," I say.

"Hey." Navi pokes my cheek, presses the muscle upward with her finger. "Smile. Nobody died. It's only color guard."

We both laugh and then I say, *"Right."*

As we approach the spectator entrance to the gym, two girls in dark purple guard uniforms with sloppy eye makeup barrel out of the double doors, caught up in their own conversation.

"Oh, my God, their show was so boring," one girl says.

The other girl nods. "Totally. They kind of suck this ye—*oh*." She almost walks right into Navi and quickly apologizes.

"That's okay," Navi says, smiling warmly.

Their eyes cut from Navi to me, and even in the dim light out here, I can see their faces flush. They offer another quick "Sorry" and scurry around us. Once they're a few feet away, they giggle nervously and continue talking, keeping their voices at a loud whisper.

I scrunch up my face. "Uh, were they talking about us?"

Navi shrugs. "Probably not. There were two more guards who went on after we did." She tugs my waist in the direction of the entrance, but I stand still, thinking about how much I don't want to face all those people inside right now—including my parents. Luckily, Navi knows how to read my mind. "Hey, why don't you skip this? You've got bigger things to worry about tonight than sitting around a gym waiting for scores to be announced."

I consider this for second. "Yeah, but Andrew—"

"I'll cover for you," Navi says, waiving a dismissive hand through the air. "And it's not like you don't already know what place we're going to get."

"True," I say, realizing that if someone who didn't know our group overheard us right now, they'd think we were such big-headed bitches. It's just a matter of fact, though.

To be clear, our local winter guard circuit does have a lot of different teams in it, but they're mostly groups in the lower Independent and Scholastic classifications. There are a ton in the Independent and Scholastic A Classes, which is sort of like beginner level, and lots in the intermediate Open Class for both levels too. But since we're in Scholastic World Class, we don't compete against any of those groups. And yes, while there are a handful of Scholastic World Class guards here tonight—and you'd technically be correct to say they're competing against us—they're not really competition.

Even with a horrible performance like the one we had tonight, the Landon Winter Guard is just on another level. We probably won't see anyone who even comes close until we're at World Championships in April.

Still, Andrew is always harder on us at smaller shows like this because he says, "The impression you leave with the audience and the judges is more important than the score you'll get." So, while we already know we're taking 1st place tonight, none of us are going home feeling like a winner.

"Go on. You don't want to keep Mr. Cutie McCuterson waiting," Navi says, suggestively raising her eyebrows. "Besides, if you hurry you can sneak in a quick shower before they close up the locker rooms."

"Cutie McCuterson? Really?" I ask, smirking, trying to sound like I'm way cooler than I am.

Navi playfully slaps my arm and smiles. "Yes, really. He's fucking hot, okay? And you know it, you lucky bitch."

A giddy sensation starts in my middle, then quickly works its way up my spine. Okay, so maybe I will be leaving here feeling like a winner after all.

"He is hot, isn't he?" I ask. It's not really a question, though. My face heats up and I giggle happily to myself because—wow. I have an actual date with an actual hot guy—wait, no—a fucking hot guy.

Navi smacks me again. "Don't rub it in. It's bad enough I'll have to suffer through Micaela and Liam being all gross lovey-dovey on my own for the rest of the night. You know how clingy they get at shows. So, you better not fuck this up. I'm making a big sacrifice here."

She rests her head on my shoulder.

"All right, all right," I say, laughing. "Thanks." I dig my phone out of my pocket to check the time and feel another pulse when I see I have a text waiting from Danny. "Holy shit, Navi, he texted me." I open the message, which includes a selfie of him holding a first-place trophy with two other boys on either side pointing at the award. They're all dressed in matching black and gray school jackets and have super-big smiles on their faces.

God, that smile of his. Those lips. I swear I am *this close* to licking my screen right now.

Danny's text begins and ends with two star-eyed smiling emojis. I read it aloud to Navi. *"Thanks for wishing us luck earlier. It worked! First place!"* I show her the picture. "Check it out. His guard won their show tonight too."

"Aww, so cute," Navi says, then shakes her head. "And, of course, his friends are hot too. Look at that—wait a sec." She taps the image and zooms into the name of the school on Danny's jacket. "Ethan, you didn't tell me he was from East Valley High."

"Uh, is that bad?" I ask.

"No, not bad at all. East Valley Winter Guard is really good. Like really, *really* good. They were actually one of my favorite shows at WGI last year," Navi says.

"Wait, they were at WGI?"

"Yeah, and I thought they should've placed way higher than they did after I watched all the finalists on video."

I'm so confused. "In what? Open Class?"

"No, stupid. In World Class. With us." Navi looks at me like I'm from another planet. "Ethan, they took seventh place right behind Centerville High."

"Hold on, you mean to tell me this gorgeous guy

was at World Championships last year and I never even noticed him?" I ask, pointing at Danny's picture. "What's wrong with me?"

"Um, do you really want me to answer that?" Navi teases.

I give her a half-hearted smirk. Normally, I'd have a better comeback ready, but I'm too busy picturing how awesome it would be to walk around the arena at finals this year, holding hands with Danny between performances and—okay, I have to stop. I hate how my brain goes from finding out he'll probably be at WGI to us instantly being happy-in-love boyfriends there. We haven't even had a date yet.

Navi softens. "Well, in all fairness, it's not like you could easily tell one person from another. They were the ones with all the red and gold face paint. They had those uniforms with the feathers and did that show about the phoenix rising."

"That was them?" I ask, lightbulb finally going off over my head. "You're right, they were pretty goo—"

"Shit. Andrew alert," Navi announces, gesturing with her chin at our instructor as he walks by in the distance. We stand perfectly still, quietly watching as he walks through the entrance inside the gym. Navi exhales. "Thank God." She turns to me and smiles. "Now would you get out of here before he comes back and starts in with some lecture about how we should be sitting together as a team?"

"Already going," I say, backing away. "Text me our score?"

"Yes!" Navi laughs. "Go!"

"Gone," I say, turning to run in the direction of the parking lot and the change of clothes I have sitting in trunk of my car.

JASE PEEPLES

Chapter Five

Danny

Walking through the door of Sweet Louie's, all I can think is, *why did I let Sanjay talk me into picking this place?*

The description on the restaurant's Yelp page said it has "live jazz music and upscale French fare in an intimate, brick-walled space that dates back to the 1920s." And, sure, when you put it like that, it sounds like it would be a great place for a date, right? But now that I'm actually here, it's kind of disappointing. Just a small, crowded dining room with a tiny stage at the back. The pictures online made it look way bigger.

Everyone in here seems so much older too, including the host, who's standing behind a podium, looking at me like I'm a lost puppy that just wandered in off the street.

"Can I help you?" she asks, but it sounds more like, "You poor thing."

I seriously hate when older people do that whole patronizing, talk-to-you-like-you're-a-little-kid thing. Pop says it's because I have a baby face and that I'll be grateful for it when I'm his age, but for now, it just sucks.

I smile, resisting the urge to speak back to her with the same tone. "Uh, yeah, hi. I have a reservation for two, under Danny Wheeler-Hall."

She glances down at a tablet and starts scrolling. My reflection in the mirrored wall behind her catches my attention and I wonder for probably the thousandth time if the outfit I'm wearing—white V-neck tee, navy dinner jacket, dark jeans—was the right choice. Conner gave me a big thumbs-up and Sanjay told me I was channeling some serious Ryan Gosling and—*oh, my god.*

I'm just now putting together why Sanjay was all hardcore for me to make a reservation here. I'll bet he took one look at the listing for this place and assumed it would be like a scene straight out of his favorite musical, freakin' *La La Land*, the story of two white people who save jazz music, starring Emma Stone and Ryan freakin' Gosling. God, I hated that movie.

Normally, I wouldn't have even asked for Sanjay's help—it's not like he ever goes on real dates—but when I told the guys about my plans with Ethan, and that I was thinking of taking him somewhere in the Castro for dinner, Sanjay rolled his eyes and said bringing a date to San Francisco's gayborhood was way too cliché. So, of course, I started to second guess myself.

The thing is, that's exactly why I wanted to go to the Castro—friendly people, random drag queens, rainbow flags everywhere. I mean, the whole area just gives off a welcoming queer vibe, you know? Sweet Louie's here doesn't even feel like it's bi curious.

Plus, when I was growing up, my parents took me there so often, I know the Castro like my own backyard. If dinner went well, I was thinking I could suggest going for a walk around the neighborhood, maybe impress Ethan with a couple of fun facts about the area I've learned from Dad over the years. And if I just happened to randomly reach out to hold his hand—or maybe lean in for a little something more—we wouldn't have to think twice about who else was around.

I definitely don't feel that same kind of comfortable here in this restaurant. Why didn't I just go with my first instinct?

"Ah, yes. Here it is. Mr. Wheeler-Hall, would you like to be seated now or wait for the rest of your party?" the host asks.

Being referred to as "Mr. Wheeler-Hall" feels so weird. "Uh, now would be good, I guess."

"Big jazz fans?" the host asks, like she's quizzing me or something.

"Yeah, sure," I answer, trying not to sound as awkward as I feel.

"That's good. Looks like you got the last table right by the stage," she says, grinning as she grabs two menus. "This way, please."

I follow her to our table, which has got to be the worst location for a date ever. It's not just "by the stage," it's all the way in the back corner on the left side. We won't be able to see anything over here. This is bad. This is *so bad*. Why did I—shut up. Just shut up, shut up, shut up. You're not going to make a good impression on Ethan if you're being all aggro when he arrives. So, stop with the negative shit and make it work. Perform, Danny. Perform.

The biggest smile spreads across my face. I thank the host, take my seat, and try to, as my instructor Nikki would say, "project confidence." My body doesn't seem to want to listen to my brain, though. I can't make it more than ten seconds without nervously tapping a foot or playing with the silverware on the table. I've got that slightly nauseated feeling too … the same one I get sometimes before we go on the floor at big competitions.

I take a deep breath, hold it for a couple of seconds, then let it out slowly. What have I got to be worried about? This is just a date. Ethan is just a guy. A totally hot guy I've been crushing on for more than year, but sure, just a guy. No big deal … even though he'll be here any minute.

My stomach lurches. I decide to distract myself by giving Sanjay a little hell. I text him a GIF of Darth Vader force-choking a dude and follow it up with an

59

appropriate caption.

I could kill you for making me pick this place.
Sanjay replies almost instantly.

Um, I think you mean you could THANK me.
It has 4.6 stars and over 1000 reviews.
And here, bitch. I fixed your pic.

A GIF of Emma Stone and Ryan Gosling dancing on a street overlooking the twinkling lights of LA pops up on my screen. This actually makes me laugh a little, because, I knew it.

Nope, pretty sure I meant MURDER!

I follow that text with another of three devil emojis and then do a search to find the bloodiest, grossest horror movie GIF. I'm scrolling through a list of the best kills from slasher films when I hear, "Um, hi, Danny?"

I look up to find Ethan with a concerned expression, staring down at me and my bright-as-hell phone screen.

Fuck!

I try to stand up so fast, I bang my knee on the table and my butt ends up falling right back into my seat. A bolt of pain shoots up my leg and I clench my jaw to hold in the string of four-letter words that wants to come out. Then I put on my I-totally-meant-to-do that-face, scoot my chair back, and calmly rise to my feet.

"Ethan, hey, man—I mean, hi." Automatically, I move to offer him my right hand to shake and realize it's still gripping my phone, which is still displaying dozens of bright, bloody images. I jerk my arm back, shut off the screen, shove my phone in my pocket and my entire body basically bursts into flames. "So, that was just a stupid, uh … thing … for a friend."

Ugh, where do I even begin? I offer him my palm again, but he just looks at it. What if he thinks I'm some kind of psycho now? "Swear to God, I'm not like a serial killer or anything."

Oh, for fuck's sake. Serial killer? Really?

"That's ... good to know," Ethan says, nodding. Then he laughs this adorable little laugh, shakes my hand, and I forget how to breathe, how to think, how to do anything except feel the warmth of his fingers wrapped around mine. Touching him gets my heart doing some noticeable thudding. He's really here. That's really him, standing in front of me, wearing the cutest blue and green plaid button-up shirt, gray Chinos, and—holy shit. I'm officially on a date with Ethan Decker ... and I just said the stupidest thing to him.

Our hands part and my lungs suddenly start working again. "So, I sort of hate everything I just said." I bite my lip.

Ethan grins and I feel my shoulders relax a little.

Good, good, this is good. I learned in my public speaking class last year that if you have a major dumbass moment and you own it with a little joke like that, you can usually win the audience back over. *Oh*, and that if you're really nervous, you should call it out and move on. That can make you seem more relatable and help you chill at the same time.

"I'm actually a little nervous. Can I try that again?" I ask and give him my best smile, full dimples this time. No one can resist the dimples.

"Sure. And I don't mind. Nervous is cute sometimes," Ethan says. His eyes quickly cut away, then slowly find their way back, making me think maybe he's a little nervous too.

"Hold up. Did you just call me cute?"

Ethan shrugs and gives me a look that I think says, "Maybe." His smile grows bigger.

Whoa. We're legit flirting right now—*in person*. A fizzy, happy feeling bubbles up in my chest.

"Sweet. In that case, hi … for the first time, again," I put my hand out once more, which is really just an excuse to touch him again. This time, he shakes it right away. "Glad you could make it."

"Thanks for inviting me." Ethan gestures to our table. "Can we maybe sit now?"

"Right. Yes." I shake my head to clear it. "Yeah, totally."

We both take our seats and Ethan says, "Sorry I'm a little late. Parking was not so easy to find, and I'm kind of hopeless when it comes to driving in San Francisco. Traffic here is so crazy."

"Oh, dude, you're fine. I'm the one who's sorry. I probably should've thought of that before I asked you to meet me downtown," I say and mentally curse Sanjay again. "I come to the city all the time, so I forget it can be a lot if you're not used to driving here."

Ethan nods and looks around, taking in our surroundings. I wonder if he's thinking the same things about this place that I did when I walked in, and what that might mean he's thinking about me?

I say, "How was—" at the same time Ethan says, "So, you—" and we let out nervous laughs.

"Sorry," I say.

"No, no. Go ahead." Ethan gestures at me and leans forward. The light from the flickering candle on the table dances in his emerald eyes. The way they sparkle in here. It's hypnotic. I think I'd do just about anything he wanted right now.

"I was just gonna ask, how was your show tonight?"

Ethan grimaces. "It was … a show."

That's not at all what I expected him to say. "Not good?" I ask.

He scrunches his lips to one side. Shakes his head.

"Really? I'm surprised. You guys are always great," I say and I mean to stop there, but my mouth keeps moving. "I'm sure you personally had a good show, though, right? I mean, I don't think I've ever seen you make a mistake."

Ethan looks down at a corner of the table. He shifts his weight in his chair and makes a tiny groaning sound. "Not exactly."

I'm making him uncomfortable. My heart starts beating in my throat and a desperate need to steer the conversation into more positive territory takes over.

"Well ... I'm sure it was just a fluke. It's not like you're *not* going to win WGI again. You guys always win. And you should. I haven't even seen your show yet this year, but I already know that. Everyone knows that. You guys are awesome." Now I sound like a fucking fanboy. Make me stop.

Ethan nods, eyes still on the table, and says, "Thanks."

I start scrolling through subjects in my head, trying to think of something to say that won't make me sound like a total stalker, but I've got nothing.

Just then, four guys walk out on stage and take up positions at different instruments. There are pockets of applause from some of the other tables around the restaurant, and then the bass player begins.

At first, I'm super thankful for the distraction and, to be honest, the low notes filling the air are kind of soothing. But then the drums kick in at the same time as the piano and it's hella loud.

Ethan says something I can't make out over the music and I have to holler, "What?" like I'm a freakin' grandpa.

He holds up a menu, points at it, and yells, "I said, any suggestions?" He looks a little annoyed and I can't even blame him. The volume is on the cusp of painful.

"Oh, you mean the food?" I'm practically screaming at him now. "I'm not really sure."

Ethan makes a confused face.

I wince inside. I'm such an idiot. When I texted him, I told him I knew this place already—and that it was cool. I've gotta fix this. Like, now. "Uh, I mean, I haven't—"

Our waiter appears and sets two glasses of ice water on the table. I swear to God. Why do waiters always show up at exactly the worst time?

"Welcome to Sweet Louie's," he yells. "Can I start you gentlemen off with drinks or appetizers?"

The drummer on stage is going to town now, banging away, but my pulse is pounding even louder in my ears. I should just pick something, anything, so I don't look like I have absolutely no idea what I'm doing here.

"Can we go with the..." I quickly reach for the remaining menu and clip the side of my glass. It turns, tips, and I watch in horror as its icy contents spills out back toward me. A waterfall rushes over the edge of the table into my lap. I leap out of my chair, avoiding most of it, but a big part of my left thigh gets totally soaked.

I. Am. Mortified.

"Shit! Sorry, I am so sorry," I stammer.

"You okay?" Ethan asks.

There's no way I can make eye contact with him right now. "Yeah, I'm just—shit."

"No worries. Happens all the time," our waiter says, swooping in with a white towel he pulled from somewhere.

Panic is pumping through my veins. It feels like everyone in this place is staring at me. Even the piano player is giving me side eye. I wipe at my wet pants leg, like that's actually going to do something. Cold water is dripping down my shin and my face is so hot.

"I'm just gonna … be right back," I say.

"Yeah, okay," Ethan says.

Fighting back the prickling sensation behind my eyes, I bullet into the bathroom and go from embarrassed to pissed when I see my reflection in the mirror above the sink.

"Get that pathetic look off your face," I silently tell myself and slam a fist on the countertop. "You cannot, will not, lose it here."

I yank a few paper towels from the dispenser on the wall and dry myself off as best I can. It's not much, but I feel like it's at least something.

Man, how in the world could I be screwing this up so badly? Here I am, finally on a date with Ethan and it's like I've got no game. I'm saying stupid shit, being clumsy as fuck. Failing at my first date with a guy. Big time.

Okay, knock it off. Feeling sorry for yourself isn't going to do jack.

Puffing my chest up like Superman, I look my reflection in the eye and tell myself to get back out there, step it up and meet this challenge. I'm out the door and down the hall before I realize I have no idea how I'm going to do that. I stop short and my mind starts spinning, scrambling to come up with a plan.

What am I going to say, do? Just sit down and pretend like nothing awkward happened?

I scan the dining room, spot Ethan at our table on the other end. His red hair is like a spark of fire in the sea of people. He's also the only person staring at his phone instead of the stage—and he's frowning.

Every muscle in me deflates a little. He's obviously not feeling any of this. For all I know, he could be texting his friends right now, telling them he's not really feeling me either. But then, I guess I haven't really given him much of a reason to yet, have I? None of this is me.

Dad's advice replays in my head. *It's not about where you go as much as who you're with. Just be yourself and have fun. The rest will fall into place.*

I pull my phone out of my pocket to check the time and see I've got another unread text from Sanjay. Out of habit, I tap the icon. All it says is, "You're welcome," along with yet another GIF of Emma and Ryan overlooking the city.

An idea lights up my brain. I'd die before I'd tell him this, but damn, Sanjay might be a genius.

I march back to our table and smile so big when Ethan looks up at me. "Hey, how about we ditch this place? Go somewhere else?" I holler over the music.

"Huh? We just got here, though," Ethan says, sounding confused. He's just so freakin' adorable.

"I know, but this will be better. Promise." I offer him my hand again. "Come on. Trust me."

Ethan looks at my outstretched palm and his forehead wrinkles, like he's giving it some serious thought for a second. I'm thinking he's going to shoot me down, but then the corners of his mouth curl up. He takes my hand and says, "Sure. Why not?"

Chapter Six

Ethan

I don't want to assume I know whatever else the universe has planned for me tonight. I already made that mistake once today. Okay, maybe twice. But at this point I think it's safe to say that this has officially gone from a fuck-my-life kind of night to an I-fucking-love-my-life sort of one.

I'm not gonna lie—it was a little weird when Danny suddenly wanted to leave the restaurant five minutes into our date. (Who does that?) There was just something about the way he looked at me that wouldn't let me say no—even when all he'd tell me about where we were headed was that it was a "surprise," and then he asked if I'd be cool with us taking his car.

Now, I know what you're thinking, and if it were a big, white, creepy cargo van, I would've totally been like, "Hard pass," but let's be real—nobody gets kidnapped in a yellow Volkswagen Beetle. Plus, it was super obvious how hard he was trying, so I figured I'd be safe. There's no way I could've guessed this is what he had in mind, though.

We're at the top of Twin Peaks, which is apparently a set of hills in the middle of San Francisco with an amazing 360-degree view of the city. From here, buildings with thousands of tiny lit-up windows seem to stretch for miles, a field of square-shaped stars twinkling in the dark. It's magical. Even the patches of fog hanging in the air above rooftops glow in soft shades of orange and blue.

"This is so cool. I can't believe I've never been here before," I say, finishing my third attempt at taking a decent panoramic picture. I keep moving my phone too fast. "I feel like a Greek god looking down from Mount Olympus." Oh, jeez. Did I really just say that out loud? Great. I'm sure that didn't make me sound stuck up at all.

Danny laughs, shakes his head. "A god, huh?"

Let's walk that back real quick. "I just mean, the city looks so small and different from here."

That's not all that seems different up here. Danny does too. I can totally tell he's a performer, same as me, because I thought I was nervous when I walked in that restaurant earlier, but he was operating at a hundred there for a minute. (Not that watching him have a mini meltdown wasn't super adorable.) Then he left the table and when he came back, it was like, *showtime*, he was a whole different person. Well, the same, but less uptight, more real.

For example, I love how excited he got when we stopped at this pizza-by-the-slice place on our way here and he started telling me how it was the best in the city and that I had to try the Castro Special. At first I was like, okay, so the surprise is we're having our date here. That's fine. He obviously thinks it's great. I'm in. But then he ordered two slices to go and before I knew it, we were back in the car driving up this winding road.

Now we're here, surrounded by all *this*, and I must be suffering from altitude sickness or something, since I don't even know what I'm saying.

"Like, look, I can fit the whole Golden Gate Bridge in the palm of my hand," I say, reaching out to cup the space beneath the bridge in the distance.

"Oh, I get it," Danny says. "That's part of why I love this spot. You sort of feel like you're king of the world up here."

He steps up behind me and rests his hands on my shoulders, sending an electric sizzle down the length of my body. "But if you're going to be a good king, you should probably know," he leans in close to my ear and whispers, "that's not the Golden Gate."

Heat balloons across my face. "It's not?"

"It's the Bay Bridge," he says, and I can hear his grin. He points over my left shoulder. "See those two towers sticking out of the fog there?"

I nod, feeling the dumbest I've probably felt in my entire life.

"That's the Golden Gate," Danny says. His finger begins drifting to the right as he continues pointing out different landmarks. "Alcatraz is there, and the tall triangle-shaped building? That's the Transamerica Pyramid. The taller building to the right is the Salesforce Tower, and if you look here," his arm ropes around my chest as he points to a spot further down, "you can just barely make out the big rainbow flag that marks the Castro."

When he finishes, he continues holding his arm there, pointing to the pride flag flapping in the wind.

As excited as he sounds to be showing me all this, I can't help wondering if that was partially an excuse to get us all tangled up like this, the same way some people pretend to yawn and stretch in movie theaters, so they can drop an arm around their date's shoulders. At least, I hope that's what's going on here. *Please, be what's going on here.*

I relax into him, just the teensiest bit, testing, signaling.

Danny wraps his other arm around me and, holy shit, it's as if every organ in my body starts doing a celebration dance.

"Amazing," I say, gesturing with my chin at the horizon. But I don't just mean the view. I mean him. This. All of it. Feeling his chest pressed against my back, the heat of his body, the warmth of his breath on my neck. It's frightening and exhilarating, uncomfortable and comfortable, all at the same time ... kind of crazy too.

Is there such a thing as trust at first sight? There must be, because I'm not sure how else to explain what's going on. All I know is, if any other guy would've brought me here, I'd probably be freaking out right now.

"You know, I wasn't exactly having the best night earlier." I laugh lamely to myself, regretting the words the second they fall out of my mouth. "Wait, that sort of came out wrong. I just mean," I crane my neck around, lock eyes with him, and it's suddenly so hard to form words with his mouth so close to mine. "Thanks. This is ... all, um ... really cool."

Danny smiles and I'm under a spell.

He licks his lips. Then I do too. His face drifts closer and then I feel his stomach rumble against my back as a loud growling noise fills the air.

He squeezes his eyes shut, uncoils his arms, and takes a step back. His sure posture sags and then his expression twists into just about the cutest grimace I've ever seen.

"So embarrassing," he groans, laughing nervously and I do the same, watching as his face turns bright red in the dim light. "Obviously, I'm starving."

He glances over at a big rock sticking out of the ground a few feet away and the pizza box he set on top right after we arrived. The thought of the two uneaten slices waiting inside that box makes my stomach growl even louder than Danny's and we crack up.

A couple seconds later, I get ahold of myself and say, "Well, then, I guess that means we should probably eat?"

"Definitely. Come on." Danny motions me over to the rock, where we sit with the pizza box between us, and it's almost too perfect, the way this boulder just happens to be sticking out of the ground in the middle of the hill like a tiny table.

Before tonight, I thought this was the sort of thing you'd only see in movies.

Danny opens the pizza box, passes me a slice of Castro Special, and the rich, herby smell of pesto and cheese has my mouth watering before I even take a bite. It's salty and sweet with a crust that's crunchy on the outside, but slightly doughy in the middle.

"Holy shit. This is so good," I say, holding up a hand to cover my mouth as I chew. "I don't think I've ever had pesto on pizza before."

"It's my favorite. I mean, it's better when it's hot, but still," Danny says around a mouthful. "The best."

"So, how do you know so much about San Francisco? Did you live here before or something?" I ask.

Danny nods, swallows, and says, "When I was really little, yeah. We moved to the east bay when I was around seven." He smirks at the memory. "*Oh*, I was not happy when that happened. My dads would still bring me back all the time, though, for like, street fairs or concerts in the park or whatever. And I hang here a lot with friends too, or sometimes by myself, if I need to get away from everything and think for a minute. I've always loved San Francisco. It's like, where I'm from. Where I belong, you know? Like home, sort of. If that makes sense."

He looks away and shakes his head. "That probably sounds so stupid. I'm sure that was way more than you wanted to know." He laughs and takes another bite.

"It's not stupid. I think it's cool actually," I say, studying him. He's totally blushing again.

The way he keeps shifting between self-assured and self-conscious is so ... sweet. He knows things, and he's not afraid to show off a little, but he's not full of himself either. I really like that and—wait, wait, wait. Hold on.

"Uh, did I hear you right? Did you say dads, with an S?" I ask.

"Yup. My dads are gay," Danny says and his tone is so matter-of-fact.

"Oh," I say, which is probably the absolute worst response, so I add, "that's cool," like it's no big deal. Because it's not. But I feel like it is. It's the biggest kind of awesome deal—exactly what I dream about having some day in the future, a family of my own with a man I love.

I try to picture what that kind of future might look like with Danny, the two of us walking in the park with a little boy or girl of our own, and then I mentally slap myself because that's seriously insane. *I just met him.*

There are hundreds of questions crowding my brain, all pushing and shoving their way to be the first out of my mouth. "So, is ... I mean, have, uh ... are you—"

Danny let's out a small, exasperated sigh. "Let's see ... I'm adopted. My dads have raised me my entire life. Neither of them are my biological father. No, I don't know who that is, and no, I've never really met my biological mom either. Does that cover it?" He smiles and I think he's sort of teasing me, but there's a bit of a sharp edge to his voice that tells me he's a little annoyed too.

I'm such a moron. *Of course* he's been asked all those questions millions of times already. I can't believe I was about to be a complete basic bitch and do the same thing, even though that's not how I would've meant it.

I nod, because I have no clue what else to say.

"Sorry for the big info dump there," Danny softens. "I've learned it's just easier to get all that out of the way. Then people can stop thinking about it, right?"

"Right," I agree, like what he just said is something I hear every day.

An awkward silence descends on us and then Danny says, "I have started looking for her, though."

"Who?"

"My birth mother," he says, staring at some point beyond what I'd thought was the Golden Gate Bridge a few minutes ago. "Nobody knows, but I have."

He puts it out there so casually, it takes a few seconds for me to process what he said. "Really?" I ask. "You haven't told anyone?"

"Well, I guess now there's you, so that makes someone. But you're the only one." He turns and gives me a tentative half-smile that makes him seem so unsure again, like he's wondering if maybe he's said too much.

The fact that he'd confide in *me*, with a secret like *that* is so—I don't even know. Maybe there's something to this trust-at-first-sight idea after all. I smile back at him, letting him know it's all good and say, "Thanks."

"So, can I ask you something?" And just like that, his tone goes from heavy to light.

"Sure."

"Before, when you said you were having a bad night, did you mean..." Danny points back and forth between us.

"You? Our date? Oh, God, no," I say quickly. "This has definitely been the best part."

"Phew," Danny says. He makes a silly face and dramatically mimes wiping his forehead with the back of his hand. Him overacting, being all goofy right now, totally makes him seem even hotter. I'm not sure why.

"No, no, if I made you think that, I'm so sorry. It was," I shrug, "nothing. Not even important."

"That's okay. I want to hear," Danny says.

After all the personal stuff he shared with me, I

73

feel like this is going to sound so dumb, but here it goes. "We had a really bad show tonight and I got totally reamed by our guard instructor in front of everyone."

"That sucks," Danny says, "But come on, it couldn't be that bad."

"Trust me. We blew up. The gym was basically a nuclear wasteland when we were done," I say, suddenly feeling the need to prove the scope of our disaster. "I missed a rifle toss that slid several feet away and came close to taking out a couple of freshman trying to get it back. And I totally fucked up our ending flag feature. Basically, I was the biggest mess in the history of winter guard tonight."

"*Pff*," Danny waves a hand through the air. "That's it? Not even close. You want to know who already won the biggest mess award?"

He starts telling me this story about how, last year, at the Fresno Regional, he accidently stepped on the fabric of his flag in the middle of some intense choreography. He nearly lost his grip on the pole and almost dropped it, but he was fast, and moved to yank it back in the other direction. Only, he did that at the exact second his foot came off the silk, and the force of his pull sent the flag shooting out of his hands like a javelin. It sailed through the air, finally landing all the way on the other side of the floor.

Danny's standing up, laughing as he continues acting out the moment. "So, I'm like, *What the fuck?* And I take off for it—'cause, I need to recover, right?—and then I slip and fall, totally eat it in front of everybody."

I'm cracking up so hard, my stomach hurts, but Danny keeps going.

"Then after all that, *after all that*, I finally get to my flag and there's a big-ass rip right down the middle. Ever tried to spin with a silk that's nearly torn in half? It looks like this." He starts air-flagging choreography like a panicked cartoon character, all wavy arms and legs.

"Stop. Stop," I beg, wheezing. "I can't." I've never laughed this hard.

"Yeah, so, don't come at me with your little drop-and-slide story. You're in the presence of a champion mess here," Danny says, striking a cheesy proud pose.

When I can finally catch my breath again, I wipe at my wet eyes and say, "Oh, my God. I think I needed that."

"Glad I could help," Danny says, and what's kind of weird is, I believe him.

It's like, you know how when most people ask you how you're doing and you just say, "Fine," because, really, you know they don't care, and you don't want to tell them either? Right now, though, staring at Danny staring back at me, I get the exact opposite feeling and something lets go deep in my chest.

"Okay, so maybe it wasn't that bad, but still. There's so much pressure this year," I admit.

Danny sits back down on the rock, giving me his full attention. "Understandable. You guys are the defending world champions," he says. "Hell, I'm feeling the pressure and we're just hoping to make top five this year. I mean, I don't know what it feels like to try to win a seventh gold medal for your school, but I think I get it. WGI can be stressful."

"Exactly. There's that, but also, more than that," I say.

"How so?"

"Winning WGI isn't exactly something new in my family," I say.

Danny raises an eyebrow and I feel like such an asshole.

"Wow, that sounded so conceited. I'm not. I swear. What I mean is, that's sort of the problem."

I inhale through my nose, exhale through my mouth—a smaller version of the breathing exercise Andrew takes us through before every show—and start again.

"Color guard is like football in my family. The sport above all others. My mom and dad did it when they were in high school, then they were in the Blue Devils Winter Guard in the '90s and then—"

"Hold up," Danny says. "*Both* of your parents were in Blue Devils? As in, the Independent World Class Guard that still holds the world record for the highest score ever at WGI?"

I shrug. "Yup. That's actually how they met."

"Whoa, that's crazy," Danny says, beaming. "You're like, a legit descendent of winter guard royalty. Should I bow? I should totally bow."

"Don't even," I warn, trying to sound serious but I end up smiling despite myself.

"Just kidding," Danny says. "That is kind of cool, though."

"You might think so, but no, not really," I say.

Danny seems to consider this for a second, tilting his head from side to side and says, "I guess I could see that." He doesn't really sound convinced, though, so I try to explain a little more.

"I mean, my parents won twice a long time ago, then my sister—who does everything right—won three gold medals before she graduated. By the time I got to join the Landon High School Winter Guard, winning WGI again had become this thing we were just expected to do. And yeah, it's been awesome, but our guard instructor is always going on and on about how we're trying to make history and it just feels like I have to be *perfect* all the time or I'm going to let everyone down." I stop, needing to take a breath and feel a little embarrassed for babbling so much. I scrunch up my face and groan, "Sorry, that was probably TMI."

"Nah," Danny says, gesturing around us. "This is a safe space." He pushes the pizza box aside and scoots next to me. His leg rests against mine. Heat spreads up my thigh, straight to my groin. "You don't have to worry about being perfect here." He puts a hand on my knee. "Besides, I sort of think you already are."

My whole body goes numb.

No way. There is no way he really just said that to me. This guy—this funny, smart, incredibly good-looking guy, who seems to know so much and has done so many things—thinks *I'm* perfect? Okay, I've dreamed someone would say something like that to me someday, but it sounds so strange to actually hear it in real time.

I turn to look at him and the only word I can manage is, "What?" I can't stop smiling.

Danny keeps his face forward for a second, a subtle pinkish vibe on his cheeks as he stares out at the sea of lit-up buildings. Then his mouth slowly morphs from a straight line to a curved one, changing his expression from shy to sure. He turns to me and shrugs, giving me a look that says, *Sorry not sorry.*

I pull Danny into me and kiss him, because if this is a dream, I'm not waking up before we get to the good part. His lips are soft and warm, and I can taste pesto on his tongue, can smell the clean spicy scent of his cologne.

He kisses me back. Then I do the same, again and again. Our timing is clumsy at first, me moving too slow and him too fast, but it's not long before we find our rhythm, steady and synced, with his mouth studying my lower lip, and my mouth exploring his upper.

I never imagined simply kissing someone could

feel this epic. It's like every one of my cells is spinning, performing the most awesome winter guard show inside my skin.

For the first time in my life, I think I'm experiencing a genuinely perfect moment in time, here on this hill with the sweetest boy in the universe, surrounded by a city of stars. And I don't ever want it to end.

Chapter Seven

Danny

When I was eight years old, my parents brought me to the top of Twin Peaks for the first time to watch the city's Fourth of July fireworks show. I thought I knew what to expect—bright colors, sparkling lights, big booms—but I had no idea my little mind was about to be blown.

After those first few rockets shot up over the San Francisco Bay, my dad told me to look to my right. That's when I realized it wasn't just the one show we could see from our hilltop spot. They were going off all around us, for miles. Dozens of dazzling explosions, splattering the sky with brilliant reds, whites, and blues, starbursts of energy that hung in the air like dandelions, defying gravity for a moment before drifting back down to Earth in tiny showers of glittering light.

It was the greatest fireworks event I'd ever experienced, and yet, it pales in comparison to what happened when Ethan's lips touched mine.

Now, I've kissed plenty of girls, and my fair share of boys too, but none of them ever made my insides vibrate like a guitar string. I mean, finally getting to kiss (and kiss and kiss and kiss) Ethan was ... well, it was kind of everything.

I totally could've stayed there, kissing him all night, but when a freezing wind began kicking up, it kind of killed the mood. San Francisco winds are always on the cold side at night. But at the top of Twin Peaks? They can be brutal. Once Ethan's teeth started chattering, I knew it was time to go.

I'm also sure that if I include that detail when I

tell Sanjay and Conner how my date went, one of them will definitely make a joke about how I basically got cockblocked by a stiff breeze. For the record, though, I really don't care. Fine, maybe a little, but honestly, I feel like ending the night in a good spot is the smarter thing to do. I'm playing the long game here. I don't want this to be a one-and-done kind of thing, and I'm getting the same vibe from Ethan, too.

I mean, he did ask if we could take a selfie together before we started making our way down the hill (good sign), and now we're even holding hands as we walk along the street back to my car.

"So ... I'm really glad you were down to go on this little adventure with me," I say. It's taking a lot of work to sound chill on the outside when there's a freakin' dance party still raging inside my body. "I'm sure at first you were probably like, *Where the hell is this guy taking me? Right?*"

"For like, a second, yeah," Ethan says, chuckling. "But seriously, no, it's cool. This was awesome. Thanks."

"Awesome enough to do again, maybe?" My eyes automatically snap forward, focusing on the city's skyline. It's hard to look directly at Ethan while I'm putting this out there, which is so weird when you think about it. We were literally touching tongues a few minutes ago. So, I don't get why just making eye contact while I ask him out on a second date feels way more stressful and embarrassing. "I mean, hypothetically, if someone were to ask, like possibly next weekend?"

In my peripheral, I watch Ethan shrug and his warm smile makes me forget all about my freezing ears.

"Hypothetically ... I could maybe be down for that," Ethan says playfully. He gives my hand a small squeeze and gently tugs, making our interlaced fingers rock back and forth like a swing.

"Yeah?" I ask, grinning as I turn to look at him.

"Yeah," he says, but then his face suddenly twists. "Shit, wait."

"No?"

"I can't. We have rehearsal Friday night and a show all the way out in Modesto on Saturday. I probably won't be back until after midnight," Ethan says. "I could do Sunday, though, if you don't have any plans then."

"We have a movie thing we're doing at my place that day." My mouth shifts into high gear, racing ahead before I think about what it's saying. "Hey, why don't you come too?"

Ethan shoots me a questioning look. "A movie thing? At your house?"

My brain hits the brakes, leaving behind a long black streak inside my head. You don't ask someone to come hang out together with your parents and your boys on your second date. You just don't. That's gotta be like, Dating 101 or something. Dammit!

I shake my head, shrug, and try to play it off. "It's just this stupid thing my friends and I do once a month. Best Worst Movie Night." My heart is fluttering and the more I talk, the stupider I feel, but I can't stop myself. "See, we pick a really bad movie and my dads make some kind of crazy themed dinner and we just eat and laugh at the…" I trail off when I see Ethan's forehead wrinkle in concentration, like he's trying to figure out what nerd language I'm speaking. I grimace. "Uh, sorry. Yeah, it's dumb. That probably won't work. We could—"

Ethan laughs and I freeze in place. Is he laughing at me?

He stops, turns to face me and leans his head to one side, all cute, like a curious puppy. "Danny."

"What?"

"Are you inviting me to meet your parents?" Ethan asks.

My pulse freaks the fuck out and I let go of his hand. "Wait, no! Not like that. I mean, yeah, they'll be there, so I guess that means you'll technically be meeting them, but it's not like *that*, that. I swear. Not that I wouldn't. It's just, my friends Sanjay and Conner will be there too and we always—"

Ethan cracks up. "I'm kidding!"

"Oh," I say, stupid relief washing over me.

"I'd love to, actually," Ethan says in a softer voice. His gaze drifts down to the street.

"Wait, what? Really?" I ask.

"Really. Best Worst Movie Night sounds pretty cool," Ethan says, his eyes floating back up to meet mine. They're smiling so big, but his mouth is only slightly turned up on one side.

There's no way he could know this, but it's an expression I've seen on his face so many times before—the same restrained, boyish coyness he usually projects just before he begins every winter guard performance. It's the same expression that grabbed my attention two years ago, and it's still got me.

"Great, I mean, cool," I say, and before my mouth can screw anything up, I move in and kiss him again, gently, more tender this time.

Ethan whimpers against my lips as another sharp gust of wind blows past us. We pull apart.

"My car heater is totally calling our names right now," I say, wrapping an arm around his shoulders, doing my best to shield him from the cold.

Ethan nods emphatically.

"Come on, let's make a run for it," I say. We do, both of us smiling.

Chapter Eight

Ethan

It's nearly forty minutes past midnight when I get home, which, I admit, is pretty late for me. My mom and dad used to be total drill sergeants about my curfew—12:00 AM, sharp—but they've been so busy lately, they barely seem to notice what time I come rolling in anymore.

So, I'm kind of surprised when I walk through the front door and find the two of them snoozing away on the couch, lights down low, as that Netflix show about the British Royal Family plays in the background. They're usually in bed by now, even on weekends.

My parents are early risers. Especially Dad, who's been on a big health kick these past few months, going on 5:00 AM jogs to help get his blood pressure under control. They've both been killing themselves since they quit their jobs as software engineers at Apple and Google to join this new startup company, Stream Box, that offered to nearly double their salaries.

They're part of a team that's designing some new technology that'll allow people to access content from every streaming service they've signed up for, all in one place without opening and closing different apps. Mom says it'll be "like cable TV, but for the streaming era," if they ever get it launched.

It all sounds really cool, but I'd give up the potential convenience of never having to jump from Disney+ to Amazon Prime again if it meant my parents were around more often. Sometimes I don't see one, or both, of them for days at a time. All they seem to do is work, but they never miss a winter guard show, which is kind of reassuring, I guess. Even if sometimes I'd rather they literally did *anything* else with me.

They look so peaceful like this, all curled up together with the soft light from the TV glowing on their faces. I hate to disturb them right now.

I'm deciding whether I should let them sleep where they are when Mom stirs awake.

"Hey, son," she says, lazily squinting in my direction. "What time is it?"

"It's late," I say softly. A smile starts to form on my lips and it takes every ounce of energy I have to fight it back. I don't want to come off as any kind of excited right now, but it's nearly impossible when my head is still swimming with thoughts about Danny.

Dad opens one eye, looks at his watch and then gives me his *Don't you think you're pushing it?* look.

"Sorry, we went out after the show and sort of lost track of time," I say, which is mostly true.

In theory, I'm sure my parents wouldn't have a problem with me going on a date tonight. But they'd probably ask way too many questions if I told them, and I know for a fact they'd have a total shit attack if they found out I drove all the way to San Francisco to hang with a guy I met online. So, if they want to think what I just said means I was chilling with my friends at the diner, I won't stop them.

"Drowning your sorrows in French fries and ranch, huh? Can't say I blame you," Mom says, giving me a sympathetic frown as she sits upright.

Fries drowned in ranch dressing was her go-to cure for feeling shitty after having a bad show back when she was in guard. She shared that little ritual with me when I was in 7th grade after the first time I dropped a toss during a live performance. And, yeah, that seemed to work just fine when I was twelve, but things haven't been that simple in years.

"You definitely get your taste buds from your mother," Dad—who's disgusted by even the sight of ranch—teases. He pretends to gag.

In some ways, my mom and dad are almost clones of one another. People make jokes about it all the time. They both have red hair, are brilliant engineers, and even enjoy the same TV shows. Then there's the whole color guard thing too. But just when you start to think Dad is basically a male version of Mom, something like this pops up to prove there are areas where they couldn't be more different. They're weird, I know, but it's a kind of weird that seems to work for them.

Mom playfully jabs Dad with a foot. "Hey, you hush." Her eyes cut back over to me and her smile melts into a concerned expression. "I'm so sorry you had such a rough show tonight, honey. How are you feeling?"

I let out a long sigh and shrug. "Fine, I guess."

"Fine? Andrew looked like he was ready to spit nails when you guys were done. I told your mom, *I would hate to be in their shoes right now.*" Dad chuckles and turns to her. "Man, the look on his face. Totally gave me flashbacks to Scott and Jay at the Vegas Regional in '96, right after that God-awful prelims performance we had. Holy shit, I thought they'd never stop screaming at us. Sure did light a fire under our asses for finals the next day, though."

Mom shakes her head and lets out a small laugh. Dad does too. Then they're both quiet, as if lost together in the past for a beat before returning to the present.

I must look completely over it because when Dad finally focuses on me again, he gives me an encouraging smile and shifts into his coach-Dad voice.

"Anyway, I know it's no fun when your guard instructor is going off, but try not to take it personally.

He's just pushing you guys to be the best you can be."

And hello familiar heat rising in my chest.

This is one of my biggest pet peeves about having former guard performers for parents. It's so irritating that I haven't said a word to them about what actually went down, but here they are, acting like they were right there next to me when Andrew pulled us aside after the show. What really gets me the most is that they're pretty spot on too. I hate that. It's like, I can never have an experience in this sport that's just mine—not even a bad one. There's nothing they haven't already done before and don't have a story about.

Also, I'm a fucking senior who's been spinning since before middle school. Do they really think I don't know all this already?

"I never take it personally, Dad," I say. It comes out a little sharper than I mean, but whatever. I was feeling great until they brought this up.

"Well, that's good—and we absolutely love this year's program by the way," Mom says sweetly, making an obvious effort to change the subject to something more uplifting. "Your costumes are gorgeous and I thought the whole dancing across the stars motif was brilliant. I can't wait to see how it evolves over the season."

"Yep, very impressive," Dad agrees. "Andrew's really challenging you guys with some complex choreography this year. Once you get all that locked down I think you're going to have one hell of a show on your hands."

"Thanks," I mumble.

"And you know, Ethan," Dad begins and I can already tell from his tone what he's about to say, "if you're having trouble with a couple of tosses, we can spend some time in the back yard going over—"

"I can handle it, Dad." I've seriously reached my limit with this for the night. "I'm kind of tired. Can we talk about this later?"

He puts up his hands in a *whoa there* gesture and nods, but he doesn't say anything else, thank God. I know they mean well, but I am perfectly capable of doing this on my own. I don't need or want their help.

"Sure, honey," Mom says.

I mouth an exasperated, "Thank you," and turn to leave.

I'm halfway up the stairs when Mom adds, "Oh, and your dad and I have to go into the office tomorrow to run some tests, so you're on your own for food, but I made sure the fridge is stocked."

Really? On a Sunday? Of course they are. Whatever. "Okay, fine. Goodnight."

"Goodnight," I hear them say in unison as I shut my bedroom door behind me.

I flop onto my bed and let out a long exhale. I don't think I realized how completely exhausted I am until just this second. Even my hair feels tired. What a fucking rollercoaster of a day this has been. But even with all the shitty downsides, the upsides with Danny? Oh, my God, so worth it.

I close my eyes and picture myself back on that hilltop with him, replay the memory of his soft lips brushing mine. It sets off a pulse that radiates from my ribcage, making me shiver as the sensation rushes down my arms and legs, leaving behind a tingly, ticklish feeling that literally makes me giggle out loud.

Suddenly, I'm not so tired anymore.

I open the House Bitchindor group text thread on my phone and start typing.

Me: **You awake?**

Navi: **I am now.**

Me: **Good!!! I have news.**

Me: **Ducking amazing news.**

Me: *****ducking!**

Me: **GODDAMNIT!** [angry face emoji, angry face emoji]

Me: *****Fucking amazing news.**

Navi: [skull emoji, duck emoji, skull emoji, duck emoji]

Micaela: **It's 1 in the morning!** [angry face emoji] **I'm shooting a makeup tutorial first thing tomorrow.**

Micaela: **If I wake up with bags under my eyes I swear to Goddess I will lose my shit. Someone better be dying.**

Me: **Sorry! No. But it's important.**

Navi: **Apparently it's** [duck emoji] **ing amazing.**

Micaela: **Oh, well in that case.** [sends a GIF of Rihanna rolling her eyes]

Me: **You know what? I can't even be bothered to respond to your bitter bait because**

Me: **WE KISSED!!!!!!!!**

Navi: **OMG! Ethan I'm so happy for you!**

Micaela: **Me too. But just a kiss is not worthy of a 1AM text.**

Me: **Well it was more than just 1 kiss.**

Navi: **Like how much more?**

Me: [Two men kissing emoji, two men kissing emoji, two men kissing emoji, two men kissing emoji, two men kissing emoji, two men kissing emoji, two men kissing emoji, two men kissing emoji, two men kissing emoji, two men kissing emoji, two men kissing emoji,]

Micaela: **Okay. Happy for you. But I'm going back to bed now.**

Me: **Wait. There's more.**

Micaela: **Unless you're about to tell me you [eggplant emoji, eggplant emoji] it can wait until morning.**

Navi: **Don't let her kill your joy. She's probably just pissy cuz her parents made Liam go home and she didn't get to ride the boyfriend train tonight. But I'm here for you.**

Micaela: **Bitch, you don't know my life.**

Me: **ANYWAY!!!!**

Me: **He invited me over next Sunday for a movie night at his house.**

Me: **With his friends.**

Me: **AND HIS PARENTS!**

Navi: **[exploding head emoji]**

Micaela: **Okay, this just got 1AM worthy.**

Me: **I know!!! I'm kind of freaking out about it.**

Navi: **Sounds kind of weird. Did it seem like he was moving you to the friendzone?**

Me: **I don't think so. Since our guard has a late show next Saturday, Sunday was our only option to hang out. He already had his thing planned. Then invited me to join. But that's a good thing, right?**

Micaela: **Definitely a good thing. Maybe a little strange, but mainly sweet. Congrats, honey. It sounds like this guy really likes you. Don't fuck it up.**

Navi: **Shit! Sorry, Ethan. I totally forgot to text you our score from earlier.**

Micaela: **Girl, nobody cares about that right now.**

Me: **Girl, that's the last thing I want to think about right now.**

Me: **But what was it?**

Navi: **78.2**

Me: **We're usually around an 80 at our first show. That seems kind of low.**

Navi: **It is. But Andrew said everything will work itself out next week.**

Micaela: **Okay, love you both, but the only numbers I care about right now are the ones on my clock telling me it's too late to be talking about this shit. Officially going back to sleep now.**

Navi: **Okay, okay. Sorry. Going back to bed too. And congrats again, Ethan. Sounds like next weekend is going to be a busy one. [winking face with tongue emoji, face blowing a kiss emoji]**

Me: **Hope so. And thank you both. [hugging face emoji] I think I'm really, really, really starting to like this guy.**

Chapter Nine

Danny

A few days ago, I Googled "best ways to find your birth mother" and came across a pretty interesting thread on Reddit. It was between a bunch of adoptees like me who were sharing the experiences they had searching for their own bio parents.

Some people had zero luck and eventually gave up while others said they did more complicated things like hiring private investigators. Then I saw this one dude who said he'd found his birth father using a home DNA test, which seemed as legit a place as any to start. So, I picked two of the highest rated services and ordered test kits from AncestryDNA and 23andMe.

They arrived yesterday (Thanks Amazon two-day shipping!) and I spent the morning hiding in my room, secretly spitting saliva into plastic bottles, so I could mail the tests back before rehearsal.

When I dropped them off at the post office, I figured that would be the end of it for a few weeks while I waited on the results. Out of sight, out of mind, you know? Full disclosure, though, it kind of put me in a weird headspace.

I'm super glad we didn't have a competition last night because I couldn't really focus during rehearsal. I kept thinking about things like what I'd say to my birth mother if I really did find her? And how would I tell my dads? Would I just be like, "Hey guys, wish me luck. I'm off to meet my mom!" And should I even call her Mom in that situation or would Ana be more appropriate?

Also, if I did meet her, what would she think of me? Would she be cool with knowing her son likes dudes? I mean, she'd agreed to let Dad and Pop adopt me, so I assume she's cool with queer people. But what if she, like, joined some crazy conservative Christian church or became a right-wing, MAGA-loving homophobe? What would I say then?

All day, my mind just kept spiraling like that. Then, right when we started our final run-through at the end of rehearsal, I found myself actually daydreaming about how it would feel to look up in the stands during a competition and see my mom in the audience.

That tied my stomach right up in knots. Kind of pissed me off too. Thinking thoughts like that doesn't exactly get you ready to nail your best run. I should know better.

Let's be real—the chances of me finding anything out this way are super slim. It's only going to work if she's also done one of the same tests I did, and even then, I may not learn much more than what I already know.

Then again, it's also possible I could find a connection to some other branch of my family tree that eventually leads to her.

Or I may learn nothing at all.

Ugh. See, here I go again, getting way ahead of myself. I've gotta stop. A person could go crazy thinking about all these possibilities.

Bottom line is I have no idea what I'm going to find out, so I can't be getting my hopes up. For now, it's just best not to think about it—especially not on what could be the greatest Best Worst Movie Night of all time. *I hope.*

"Danny, can I get your help with something real quick?" I hear Dad call from the kitchen.

"One sec," I say as I finish putting on deodorant for the third freaking time. Seriously. The front of the container claims this stuff is supposed to have "clinical strength sweat block," but it feels like it ain't doin' shit. I hate, hate, hate how much I sweat when I'm nervous, and this might be the most nervous I've ever been.

Ethan Decker is going to be in my house ... with my parents ... and my best friends. All at the same time.

The thought makes my heart jump into my throat. I made everyone swear to me—under penalty of death—that they will NOT do anything to embarrass me tonight. But we're talking Sanjay, Conner, and my dads, so, who knows?

I take a deep breath and tell my reflection in the bathroom mirror, "It's going to be awesome. It's going to be awesome. It's going to be awesome." Then, I slowly exhale.

"Danny," Dad impatiently repeats.

"Coming," I say, doing another (last one, swear to God) hair check before hurrying down the hall. I slide into the kitchen, making an overdramatic entrance like I'm in Pop's favorite old Tom Cruise movie. I can't pull it off nearly as well, but when my parents both stop what they're doing around the kitchen island and crack up, I instantly feel my shoulders relax a bit.

"You are such a ham," Dad says, shaking his head as he resumes arranging something on a tray.

"If anyone would know, babe," Pop teases Dad before giving me a quick once-over. "Lookin' sharp there, Danny-boy. I'm likin' the short-sleeve black button-up. Simple. Classic. Good choice."

Dad cups the side of his mouth with one hand and whisper yells to Pop, "And it's only the fifth time he's changed his shirt."

Pop leans in closer to Dad, playing along. "I thought it was the sixth."

"Uh, hello. I'm right here," I say. "And please, promise you won't call me 'Danny-boy' in front of

Ethan."

He gives me a cheesy army salute and grins. "You got it, Dan-O."

I drop my chin at him. "Can you not?"

"Relax. I promise I'll make sure he behaves," Dad says, gesturing to the cabinets behind him. "Now, can you grab the small square plates off the top shelf and put them on the table for me? We're setting up buffet style, so just place them on the end, please. It'll help you work off some of that nervous energy."

"I'm not nervous," I lie, as I open the cabinet.

Pop chuckles and I can practically hear Dad's smirk as he says, "Mmm hmm."

Pretending I didn't hear that last part, I take the plates to the kitchen table and my eyes go wide when I see what they've set up. It's not just an impressive spread of Japanese food. In addition to the perfectly arranged trays of sushi rolls, pot stickers, and various appetizers, they've also set out a small bonsai tree in a ceramic pot as a centerpiece.

When it comes to throwing dinner parties, let me tell you, my dads do not mess around.

"Did you make all this food, Dad? It looks so good," I say, setting the plates down. I notice the usual wooden chopsticks we use for meals like this have been replaced with plastic ones shaped like samurai swords.

He walks in carrying a small tray of California rolls and sets it in the one remaining empty spot on the table. "Oh, God no. I'm a little embarrassed to say it's all takeout this time. But I'm afraid it would require a bit more skill than I gained from that two-week sushi making class last year to pull all this together."

I hold up one of the sword chopsticks and give it a judgmental frown. "I take it these were Pop's idea?"

Dad rolls his eyes and waves a hand through the

air dismissively. "I know. I tried to tell him they were overkill, but he insisted they went perfectly with the theme of the movie."

"What? Come on. They do," Pop says, clearly amused, as he puts a small pile of paper napkins next to the stack of plates on the table. He makes a big show of fanning them out so we notice the cherry blossom artwork printed on them. "And any theme worth doing is worth overdoing, right?"

I offer him an arched eyebrow. "Now I'm almost afraid to ask which—wait. Swear to God, Pop, if you picked that stupid Tom Cruise samurai movie for us to watch tonight..." I finish my half-hearted warning by wagging the sword-shaped chopstick at him. He cracks up and snatches it out of my hand.

"Don't worry," Pop assures me. "We've got the cheesiest of cheesy '80s action flicks on deck. The guys are gonna love—"

The doorbell rings and it's as if I'm on a roller coaster, careening over that first big drop, a thrilling mixture of fear and excitement speeding through my body. "I'll get it," I say in a surprisingly high-pitched voice and bullet over to the door before either of my parents can answer it. I take a deep breath, pausing just long enough to compose myself before pulling it open.

Ethan and I have been texting back and forth all week with no shortage of things to talk about. But when I see him, standing on our front porch, smiling that perfect Ethan-smile of his, it's like I can't get my mouth to form words.

"Hi," Ethan says.

My eyes instantly start studying the sight of him, tracing every curve and line. They follow the map of freckles on his neck, leading down to the smooth skin of his chest peeking out below his collar. I want to undo the buttons on his shirt and find the treasure buried underneath.

"Hey," I finally manage, reminding myself to stop staring like a creeper. It's just, *damn*, between his deep red hair and bright pink shirt, he looks so beautiful, like a sunset come to life. Also, incredibly hot. Definitely. Ethan is super, crazy, scorching hot right now. I shake my head and wave him inside. "Come in."

I lead him to the living room where my parents immediately swoop in to greet us.

"Well, hello there. You must be Ethan," Dad says, extending his hand and I low-key cringe. Somehow, I'd failed to notice earlier that he has on his Wonder Woman cooking apron—the one where it's full-on her body from the neck down printed on the front. So, yeah. Dad's head on an Amazon's body. Great. Just how I always pictured introducing him to the first guy I bring over.

"Nice to meet you, sir," Ethan says, shaking Dad's hand.

"Please, call me Glenn," Dad says.

"Sure thing, Mr. Gle—um, I mean, Glenn," Ethan says, and I'm just now realizing he seems a little nervous too. "I, uh, love your apron, by the way. Next to Scarlet Witch, Wonder Woman is my favorite superhero."

Dad does what Pop calls his "gay gasp" and grins. "Well, you are going to get along famously in this house." He turns to me and says, "I like this one already."

My face gets toasty. "Okay, then," I say, butting in, gesturing to Pop. "And this is my other dad, Clayton."

They exchange handshakes and hellos. Then Pop starts in with, "Well, Ethan," and I can already tell by his corny, game-show-host tone that this is headed in a bad direction, "if you like fun movies about strong female superheroes, I think you're gonna love the one we're watching tonight."

"Oh, yeah? What's it about?" Ethan asks.

"In *Ninja 3: The Domination*," Pop begins, shifting from game-show host to movie-trailer-announcer, "the spirit of an evil ninja possesses the body of an innocent aerobics instructor, transforming her into a lethal assassin." He emphasizes the last two words with the sword-chopstick that's still in his hand, swirling the tip in a circle at Ethan and then stabbing the empty air in front of him.

Ethan politely laughs, but I literally facepalm and mumble, "Jesus, Pop."

Fortunately, Dad quickly intervenes. "Hey, honey, let's not give away any spoilers now. How about we finish getting dinner ready and let these boys catch up?"

Pop agrees. Dad ushers him out of the room before he can reenact any more scenes and my next breath comes a little easier.

"Sorry about that," I say when they're out of earshot. "My parents can be a bit much sometimes."

Ethan shrugs. "Oh, no worries. They're great."

"Yeah. Great," I say flatly.

He smiles a perfect Ethan-smile, then I do too, and when our eyes connect there's this honest-to-God tugging sensation in my chest, like a magnetic field has turned on between us.

"Anyway," I say, looking down at my feet to make sure they're not actually sliding across the floor toward him. "Shall I give you the tour?"

Ethan raises his eyebrows and his smile grows wider.

Chapter Ten

Ethan

This might sound kind of lame, but as Danny shows me around his place, I feel so seen. Okay, maybe not *seen* so much as *inspired*.

I mean, I've watched TV shows about families with queer parents. My love of *The Fosters* was a borderline-obsession for a little while. But there's something about actually being in the real home of a real married gay couple, raising a real family, that makes me stand a little taller.

And yeah, I know, things like that aren't supposed to matter, and I'd never say this to anyone out loud, but the family photos and vacation snapshots that line the walls here, they remind me that the future I dream of really is possible—and not just on TV.

Also, I love getting a peek at all these pictures of Danny that he'd probably never share on Instagram. Can I just say, baby Danny and his dads? Adorbs.

"And this is my room," Danny announces as I follow him inside.

I catch a whiff of his cologne and the scent instantly fires up memories from last week of Danny's arms wrapped around me with his lips pressed against mine. I'm sure that's why the first thing my eyes are drawn to is his bed and then my pervy brain immediately starts picturing all the things we could do there.

And now it suddenly feels way warmer in here.

I hear the door click closed behind me and force my eyes elsewhere, ignoring his bed for now, as I take in the rest of his room—the dark wood desk and bookshelves, the baseball bat-shaped hat rack on one wall, an old-school *Star Wars* poster on another.

"Cute," I say, trying not to sound like my pulse has been beating double-time since the second I walked in here.

"Thanks," Danny says. "Oh, and check it out." He taps buttons on a wall panel next to his door, diming the overhead light and turning on a continuous strip of blue LEDs that outline the ceiling. "I installed these not too long ago. Even wired the light-switch panel myself."

"I'm impressed," I say.

Danny grins shyly. "No big deal, really. I just watched a couple of tutorials on TikTok."

"Yeah, well, I'd probably end up electrocuting myself if I tried something like that," I say, continuing to look around. A framed photo on his desk catches my attention and I pick it up for a closer look. Danny and two other guys are wearing cool black and red winter guard costumes and the biggest smiles. "Is this from WGI last year?"

"Yup," Danny says, walking over to me. "That's me, Sanjay, and Conner—the other guys you'll meet tonight." He points out each of his friends in the photograph. "This was taken right after we found out we made finals."

"No wonder you all look so happy," I say.

Danny laughs lightly to himself. "Yeah, plus our semi-finals performance that day was, like, our best of the season."

I can practically feel the joy radiating from him right now and, honestly, I think I'm a little jealous. Now, don't get it twisted, winning world championships is pretty damn exciting. But the last couple of years, what I feel most at times like that isn't so much joyfulness as relief.

I mean, even at last night's competition, our guard

totally redeemed ourselves with a strong performance, and when we were announced in first place, all I could think was that our score should've been higher than an 80.1.

Seeing the light in Danny's eyes, the smiles on the faces of the three boys in the picture I'm holding, it's obvious that moment wasn't tainted with expectations or tons of pressure for them to "make history" or anything. It was just pure happiness. That's got to be an amazing feeling.

"Do you have a video?" I ask, placing the photo back on his desk.

"Of semis? Of course." Danny says.

"Want to show me?"

"Now?"

"Yeah, why not? I've seen your finals performance on YouTube before, but if you say your semis run was your best, I'd love to watch it with you."

Danny's face lights up. He shrugs and says, "Sure." He grabs his laptop off his desk, sits on the foot of his bed, and motions for me to join him there. The second I do I can feel the tips of my ears and nose heat up, because, well, *hello*, you already know what I'm thinking.

I scoot right up next to him. An electric current runs through me when our legs and shoulders touch and I have to bite my lower lip to keep from giggling out loud. Being this close to Danny makes me feel kind of euphoric. But also, it's funny. Of all the things I pictured us doing on his bed, watching a winter guard video together wasn't one of them.

"Hey, so, I just want to remind you we're not, like, Landon High School good or anything," Danny says, turning to look at me.

God, the apprehensive expression on his face is so

cute it nearly kills me.

"Stop," I say, playfully bumping his shoulder. "I want to see. Really."

Danny looks directly into my eyes, then his gaze slides down to my mouth, holding there for a few seconds before he turns his attention back to his laptop. "All right," he says, grinning. He types in his password, unlocking the computer, and the Ancestry.com website fills the screen. Near the top of the page it reads "Hello, Danny" along with a prompt to build his family tree.

"Oh, cool," I say. "My family did that same DNA tes—"

Danny inhales sharply and jolts upright. He quickly closes the browser and whips his head in the direction of his bedroom door. He seems a little panicked, like he's just seen a ghost or something.

"You okay?" I ask

Danny swallows hard. "Yeah," he says, tone clipped, still looking at his closed door.

"Should I—"

"No, no, you're fine," he says, turning back to me, then under his breath he adds, "Didn't mean to leave that up."

"Sorry," I say, shaking my head. "What?"

Danny's shoulders relax as he exhales slowly. "Remember when I said I started looking for my birth mom?" His voice is barely above a whisper.

"Yeah," I say, still confused.

"Well, this is part of that." He taps his laptop with his thumb. "And I don't want to tell, you know," he jabs the same thumb toward his door, "unless there ends up being a reason to."

"Oh," I say, finally putting it all together. Wow, I am so slow. He's trying to keep this quiet and the second I see it, I nearly announced it to the whole house. "I am so, so sorry, Danny. I didn't mean—"

"You didn't know. It's all good, really," Danny says. "Look, I know I sort of freaked out there for a sec, but seriously, I don't mind. It's kind of nice to tell someone, actually. Well, it's nice to tell *you*." He glances away and that damn self-conscious smile of his burrows into my chest.

His words hang in the air as I nod over and over, trying to think of something to say, because how should you respond to something like that? I'm used to meeting boys who use fake names on their profiles and can't admit out loud that they like dudes, even after they've made out with you. But Danny is something altogether different.

He turns back to me, his expression more serious now. "But just you. I'm not ready to say anything to anyone else about that yet. Cool?"

"Yeah, totally. Lips sealed," I assure him, making a motion like I'm zipping my mouth closed.

With a sly grin, Danny says, "Well … let's not get crazy now." He reaches up, pretends to undo the imaginary zipper across my lips, and raises his eyebrows suggestively.

Oh, I know exactly how I'm responding to that.

I place my hand across the back of his neck, gently pull him to me. He pushes his laptop aside and then his mouth is on mine, body pressing into me, guiding me to lie back on his bed. There's almost none of the clumsiness between us from before. This time, our hips, hands, lips and tongues all seem to know where to go, how to dance together, and I love how this all feels so familiar and still unlike anything else I've experienced in my life.

Danny's mouth moves from my lips to my chin, over the line of my jaw, then down, down, where he whispers my name into my neck, melting me into a puddle beneath him. This feels so right it almost hurts and a need for more, more, more is consuming every part of me. God, I could do this with him all day, all night, all week, and it still wouldn't be enough. But then I hear the doorbell ring and I know it'll have to be for now.

"My friends have the worst timing," Danny groans, head hovering over me. He lets out a frustrated sigh. The spot where he was kissing my neck tingles as his cool breath rushes over my skin, leaving traces of mint mouthwash in the air.

I smile, surveying Danny's features, and when our eyes lock, I think how much I'd love to wake up next to him, have his face be the first thing I see in the morning. That's not a thought I've ever had about anyone and it fills me with a strange syrupy sensation.

The doorbell rings again. Danny rolls off me, vaults from the bed, and opens his door just as I hear one of his parents call out, "Danny. Sanjay and Conner are here."

"Okay, one sec," he hollers back, then gives me another self-conscious grin, blushing as he impatiently bounces on his toes. Now my cheeks are totally heating up too because I know exactly what he's doing, and yeah, I could also use a few seconds for a certain body part to calm down.

A long moment later, I follow Danny into his living room where his friends are waiting. I immediately recognize them from their photo. As Danny walks in, Sanjay says, "There you are. We were beginning to wonder what you were doing back there." When he sees me file into the room behind Danny, he purses his lips, folds his arms, and adds, "Or should I say *who* were you doing back there?"

"Um … uh," I sputter.

Danny sucks his teeth loudly and backhands his friend's bicep. "Stupid. Shut up," he whisper-yells, then looks around as if he's worried his parents may have overheard.

"Ow," Sanjay exclaims, rubbing his arm. "Really, bitch? One afternoon of passion with the enemy and you're already hate-criming your sister?" He delivers that line with all the drama of a drag queen. Everything about what he said is so shocking, so unexpected, I'm genuinely surprised at the size of the laugh that busts out of me.

"Ignore him, dude. He's obviously off his meds again," Conner says, extending his hand and introducing himself.

I grab his palm, shake it. "Hi, I'm—"

"Ethan," Conner finishes. "We know. We're all big Landon Winter Guard stans here, despite what some people pretend." He smirks at Sanjay.

"Bitch, please. He knows I'm just kidding," he says, then sings, "And everyone loves a winner." Sanjay leans in closer to me, conspiratorially, and adds, "Especially that one there." His eyes dance over to Danny.

I can't tell if he's trying to be funny or shady.

"Dude, seriously?" Danny says, readying another backhand, but this time he's smiling.

Sanjay squeals, "JK, JK—sort of." He throws his arms around me and says, "I'm a hugger, not a fighter."

"Oh, wow, uh, okay, hi," I say, limply hugging him back.

Over my shoulder, Sanjay announces, "And no, Conner, I already told you, I don't hug straight boys, so stop asking."

"Yeah, I'm good. Thanks," Conner says flatly. "How about next time you catch that saber seven you dropped in rehearsal today and we'll call it even?"

Sanjay gasps. "How dare you," he says, indignant, and then hisses, actually hisses, like a cat.

Everyone laughs, myself included, but it's uncomfortable at first. Then Sanjay releases me, drops his extra energy, and sincerely says, "Nice to me you, girl."

It dawns on me that, in some ways, Danny's friendship with these guys is a lot like mine with Micaela and Navi. We all love to tease each other, but at the end of the day, nobody means anything by it.

"Thanks. You too," I say, deciding everyone here is what Navi would call "good people" after all.

"All right, boys, who's hungry?" one of Danny's dads calls from the kitchen. "Come and get it."

"Hell, yeah," Conner says, as he and Sanjay bounce out of the room, play-pushing one another.

The look Danny gives me is one hundred percent apology. I smile back at him, letting him know all this is totally fine with me. We follow his friends into the kitchen and my eyes widen when I see what his parents have prepared.

"*Oh*, category is ... Sushi Extravaganza," Sanjay exclaims. "This is gorge. Tens across the board."

He's not kidding. Everything looks delicious, plates of assorted sashimi, fried tempura, nigari, California rolls, tuna rolls, dragon rolls (my favorite), and other things I can never pronounce correctly. It's all beautifully arranged with tiny ceramic soy sauce dishes shaped like fish and a row of little plastic swords like the one Danny's dad, Clayton, was playing around with earlier—which I now realize are chopsticks. Super cute.

"You're too kind," Danny's other dad, Glenn, says as he curtseys.

"*Yaass*, honey, and extra points for these." Sanjay picks up one of the chopsticks, pretends to spin it like a saber for a few counts.

"You kids crack me up," Clayton says, chuckling, then he turns to Glenn. "See, I told you those would be a hit."

Glenn rolls his eyes.

"Well, don't be shy. Fill your plates and grab your seats in the living room, boys. We'll start the show in about five minutes," Clayton says.

We dig in. I thoughtfully choose each piece I take, remembering Micaela's advice about dinner dates where you meet someone's parents for the first time: *Don't eat so much you look like a pig or so little that you look like a picky bitch. Keep it balanced.*

"So, Ethan, how is your team doing this year?" Glenn asks.

"Great," I say. "Our first competition was a little rough, but we all felt good about the performance we had last night."

"Yo, you guys were sick, man," Conner says, placing two tuna roll pieces on his plate. "We caught a video of that performance this morning."

"Thanks. I'm so glad you all saw that one, 'cause the first show we had…" I wrinkle my nose, then give Danny a grin, thinking about how sweet he was trying to cheer me up that night.

"Well, Conner and I checked it out, but Danny has this rule. He refuses to watch his favorite guard on video until he's seen your show live at least once," Sanjay says, dramatically dropping a dragon roll piece on his plate.

"We're your favorite guard?" I ask Danny, trying and failing to hold back an enormous smile.

Danny's face goes bright red.

Conner snorts. "For real. We're scheduled to perform *after* you guys in prelims at the regional next week, and dude, you should've seen Danny's face when he realized he wouldn't get to watch Landon." His expression wilts and he sticks out his lower lip.

"Shit, you should've seen *my face*," Sanjay says, frowning. His tone is more serious now. "I don't understand why performance order for prelims has to be a random draw at regionals. Nobody wants to go on after the six-time world champions, girl. You're gonna set the gym on fire before we even get in there. It's so not fair."

Normally, I love being in the spotlight, but this is starting to feel uncomfortable.

"I'm sure you guys are going to be amazing," I say, a little too enthusiastically, and then immediately try to change the subject. "So, the movie tonight sounds like fun."

"Oh, it's a riot," Clayton says. "An unintentionally funny cult classic—and it's starting in T-minus sixty seconds, boys, so *chop, chop.*" He holds up a pair of chopsticks in one hand and pinches the air with them twice, making the plastic tips click.

It's such a goofy dad joke, I can't help but laugh. Everyone does a little, except for Danny.

"Ugh, Pop," he groans, obviously embarrassed, which ... *aww.*

"I'll bet you've been waiting all day to make that joke, haven't you?" Glenn says, shaking his head.

Clayton shrugs, whistling an innocent tune, as he strolls out of the kitchen.

The couch in the living room is a large sectional, arranged in a U shape around a circular coffee table. It's set up in a way that makes it look more like three little couches (love seats, I think they're called), broken up by two end tables where each section meets. Danny insists we take the middle section while his dads sit at the one on the left, leaving the one on the right for Sanjay and

Conner.

When the movie begins, Danny bumps my leg with his and I become acutely aware that, with everyone's eyes on the TV at the other end, he's fixed it so we actually have the one seat in the room with a little bit of privacy. I mean, it's not like we can pick up where we left off in his bedroom or anything, but it's enough that a foot tap here and a shoulder bump there go unnoticed by anyone else.

At first, I'm a little freaked out, because, come on, other people (his parents) are right there. But soon it becomes kind of thrilling, us playing this flirty game of tag on the DL between bites of sushi.

After everyone has finished eating, Glenn turns off the lights, I assume so it'll be easier to watch the rest of movie, but I'm not really paying much attention to what's happening onscreen. Danny and I are sitting right next to each other, not touching, not touching, not touching, and I've never been so aware of someone's body heat before.

He inches closer and the space between us hums with energy. I wonder if anyone else can hear it? I adjust my weight, scoot closer. My skin crackles. Shit, the anticipation is almost unbearable. Danny's finger brushes against my hand. Sparks fly from the point of contact.

Maybe it's the darkened room or the fear of getting caught—not that I think anyone here would really care—I don't know, but this feels so different from our game of tag minutes ago. Way more intense.

I inhale quietly, trying to get my pounding heart under control, then Danny slips his hand into mine and lightning strikes me dead. So dead. The deadest dead and the most *alive* I've ever been.

Then something amazing and strange happens. It's like a wave, a cool, calming wave, that washes over us as Danny relaxes into me. I exhale, slowly, loving the sensation, like the sides of our bodies are melding together.

We stay like this, unmoving, and as much as I wish we were alone, kissing in his bedroom again, in a weird way, this feels so much more … intimate. I don't think I've ever even used that word before, but I don't know how else to explain it, except maybe, that for the rest of the movie, it's as if something inside us has synced.

"That was awesome," Conner says when the credits begin to roll.

Danny releases my hand and sits up straight, and I do the same as Glenn turns the lights back on.

"Holy shit, that scene where the ninja's sword was floating around her in circles? I was like, yes, bitch, get it with your fierce saber choreography!" Sanjay says.

"Oh, my God, I was thinking the same thing!" I say, and we all crack up.

"I'm glad you boys enjoyed the movie," Clayton says. He gets up and begins clearing dishes off the coffee table, which I take as a subtle hint that we need to start wrapping things up.

"Thank you so much for inviting me to hang with you guys. I had such a great time," I say, standing up as I spread my smile around the room.

"Do you have to go now?" Danny asks. "I was—"

"Danny, it's a school night," Glenn gently warns. "We should let your friends get home at a decent hour."

"Fine," Danny sighs.

"Yeah, I've actually got a ton of homework I need to finish tonight. But seriously, dinner, everything, was just so great. Thank you."

"You're very welcome," Glenn says. "Danny will have to have you over again soon."

Why, yes, Mr. Wheeler-Hall, I would love to have your hot son invite me here again. "I'd like that."

We all finish saying our goodbyes. I get another hug from Sanjay and a fist-bump from Conner on their way out. Then Danny insists on walking me to my car. We make small talk about how nice the temperature is outside while we slowly stroll to where my Toyota Prius is parked on the street. I don't think either of us really want this night to end.

"So, about next time," Danny begins, "that is, assuming my friends and family didn't just scare you off for good and there will be a next time?" His tone is more flirty than unsure.

"I think it's safe to say that's definitely going to happen," I say, trying to match his flirty pitch.

Danny's eyes twinkle. The straight line of his lips becomes a curve. "That's good to know." He studies my face for a few seconds before he adds, "This week?"

"Argh, this week is going to be tough," I say, scrunching up my face. Landon is a little over an hour away from East Valley. Just far enough to make it a bit harder to hang during the week when you've gotta get up early the next morning. "Andrew always adds an extra night of rehearsal the week of a regional, so we'll have Monday, Wednesday, *and Friday* night booked."

"Well, we'll both be at the same show Saturday," Danny offers.

"Yes, we will," I say, playfully. Then an unpleasant thought slams into me. *We're going to be competing against each other.* Sanjay's comments about how unfair Saturday's performance order is, and how Landon is going to basically burn the floor before their guard gets a shot, play back in my brain. I grimace.

"What is it?" Danny asks.

I shrug. "It's just, kind of weird, knowing I'm

going up against you, your friends."

Danny chuckles. "Ethan, we've been competing in the same classification with you since our freshman year. How will Saturday be any different?"

God, I hope that didn't just make me sound super conceited, like I think we're so good I never even noticed his guard existed before. I didn't mean it like that. He's right. Don't make this weird.

I shake my head. "Right," I say, smiling as I literally wave those thoughts away.

"So, how about after finals? We can go out. Celebrate your win … and hopefully a second-place finish for East Valley too?" Danny's laugh is so sweet, so disarming, I have no choice but to do the same.

"Yeah, that'd be great," I say, feeling warm all over. "Oh, and uh, we'll have a couple hours of downtime between prelims and finals. If you'd be down to grab lunch, I'll be around." I'm so glad that came out as cool and casual sounding as it did, because inside I am squealing with excitement.

"So, two dates on Saturday, huh?" Danny says, beaming. "Sounds perfect."

Chapter Eleven

Danny

God, I love show days. From the minute you wake up, it's like you're running on supreme gasoline. Today isn't just any old show day, though. It's the West Regional and, oh man, right now I'm feeling like the stuff pumping through my body could fly me to Mars—for a couple of reasons.

First, East Valley Winter Guard just killed it in prelims competition. *Killed it.* I knew we were going to do it too. Our rehearsal earlier this morning was laser-focused and everyone's energy was through the freakin' roof. When you start the day off that hyped, you know you're gonna serve up something good.

"Slow down, girl. They probably don't even have our score posted yet," Sanjay says, trying to keep pace with my sprint across the parking lot of Buchanan High School, the location of today's big competition.

"That's not why he's suddenly in such a hurry," Conner teases.

"Let me guess; does that reason start with an E?" Sanjay asks. I don't need to see him to know he's totally rolling his eyes right now.

"It could be both," I say.

It's not. Not exactly.

Of course, I want to see the number we got. I'm the one who suggested we bounce as soon as we had everything loaded back on the equipment truck. But, yeah, okay, fine. Maybe the bigger reason I'm in such a rush to get over there is because I got a text from Ethan letting me know that's where he's at.

I've been living for his texts this week, especially

all the pictures and videos he's been sending. Mostly G-rated, but there've been a few not-so-innocent ones too. Still, though, as nice as it's been getting to know him one message at a time, viewing selfies I know he snapped just for me, I'm seriously dying to see that face of his in real life again.

"Bitch, that boy has got you dickmatised already," Sanjay says.

"Does not," I say defensively.

"Really? Then why are we running?"

I slow down and try not to let it show that I'm breathing a little heavier as we near the gym.

"Mmm hmm," Sanjay says, "that's what I thought."

Shaking my head, I mumble, "Whatever."

"Hey, no shame here," Sanjay says, his voice raising in pitch and volume. "We all get hypnotized by the D sometimes."

Conner clears his throat loudly.

"Or the V," Sanjay adds.

It's at this exact moment, an older woman—who I'm positive is the mother of someone here—comes around the nearest corner of the gym. She gives us a dirty look, making it clear she overheard a little more of our conversation than she should've. Sanjay's lack of inside voice is a serious problem sometimes.

Conner and I drop our heads in embarrassment, but, naturally, you-know-who does the exact opposite.

"Please, Miss Karen over there, lookin' at us like she's never been thirsty a day in her life," Sanjay says, all indignant. Then, even louder, he adds, "She knows what I'm talkin' about!"

"The fuck, man?" Conner says at the same time I grumble, "Dumbass," and our steps get faster. I can hear Sanjay behind us, cackling at our discomfort, but by the time we're walking though the main entrance, we're all cracking up about it.

Inside the gym, there's a large foyer twice the size of the one at our high school. The air is thick with the smell of popcorn and nacho cheese coming from a snack bar at one end of the room. At the other, a big crowd has gathered around three poster-sized printouts that list all the guards performing today—the scoreboard.

See, at regular competitions, you do your thing and at the end of the show there's an awards ceremony. Scores are announced, trophies are handed out, and that's it. But at regionals, every team is ranked in prelims first. Only a few guards in each class get to advance to finals.

Throughout the morning, every three to five performances, an official comes out here and writes a few more scores in the blank boxes by each group's name.

If you were to just hang out in this spot all day, you'd catch a whole different kind of show with people crying, cheering or getting all pissed depending on the number they get. Trust me, it can be a real fuckin' nail-biter if you're one of the groups whose ass is on the line, waiting to find out if you make finals or not—particularly in the A and Open classes where there are a lot more groups competing.

"Danny!" I don't think I'll ever get tired of hearing that voice say my name.

My eyes immediately find Ethan. His smile is so bright it stands out like a flare above the crowd.

I'm moving before my brain even sends the signal, swimming through the sea of people, scooping him up off the floor into the biggest bear hug. Ethan makes a small surprised noise as I spin him around, and then we're laughing and he feels so good in my arms.

The tank-top style of both our costumes exposes our arms and a bit of our chests near our collarbones. I squeeze him tighter, loving the skin-to-skin contact, breathing in the smell of him—a sweet mixture of sweat and fruit-scented hairspray—before returning his feet to the ground.

"Well, hello there," Ethan says, breathless and beaming.

My heart is like a caged animal, clawing at my ribs. "Hi," I say, grinning.

"Hey, girl, hey," Sanjay says in a blasé tone, appearing beside us with Conner, who throws Ethan a what's-up nod.

"Hey guys," Ethan says, giving them both quick hugs. "A few of us tried to get back here to see your show, but by the time we got our stuff put away, it was too late. How'd it go?"

"Oh, we delivered the goods," Sanjay says, pretending to toss and catch a saber.

"Nice," Ethan exclaims and gives him a high-five.

"Yo, we didn't just deliver, we Amazon-Primed that shit," Conner says, putting his palm up for Sanjay to smack too, but he's left hanging.

Sanjay looks at him like he's from another planet and wags a finger at him instead. "Um, no. That's not a thing."

"It's okay, I totally got it," Ethan says sweetly to Conner. They bump fists.

Conner turns to Sanjay, sticks out his tongue and makes a "nah" sound, because inside my friends are both six-year-olds.

"We did awesome," I interject. "How about you?"

"A little shaky in the beginning, but overall, pretty good. Definitely room for improvement in finals tonight, though," Ethan says. "It's just," he frowns, gesturing to Landon High School's name and the 80.9 written in Sharpie next to it on the scoreboard, "the judges have been lowballing us all season. I mean, that's only eight-tenths higher than we got last week, and this year we're doing the hardest choreography we've ever done. I don't get it."

I scan all eight names of the Scholastic World Class guards on the board. Scores for three groups still haven't been posted (ours is one of them), but of the other four that have been, the closest one to Landon is still more than seven full points away.

This makes me feel confident about our chances of taking second place today, but I think about how weird this must be for Ethan and his guard. Nobody is going to get anywhere near them at this show, true, but their biggest competitors aren't here. They're at other regionals happening in other states right now.

By tomorrow morning, all the final scores from every regional will be slapped up on the WGI website, ranked in one big international list for the whole world to see. So, even though they aren't technically competing with the rest of the world today, in another way, they are. That's gotta feel like a lot of pressure.

I point to the other groups' scores on the board here, all in the low seventies. "Looks like everyone's a little low this morning. The judges are probably just being conservative in prelims. Plus, you guys went on really early. I'm sure you'll pop a bigger number in finals tonight," I say, trying to offer something helpful, as I rub his arm. I can't help it. It's impossible for me to keep my hands off him for more than two seconds.

"Hope so. By the way," Ethan says, his smile returning as his eyes move up and down my body, head to toe, "you look really good in your costume."

"Thanks." I can feel my face flush. His tone is so flirty, I have to glance down and give myself a couple seconds to absorb the compliment. "You do too."

Ethan's costume—the way it fades from dark blue at the bottom to light blue on top with tiny rhinestones all over that sparkle in the light—looks like a million bucks compared to what we're wearing.

Ours are just basic black Spandex tank unitards with custom black and red fight shorts worn over the top. I mean, we've got a few embellishments, like two big diagonal gold stripes that run down the right leg of our shorts. Anything flashier wouldn't really work with the theme of our program this year. So, they're nothing fancy—and I wish my bare shoulders looked as ripped as Conner's do in this thing—but if Ethan thinks I look good, hey, I'll take it.

"What's your show about, boxing?" Ethan asks, pointing to the red wraps around our hands, wrists and ankles.

"Close," I say. "MMA, actually."

Ethan's brow furrows. "Huh?"

"You know, mixed martial arts, Ultimate Fighting Championships, that kind of stuff," I explain quickly, suddenly wondering if he might think it's a dumb idea for a winter guard show. I'm not doing a great job describing how cool it is.

"Really?" Ethan says, sounding amused as he studies me again.

"I know, right?" Sanjay says. "Who knew we could look so butch spinning flags?"

Ethan runs a finger along the oversized red elastic waistband of my shorts. "Hot," he says, then leans in closer to me and adds, "I can't wait to see it," and I shiver because his hand is kind of close to my dick, and I'm pretty sure he's not just talking about our show.

My skin gets toasty all over. "Do you—"

"There she is. Coming through!" someone announces.

The crowd begins to murmur and we're jostled as people move to make room for the official approaching the scoreboard. A couple of girls in silver sequin costumes push past us, clearly trying to get a better look as the official starts writing. I go up on my toes, but it's impossible to see over all the craning necks.

A girl nearest the scoreboard bursts into tears, looking upset as she hugs a girl next to her whose hair is in an identical high ponytail. I'm guessing they're both members of a guard that just found out they're not making finals tonight. Sucks.

A commotion starts rippling through the people pooled around the official. Someone shouts, "Oh," and a few others gasp. I have the terrifying thought that maybe our score isn't good enough to make finals either, and now my heart is trying to kick its way out of my chest.

Then people are suddenly shouting excitedly, jumping up and down, cheering. I don't understand.

"Holy shit," Conner says as the official backs away from the scoreboard—and I can't believe what I see.

Chapter Twelve

Ethan

There must be some mistake. This can't be right. My pulse pounding, I read the numbers on the board again. They still don't make any sense. How could East Valley High School score an 81.2 when the judges only gave Landon High School—my guard—an 80.9?

Everything around me is moving in slow motion, but my mind is on fast-forward, racing faster and faster until it crashes into the answer.

Second place. We're in second place.

A girl wearing the same costume as Danny runs up to him and throws her arms around his neck. A shitty feeling stirs in my chest as I watch him spin her around like he did me minutes ago, looking way happier.

Sanjay is clinging to Conner, crying obviously joyful tears, and now they're all being mobbed by their teammates, cheering and shouting like they've just won a war. They aren't the only ones, either. Members of different guards from every class are all clapping, celebrating—not just because East Valley won, but because we lost.

Sweat trickles down my back. It suddenly feels like a spotlight has been turned on me, like I'm drowning in an ocean of staring eyes and pointing fingers. Panic floods my body. I can't breathe. But then Micaela is there, tugging my arm, pulling me back to the surface, out of the crowd, where I can fill my lungs with air again.

"Come on, Ethan," she says, deadly serious. "Andrew's called an emergency meeting. Outside. Now."

I tuck my phone inside the waistband of my costume and follow her out through a pair of doors where the rest of our guard is waiting, worked up in all kinds of emotional states. Some are crying and looking confused. Others seem totally pissed, arms crossed, practically growling every word they speak.

Navi gives me a hug the second she sees me, but neither of us says anything. I can tell she's as shell-shocked as I am.

Andrew approaches the group a few seconds later, his face an unreadable mask under his aviator sunglasses. My throat goes dry and I swallow hard, expecting we're about to get an earful from him, that he'll rip us for our less-than-perfect performance this morning, but he simply says, "Line up and come with me," and keeps walking.

We do as we're told, following him away from the activity surrounding the gym, all the way out to the edge of the football field where we're completely alone.

"Gather around," Andrew commands and then he's silent for a while. Except for a few random sniffs and fiery exhales, we all are. Finally, he continues in an oddly calm tone. "If you've got more tears you need to cry over this, get them out now. If you're pissed off and you want to scream, better let that out here too. You're not going to be any good to anybody if you're an emotional mess. So, go on. Out with it."

No one makes a sound.

"We're done then? Good. Because all I need to know is," Andrew pauses for what I'm sure is dramatic effect before continuing in a stronger voice, "are you ready to fight?"

Our answer is a unified, "Yes." We sound like an army, and in this instant, I can feel the vibe from our group begin to change, see my teammates snapping to attention like soldiers preparing for battle.

"Good. That's what I want to hear," Andrew says,

a sure smile forming on his lips. "Now, I haven't seen East Valley's show, but I already know we have a superior program. Scores were very tight and we left some points on the table this morning. But that's not going to happen tonight, is it?"

"No," most of us answer.

"What's that?" Andrew asks, cupping a hand to his ear.

This time we all respond with a resounding, "*No!*"

"That's better," he says, grinning. "So, let them have their moment, because if anyone thinks they can beat Landon in finals with the energy I'm feeling from y'all right now, I say bring it on, baby."

"Yeah!" we cheer.

I feel my chin rise higher as I scan the faces of my teammates. Our collective mood has completely transformed now. Tears have been replaced with enthusiastic grins, angry expressions eclipsed by determined ones.

This is part of what makes Andrew the best winter guard coach. With just a few words, he can put you in your place or have you believing you can conquer the world. He's right. It's like my parents were saying the other night, our show this year is complex, sophisticated. It's a beautifully designed program with a high level of difficulty. There's no way some guard doing a little show about boxing or whatever can compete with that—no matter how hot some of their members might look in their costumes.

"All right everyone, bring it in closer. Here's what we're gonna do," Andrew says and we all huddle up to hear his plan. "I've pulled some strings and booked us a private rehearsal space at a middle school nearby. Some of your parents are already heading over there to set up lunch. After you eat, we're going to rehearse for the rest of the afternoon. Then come right back here in time for warm-up. I want y'all away from distractions, completely focused for the rest of the day. Got it?"

"Got it!"

"Excellent. Gather your things quickly and efficiently. We've got a job to do. Let's show them how champions get it done," Andrew says, and then counts us down with an energetic "one, two, three!"

Punching our fists in the air we shout, "Landon," then break, totally pumped.

We begin heading back toward the gym when my phone vibrates against my hip. I pull it out of my waistband and check the new text.

Danny: **Hey, where'd you go?**

The pride that was swelling in my chest deflates. What do I even say?

Congratulations, probably, I know. Just shake his hand and tell him and his friends I'm happy for them. That would be such a lie, though. I'm not. Not even close.

Sanjay's stupid words from last week echo in my head. *Everyone loves a winner.*

I remember how Conner gushed about the video he saw of our show and the way Danny turned bright red when I found out we were his favorite winter guard. My stomach cramps. How am I going to face him after this?

And, shit, I don't even want to think about what people are going to say if our score isn't the highest in the country tonight. We've gotta fix this in finals. We have to.

I start typing a reply. Stop. Delete it. Start again. Stop and delete that too. I can't. I just can't. I can't deal with this kind of distraction right now.

Chapter Thirteen

Danny

"Don't sweat it. Maybe some shit came up," Conner says when I check my texts for the millionth time and find Ethan still hasn't replied.

It's 7:00 on the dot, and we're with the rest of our guard, hanging out near the equipment truck in the parking lot. We've gathered everything we need for finals and now we're just waiting on our coach Nikki to walk us over so we can begin warm-up.

"Yeah, we won, he mad. That's what shit came up," Sanjay says, sounding giddy. Hell, I should be too. We all should be. I mean, we won Scholastic World Class Prelims at the West Regional. Come on. How epic is that? But I'm in such a shitty mood right now.

Ethan ghosted me. He totally fucking ghosted me, and I feel so stupid I didn't put that together way earlier.

This morning, when he disappeared after scores were posted, I was like, *I get it. He needs to be with his guard for a minute. He'll get back to me. We have a lunch date.* But then lunch came and went and … nada.

All afternoon, every text I sent Ethan may as well have been shot straight into a black hole. I've gone from worried, to hurt, to pretty pissed, actually—mostly at myself right now. Because even though I swore I wouldn't message him again, I did. And, of course, still no response.

Shaking my head, I let out a frustrated sigh and lock my screen.

"Wait," Sanjay says, staring at me suspiciously. "You didn't text him *again*, did you?"

Pursing my lips, I do that thing where instead of

rolling my eyes I look up at a diagonal and hold them there for a few seconds.

"Girl," Sanjay says, sounding disappointed.

"What? All I said was, *Have a good show*."

"That does it. Give it to me," Sanjay says, thrusting an open palm at me.

"Why?"

"You know why," Sanjay says. "That boy hasn't sent you so much as an emoji all day, and here you are, texting him like some pathetic simp before finals? No, bitch. You are booked and busy." He makes a gimmie motion with his fingers.

"I'm not a—" I start to say, but then Conner gives me his exasperated *just do it already* look, and I shut up. "Fine." I pass my phone to Sanjay.

He powers it down, passes it back and says, "There, problem solved. Now don't turn it back on until after the show."

"Yeah, he ain't worried about you. So why are you stressin' over him?" Conner asks, then runs a palm across the side of his head in a smooth motion and adds, "You gotta play it cool like I do with the ladies, man."

Sanjay and I look at each other and snort at the same time. The absolute last thing Conner is with *the ladies* is cool. If he gets within five feet of a girl he's into, he becomes a clammed-up ball of awkward who can barely string a sentence together.

"Whatever, dicks," Conner says, grinning sheepishly while half-heartedly flipping us a middle finger. This time we all laugh. I can feel my shoulders relax for the first time in hours.

"All right, all right," I say, making a big show of slipping my phone into my jacket pocket. "See, out of sight, out of mind." If only it really were that easy.

Sanjay exhales dramatically and says, "Fucking

finally."

"Hey, West Regional Prelims Champions. You ready to give these people a show?" Nikki says, beaming as she approaches us.

We respond with affirmative cheers as we group up around her.

"Listen, before we begin, I just want to say once again how proud I am of you guys. You absolutely crushed it this morning," Nikki says, applauding and we all cheer a bit louder. "Now whatever happens tonight, whatever score those judges give you, I want you to know if you go out there and have the kind of performance you had in prelims, I don't care what place you get, you've already won in my book." There's a glimmer in her eyes and her smile grows larger as she adds, "And don't forget to have some fun while you're at it!"

My chest is fizzing with all the feels as I join in with my teammates, roaring and whooping. I'm totally not thinking about Ethan anymore. Not even a little bit. Really.

Minutes later, Nikki leads us across campus to a large quad where a few other winter guards are already doing their thing. There's lots of space here, with most teams spread pretty far apart, each group practicing near one of the tall outdoor lamps lighting the area.

Once the sun goes down, finding a spot to warm up that's well-lit is essential for practicing high rifle and saber tosses outside. Without it, you're just chucking your equipment blind, gambling with your safety. Trust me when I say getting clocked with a rifle because you couldn't see it well enough to catch is a pain you never want to experience twice.

Potential hazards aside, though, I sort of love this part at competitions, when you're surrounded by other teams, each practicing parts of their show. It's like getting access to the winter-guard equivalent of a bunch of movie trailers, little previews filled with incredible choreography and trick tosses performed live all around you. It's pretty cool to see ... and to be seen.

We're well into our warm-up, preparing to run our ending ensemble flag feature again, when I sense the loose, energetic vibe of our team stiffen. In my peripheral, I can see another guard has begun setting up next to us and it feels like they're a little too close.

Nikki is clapping out a tempo, counting us in, "...and a five ... a six ... a five, six, seven, eight."

In the fraction of time just before the downbeat, I steal a quick glance at the guard next to us and lock eyes with Ethan. My brain, my heart, all my organs ... short circuit. I freeze.

"Stop! Cut, cut, cut," Nikki commands. "Danny, you can't be late. You've gotta attack that entrance. Catalina, Conner, you guys were rushing it. Come on now, East Valley. Stay focused. Reset."

I'm anything but focused, looking every direction except one. I nod like I'm considering Nikki's instructions, but my head is filled with the image of Ethan, glaring at me with that hard expression on his face. Did I just see him sneer (At me?) just before I looked away?

Nikki is about to count us in again when the sudden whoosh of thirty flags whipping through the air next to us pulls our attention to the right. My jaw drops as I watch the Landon Winter Guard execute a flawless flag feature. Every one of them is perfectly synched, ending with a toss they throw over their heads, walk under the rotating pole, and catch behind them—not with their hands, but with one leg.

It's magic, the way they sweep their left feet back,

bring their heels up to their thighs, and trap the spinning flag behind their knees. With unwavering balance on their standing legs, they hold that final pose, arms outstretched at their sides, the living picture of strength and beauty. I mean, you can't not be impressed.

Even the way they're standing, in six perfect rows of five people each, forming a perfect block, everything about them has military precision. Unlike our guard that's scattered around the area, freeform.

How in the world did we beat them? I think, an uncomfortable feeling stirring in my gut. *They're legends.*

"What a bunch of assholes," Catalina says, making no effort to keep her voice low. "All this space and they have to be right here? Really? *Really*?"

Some of the Landon guard members nearby scowl a bit, but otherwise do a good job of acting like they didn't hear what I'm sure they did.

"I know, right?" Sanjay says. "Very sus."

Nikki quickly calls us to attention, claps out a tempo, and we run our own flag feature again. We may not have a crazy one-leg catch like Landon does, but our choreo definitely doesn't suck either.

"Yes, East Valley, that was a tasty one!" Nikki hollers when we finish. She's all about the food analogies when we rock it, but I can tell from her boastful tone that that was meant for more than just our ears. "Now let's—"

Music blares from a small speaker the Landon guard coach is holding. He barks out a quick four counts and they spring into action. Performed to music, their flag work is even more impressive, seeing how the sweeping motion of their silks aligns with the long notes of their soundtrack.

This time, my eyes go right to Ethan. Total reflex. I've always enjoyed watching him perform, the way he makes even hard shit look so easy, graceful. And truth be told, over the past few weeks there's so much more I've loved learning about him—the way his breath feels on my skin, how he tastes, and that cute little noise he makes when his neck is kissed in just the right spot.

I know what he looks like when he's feeling a moment, but the guy I'm watching right now seems like a totally different person. There's no excitement, no joy in his movement, no fun. Everything seems so forced and aggressive and … mad.

The Landon guard finishes. Their coach cuts their music and Ethan glances at me. This time, I hold his gaze and offer up my best smile, full dimples. Whatever this weirdness is that's going on right now, I want him to know, I'm still me. We're still—whatever we are.

Ethan doesn't smile, doesn't scowl, doesn't offer any kind of response whatsoever. He just turns away and sticks his nose in the air.

Oh, that just feels like a bitch slap. I mean, I *know* he saw me.

My face is totally low-key roasting now. I can't believe this. He was totally fine with us being competitors when he thought his team was going to win, but now that we're on top, he can't even look at me?

Fine. You know what? If that's how he's going to be about it, then I will too.

Nikki cues up our music and we perform our feature again. Only this time, I'm fully aware that we aren't just going through the motions; we're returning fire.

"Spicy, East Valley, extra spicy! That's how momma likes it!" Nikki exclaims on our catch. She does a happy shoulder bounce that gives us permission to cut loose and celebrate a little too. So, we do. A lot.

"Bringin' the heat!" Conner announces at the

same time I shout, Winning!" and we fist bump. Others cheer, trade high-fives, and a few teammates throw random flag tosses. Catalina, Sanjay and a couple of juniors even sing part of that song that's all over TikTok about being a savage.

I'm purposefully not paying them much attention, but at the edge of my vision I can see the Landon Winter Guard giving us full-on stink-eye now, including their coach, who's talking to them but glaring at us. And yeah, okay, we are being a bit much right now, but if we're getting under their skin—good.

Sorry, I know that's not a very sportsman-like attitude, but they started it, coming over here, invading our space when they could've warmed up literally anywhere else in the world.

"All right, let's simmer down now. Bring it in," Nikki says, motioning for us to come closer. We group up around her and she continues: "You know, I think we're done here. Let's not overcook it. You look ready to me. You feel ready, East Valley?"

"Yeah!" we answer.

Behind us, I can hear the Landon guard start up again, and maybe I'm imagining it, but the swoosh their flags make as they begin moving through the air sounds a little angry to me.

A smirk forms on my lips.

They want a fight? They've got one.

Chapter Fourteen

Ethan

The gym is buzzing with activity when we enter. Hundreds of people in the stands are excitedly chatting away, wrapped in countless conversations while dozens more—like me and the rest of the Landon Winter Guard—are hurrying to find our seats before the awards ceremony begins.

I'm sure people are talking about us—I can feel their eyes on me. Earlier today, that was the absolute last thing I wanted, but after the rock-solid performance we threw down in finals, I have zero problems holding my head high right now. In a word, we *slayed*.

We're moving up the middle of the back stands when Micaela stops, turns to me and says, "Ugh, East Valley Winter Guard is right there." She slyly gestures with her head to the area near the top left where Danny and his team are sitting.

I pretend to scan the bleachers nearby, but really, I'm looking without looking at Danny. His expression turns stony when he sees me and it's like bricks stacking up in my stomach.

Part of me wants to stomp over to him right now, explain that I wasn't blowing him off, but I can't just play around at shows like him and his guard. We have a legacy to uphold. I had a job to do. Being a real champion means sometimes you've got to make tough sacrifices, and this is important and … and … and I know that's not all. But how would I even begin to explain? No way he'd understand.

Danny leans over, whispers something (about me?) in Sanjay's ear and I lock eyes with his friend, who then smiles at me. Not the warm, happy kind. One where he squints and the edges of his mouth turn up into sharp points. A *fuck off* smile.

The bricks in my stomach melt into molten lava, reheating feelings I thought had cooled off after the great performance we had.

I'm not the one who should be feeling bad here, Danny is. He and his whole guard owe us a massive apology after the way they were acting during warm-up. So rude how they were being all loud-as-hell and just ... obnoxious. Completely, totally obnoxious.

I mean, Navi said she even heard them calling us names. What the fuck? How could Danny do that? That is *not* how champions behave. That's not how a boyfriend—*whoa.*

Okay, I can't believe I just went there.

After what happened with Jimmy Richards, you'd think I would've learned my lesson, recognize the warning signs, but nope. Here I go again, letting myself get too intense too fast. Obviously, if Danny can do what he did and then talk shit about me to his friend when I'm ten feet away, he's not the kind of guy I thought he was.

A lump begins forming in my throat. I swallow hard to fight it back.

Micaela picks up on my discomfort right away. Her forehead wrinkles with concern, but all she says is, "Come on, let's find a better spot."

"What's wrong with right here?" Liam asks, clueless. Micaela shoots her boyfriend a look. He shakes his head and shrugs.

Without missing a beat, Navi grabs my hand and says, "Good idea. Over here." She tugs me in the opposite direction of Danny, taking charge of our group before anyone else can protest, leading us to the top right side of the bleachers, where we settle in.

Thank God for Navi and Micaela. Everything has been so crazy today. We haven't had much of a chance to talk details, but enough that they get how awkward this is for me. I love them for having my back right now.

A dance beat begins playing over the gym sound system, followed by the announcer's booming voice: "Ladies and gentlemen, please put your hands together for our WGI Sport of the Arts, West Regional finalists!"

The room erupts with applause as two tables filled with trophies are wheeled to the front of the gym. In all, there are only thirty-two finalists from across the six different classifications here. Tonight, though, it feels like there are three thousand.

One by one, the captain of each team enters the floor when their guard's name is announced. They begin lining up in a long arch that'll eventually span the length of the gym when they're done. It's an endless, painful process, made even more excruciating knowing Danny is nearby, that if I turn my head just slightly to the right, I'll catch a glimpse of him.

At first, it's not that hard, keeping my face forward, only allowing myself to look left. But soon, the right side of my neck starts feeling stiff. I tilt my head side to side, try to stretch things out. It just makes it worse, though, the need to move that direction spreads over my shoulder, down to my elbow, wrist and hip.

It's weird, how the minute you know there's something around you shouldn't look at—car crashes, scary parts in horror movies, hot guys in locker rooms—it suddenly feels like you have to fight every muscle in your body to keep from doing it, like there's this invisible force that keeps tugging, tugging, tugging until you eventually give up.

Our school name is announced and I watch our

captain, Heather, walk across the floor. I decide to use the moment as an excuse to turn my head just a bit, but my eyes go sprinting off on their own, right to Danny—who is staring directly at me. He seems so … I don't know … sad or disappointed maybe? I'm not sure exactly. I mean, hey, I'm disappointed too. How did we end up in this mess? And why did his team have to be such assholes? Guh, why am I even looking at him right now?!

I snap my head forward, hating myself for giving in so easily and trying to ignore the dull ache in my chest.

Finally, the music fades and the noise in the room quiets when the announcer says, "Here are the scores for the Scholastic A Class. There were twelve finalists."

I groan. It's going to be another century before they get to us.

The plastic bleachers beneath me become more and more uncomfortable as we slog through awards for the Scholastic and Independent A Classes. By the time we've made it to the end of the Scholastic Open Class, it practically feels like I'm sitting on a medieval torture device. My legs impatiently bounce through the entire Independent Open Class and when the announcer says, "Moving on to the Scholastic World Class. There were five finalists," my breath catches.

I've never been so nervous to hear scores for our class at a regional before. For the first time ever, I have no idea how this is going to end up.

"In fifth place," the announcer begins, "with a score of 74.3 … that's 74.3 … Branson High School."

I exhale slowly, trying to get my rising heartrate under control.

"In fourth place, with a score of 75.0 … that's 75.0 … Davis High School."

I scrub at the back of my hair, crack my knuckles. Come on. Let's go. Let's go. Let's go.

"And in third place, with a score of 78.9 … that's 78.9 … "Taylor High School."

The Taylor guard captain leaves the line to accept the third-place trophy and—*god damn*, could she move any slower?

My palms are sweating. I try to swallow, but my throat has become a freaking desert.

This is it right here, I think. *Winter guard history in the making.*

Navi grabs my hand and holds on tight. She's shaking a little. I am too.

"And in second place, with a score of 82.4 … that's 82.4 …"

JASE PEEPLES

Chapter Fifteen

Danny

I don't think there's a single person in this gym who isn't holding their breath. Except for the hum of the florescent lights overhead, it's like eerily quiet, and I swear the air in the room is getting heavier every second we sit here waiting on the announcer—who must think he's hilarious, keeping us in suspense like this.

The announcer clears his throat and starts over. "Once again, that's second place ..."

Some in the audience laugh nervously, others let out exasperated groans—me included—and the announcer chuckles. He's totally drawing this out on purpose.

Under his breath, Sanjay says, "Oh, my God, this bitch is killing me."

"Seriously," Catalina murmurs.

"... with a score of 82.4 ... that's 82.4 ..." the announcer repeats before another agonizingly long pause. Then, just when I think I'm about to scream, "*spit it the fuck out already*," he says, "Landon High Scho—."

Before he can even finish saying their name, we're launching to our feet with all the force of a rocket ship, erupting in an explosion of cheering and jumping, crying and hugging. It seems impossible, exciting, and so bizarre. Landon, in second place, which means we're—wow.

"And in first place," the announcer begins. We can barely quiet down long enough to hear him confirm it. "This was incredibly close, folks. With a score of 82.5," the crowd *oohs* at the tenth-of-a-point difference in our score. "That's 82.5, your new West Regional champions, East Valley High School."

A parade of feelings travels through my body like a marching band, high-stepping to the symphony of enthusiastic applause and ecstatic squeals playing around me. Then a sour note cuts through our celebration, ringing in my ears—booing. Sounds like only a few people—the cheering is way louder, but it's definitely there, and then it stops as suddenly as it started.

Conner's eyebrows squish into a confused squiggle. He definitely heard it too, but his joy is bulletproof. He quickly shrugs it off and returns to handing out high fives.

Catalina, on the other hand, isn't so subtle. With a smirk the size of a crescent moon, she turns her attention to the area where the Landon guard is sitting in the stands and says, "Get over it, haters!"

Then Sanjay is right by her side, waving at them like he's the freakin' queen of England, which is so shady, but you know what? They deserve it. It had to be them who was booing us, right? They've been sore losers all day.

I turn to glare at them too, but when I see Ethan comforting one of his teammates who's crying into his shoulder, I don't know what to think. His eyes are glassy and he's staring off into space. Now I'm not so sure they were the ones booing us after all. No one in the Landon guard is even looking our way. They're mostly the opposite of us—still, quiet, with slumped posture and weighty expressions, like they just learned someone died.

Something crumples in my chest.

This is so dumb. Maybe if I just walk over there and… No. Ethan couldn't be bothered before, so I'm not going to be bothered now. I turn away.

"And now for the final scores of the evening," the announcer says. "Moving on to the Independent World

Class."

The crowd settles down, scores are read, and the last three trophies are handed out. Then the announcer thanks us all for coming, and dance music fills the gym again, signaling the end of the competition.

Everyone begins rushing out to the floor at once, eager to meet up with their captains and take pictures, causing an instant traffic jam in the stands.

"Holy shit, girl, I can't believe it," Sanjay says as we shuffle along, funneling into the middle stairway, slowly making our way down the bleachers with the rest of the crowd. "Do you think this means we could medal at World Championships this year?" His eyes go wide with a thought. "Do you think we could win?!"

I've been so caught up in everything happening today, I haven't even thought about what this might mean for the rest of the season.

"Hell, yeah. WGI gold medalists, baby! Get ready!" Catalina howls.

It's at this exact moment the song playing overhead ends, and before the next one begins, a voice behind us says, "I'm telling you, that show was trash. They shouldn't have won tonight."

Catalina stops dead in her tracks, halting the flow of traffic on the stairs. She whirls around, and says, "Excuse me?" only her super-confrontational tone makes it sound more like, "Ex-cu-se me?"

I turn to see who she's shooting daggers at and find a girl and guy, holding hands. They're wearing identical costumes and confused expressions. I don't know their names but I recognize them instantly. Landon Winter Guard members. The hairs on the back of my neck stand up.

"Wha-we ... uh, no," the girl stammers. "We didn't—"

141

Catalina cuts her off. "No, no. Keep runnin' your mouth. Say some more." She moves up a step closer to the girl. "Say it to my face."

See, this is another reason why it didn't work out with me and Catalina. Not only does she love to dive into drama at every opportunity, she's also got a crazy-short temper. I mean, I kind of agree with her right now, but still. She needs to stop.

"Cat, chill," I say, placing a hand on her shoulder.

She shrugs me off. "No, apparently, these bitches got a lot to say about us. Let's hear it." She tilts her head and narrows her eyes at the girl. "So, we're trash. Got it. Go on."

People around us are beginning to stare. A few heads on the steps above us are peering around others in front of them, trying to see what the hold-up is.

"You need to get out of my face," the girl says sternly, raising both of her hands and making a back-off motion.

"Micaela," the blond guy next to her warns, puffing up his chest, like he's ready to jump between them anytime she gives him the signal.

"Or what, *Micaela*?" Catalina says the girl's name like it's a swear word.

A few people begin detouring around the blockage on the stairs, bounding down the bleachers. Ethan is one of them. He stops at his teammate's side and the muscles in my back tense.

"Hey, this is a winter guard show, not a *boxing match*. Maybe you guys should try having a little class," he says, glaring right at me.

"So sorry, sir," Sanjay says, sounding a lot like a British butler. "Is the ratchet guard not behaving in a proper manner?"

There's a lot of truth packed into that bitchy little

comeback, and it goes miles beyond the fact that their guard is way better funded than ours—their whole school is. They have better teachers, better programs, better everything.

Now I'm fully aware that between Pop's dental practice and Dad's job as a hairdresser, my family doesn't exactly struggle to make ends meet, but I'm more of an exception at my school than the rule. Catalina and Sanjay come from families that have it way harder—most students at East Valley do. The last thing any of us want to hear from someone who goes to a rich school like Landon is that we need to have some "class."

Before today, I never got this kind of stuck-up vibe from Ethan. A little cocky? Sure. Confident? Absolutely. But I always thought there was also an undercurrent of sweetness to everything he said and did. That's so not the case right now.

I'll bet his comment about this not be a "boxing match" was supposed to be a middle finger at our show too. He's got some fucking nerve putting us down like this, especially after the way he's acted all day.

"Come on, Micaela, Liam," Ethan says and the look on his face, it's like he thinks we're not even worthy of breathing the same air. "Just ignore them."

That does it.

"Yeah, you're real good at that, Ethan," I snap. It comes out so harsh, even Catalina turns to look at me.

"What's that supposed to mean?" Ethan asks.

"Oh, I don't know, just that maybe it would've been nice to hear from you, get some kind of response after you ghosted … a little common courtesy, since, you know, we had plans." I'm heading into dangerous waters here, I know. A little voice inside my head is screaming *Danger! Danger! Turn back!* but I'm caught in an angry current and can't get my mouth to reverse course. I keep right on going, full speed ahead. "But maybe that's something you only care about when you're winning."

He's really mad now. I can tell from the clenched set of his jaw. Then he aims and shoots. "In case you didn't notice, I was a little busy doing something *important*. Sorry I couldn't drop everything to *play around* with you."

His words hit like a bullet, blasting through skin and bone, muscle and tissue, getting lodged in the soft center of my heart, where I'm suddenly hemorrhaging old fears and feelings I've carried there my whole life:

You're not good enough.
You're not important enough.
Even your own mother didn't want you.

"Wow, Ethan. Just playing around, huh?" I say and my voice sounds so rough. Is that really all he thought was going on between us? Fuck me for thinking it was anything more. Behind my eyes, a prickling sensation starts, threatening to turn into tears. I shake my head to clear it away.

Ethan squeezes his eyelids shut and exhales. "I-I didn't—" he begins, but then someone in the bleachers shouts, "Get out of the way!" and a chorus of impatient voices join in, telling us to "Go already!" and "Keep it moving down there!"

"Attention, guard members in the stands," the announcer says, voice cracking like thunder through the gym speakers. "Please do not block the stairways."

More people are watching us now. Some bystanders have whipped out their phones, trying to catch what they can of our confrontation on video.

"Nope. We are not ending up on TikTok like this. Let's go, guys," Conner says. He grabs me and Catalina by the wrist, forcefully pulling us away. Neither one of us resists, but as he leads us down the steps, Catalina looks back over her shoulder and shouts, "Keep your mouth shut next time."

I really wish she'd take her own advice right now.

On the floor, we wade through the crowd, thanking those who congratulate us as we make our way to the center. Finally, we meet up with the rest of our team and pose for pictures—dozens and dozens of pictures. I smile for every one of them, but they're all lies. I'm not happy.

We may have won the West Regional, but I feel like such a loser.

Chapter Sixteen

Ethan

The next few moments are hazy at best. We get a pep talk from Andrew. Random people congratulate us on a great performance. My mom gives me a sympathetic hug while Dad offers a sincere, "You did good out there, son." None of it matters.

I go through the motions, nod along, say "Thank you," but all I can think about are the last words I said to Danny and the wounded look on his face that followed. It replays in my head over and over, each loop more painful than the one before.

I've got to get out of here, fast, because if I accidentally make eye contact with him right now, even for a second, it'll break me.

A chance to escape presents itself and I bolt. I don't even say anything to my friends, I just head straight to the parking lot, hop in my car, and drive. I need quiet, space, time to think.

As I speed down the highway, a light rain begins. I flick on the wipers and get lost in their *swip-swipe* rhythm, still trying to absorb everything that went down over this clusterfuck of a day. I'm not sure how long I've been rolling along like this when an incoming call pulls me out of my hypnotic trance.

I glance at my phone, secure in its dashboard mount, and see my sister's name, Samantha Decker, lighting up the screen. I hit the decline button, but no sooner does my phone go dark than it buzzes back to life with another call from her.

"Take a hint," I say out loud, sending her to voicemail a second time. I don't want to talk to her. I don't want to talk to anyone right now. But this is my sister, so, of course, she's calling yet again seconds later.

I'm about to just turn off my phone so I can go back to not dealing with this when Danny's comment about me being "real good" at ignoring people replays in my head for the thousandth time. A sudden need to prove I'm *not* like that boils over and I hit the speakerphone button.

"What?" I growl.

"Jeez, bite my head off, why don't you?" Samantha says.

"Sorry," I say, sounding about as convincing as younger me every time our parents would force us to apologize to each other after some dumb fight.

"I saw they posted scores for the West Regional online. What happened?" she asks.

"Obviously, we lost," I say.

"Yeah, I got that part," Samantha says, matching my sarcastic tone. She takes a deep breath and when she continues, her voice is considerably softer. "But, come on, tell me, what happened, E-bear?"

That nickname. Sam and I can fight like cats and dogs, but all she has to do is call me E-bear in just the right voice and I melt like I'm five again, being helped up by my big sister after wiping out on my bike.

I open my mouth to reply and it's as if a thread is pulled inside my chest. The gnarled knot of emotions stuck there comes undone, releasing a flashflood of feelings that overwhelms my system. A guttural sound rushes up my windpipe and blows past my lips, where it becomes a full-on sob.

"Oh, E-bear," Samantha says, voice wavering.

The rain outside is falling harder now, thick water drops bursting on glass like thousands of tiny bombs. Between the downpour and the tears filling my eyes, the road ahead blurs. I drift a little into the left lane. An angry horn blares and I swerve back to the right as a pickup truck rockets past my Prius.

"Ethan, are you driving?" Samantha asks, sounding panicked. She doesn't wait for me to answer. "Pull over, Ethan. You need to pull over right now."

"Okay," I bawl, managing to get myself together long enough to make it to the shoulder. But the minute I come to a safe stop, I lose it again.

"Aw, don't cry," Samantha says.

"I c-can't believe we l-lost." I sniff. What I'm feeling right now goes way beyond that, but these are the first words that come, the easiest part of everything to articulate. "We did everything r-right and still..." I swipe at my eyes and take a deep breath, working to regain my composure. Finally, I say, "I guess that's it, the end of a freakin' era."

"Don't be so dramatic. It's just one show, one regional. In the grand scheme of things, I promise, you're eventually going to look back on this and realize it's not that big a deal," Samantha says, and I can't stand her tone right now, all dismissive and smug, like now that she's about to graduate with a psychology degree, she's so above high school winter guard.

"Says the golden girl who was always a big deal," I retort.

"What are you talking about?" Samantha asks.

"Nothing, just forget it," I say, not wanting to dig into this any deeper right now.

"No, you can't just put that out there, do a hit and run like that. You know, we didn't win every show when I was at Landon either. Freshman year, hello."

"And you still ended up getting the bronze medal at WGI that year," I say.

"Which, surprise, is not first place, Ethan."

"Yeah, well, you wouldn't know that by the way Mom and Dad acted," I snarl. I can feel my face getting hot, chest tightening, pressurizing a truth I keep buried deep inside.

"Oh, for the—" Samantha's voice shifts, becoming more intense. "Ethan, you cannot seriously still be jealous about that. Sorry Mom and Dad didn't make it all about you all the time."

"Oh, please. They always made a bigger deal out of you in guard. It didn't matter what I was doing, everyone was always all, 'Sam is so talented,' 'Sam is such a great guard captain,' 'Sam is a chip off the old block.'"

"So, this is all somehow my fault now?" Samantha asks. "You know, this is so typical of you, Ethan. Every time something happens that you can't deal with, you go on the attack. You don't care who it is or what it's about, you just look for a reason to get pissed, grab whatever ammunition you can, and fire away."

I take a sharp breath and tense up, feeling like she just pushed me into the deep end of a pool—cold shock, then a searing rage takes over.

"*I do not!*" I shout, but even as I'm denying it, I realize she's not wrong, and I hate it. "You are going to be *the worst* therapist if that's how you talk to your clients."

"And thank you for proving my point."

I feel so exposed. An instinctual need to hide kicks in. I rest my forearms, crisscross, on top of the steering wheel, burrow into the crook of an elbow, and burst into tears.

Samantha is quiet for several seconds, then, with a kinder tone, she says, "Come on now, deep breath." She demonstrates, loudly inhaling and exhaling.

I breathe along with her, trying to get ahold of my

lungs and brain again.

Neither one of us says a word for a while, so I focus on the traffic speeding by outside. Through the foggy windows, it seems more like a stream of UFOs than automobiles—sources of light that start small and soft, becoming big and blinding as they pass, then disappear.

Finally, Samantha asks, "So, do you want to talk about it?"

"About what?"

"About what's really going on with you?"

I shrug like she can see me.

"If you don't want to, you don't have to, but my ear is always open, E-bear. Anytime," Samantha says. "No judgment."

And there she is again, the warm, caring version of my sister I sometimes wish wasn't living two thousand miles away.

Over the next few minutes, I thoroughly spill my guts, catching her up on everything about Danny, from our first date to the shitstorm that went down at the show. When I finally finish, Samantha says, "Ah, now everything makes way more sense. That's ... I'm not going to lie, that's a lot, Ethan."

"I know. And now I can't stop seeing his face. The way he looked at me when I told him I was dealing with more *important* stuff, Sam, it was like I slapped him," I say. My throat tightens and my eyes begin to itch. "Why did I have to say that to him?"

"Why do *you* think you said that?" she asks.

"I don't know."

"Mmm, I think you do," she says, gently encouraging me.

Chewing on my lower lip, I mull it over, then let out a resigned sigh. "I think I was doing what you said before. He called me out in front of everyone, I got upset and shot my mouth off. I was mad at him, his team, for the way they were acting, the things they were saying."

"For winning, maybe?" Samantha adds.

It stings, but after a beat, I agree. "Yeah, maybe that too."

"And it's perfectly understandable you felt that way, but try to look at this objectively. Do you think, perhaps, Danny might've had a reason to be upset with you too?"

My defenses start to power up again. "But we weren't the ones who said anything about their show, we—"

"I'm not talking about that. I'm talking about you, specifically," Samantha interrupts. "Think about it from his point of view. What if you were texting him and he was the one not responding all day. Knowing you two made plans together, how would that make you feel?"

"Pretty shitty, I guess."

"Do you know why you might've done that?" Samantha asks, quickly adding," And before you say it, I understand you had other responsibilities, but you could've explained that to him and you didn't. Why?"

I start to respond and stop. Whatever my reasoning, whatever excuses I had, none of it seems like a fair justification now. Instead, I answer in the most honest way I can.

"I wanted to text him, but then … I couldn't. I'm not exactly sure why. At first, I tried to convince myself it was because I didn't want any distractions before finals, but that wasn't it. Not really. Then things just got out of control."

"Okay, so, walk me through this," Samantha says. "You were with him after prelims, then they posted scores. What were you feeling in that moment?"

"Shocked, confused. Then hurt and…" I pause, sifting through the mixture of emotions, trying to identify each of them.

"Anger?" Samantha offers.

"A little, but that mostly came later," I say, still searching, and then it clicks. "Above everything else, I think I was … embarrassed." Saying it out loud helps me process it in a way I hadn't until now.

I tell my sister about what I'd learned the week before, how much Danny and his friends said they admired our guard, and how Sanjay's weird "everybody loves a winner" comment made me feel uncomfortable.

"Well, that definitely gives a bit more context to why you reacted the way you did," Samantha says. "After being placed on such a high pedestal by someone you liked, I can see how taking second place in a very public setting might feel a little more humiliating."

The empathy in her voice feels so good right now.

"Do you think," she begins and then pauses, as if carefully choosing her words before continuing, "you might've also been afraid? Like, maybe a part of you was worried Danny wouldn't see you the same way after his team beat yours?"

The second she puts it out there, I don't even have to think about it. "Yeah," I say, ashamed to admit it's true. "That, plus all the people from all the other guards around, staring at me. I guess I kind of freaked out."

"Hey, *fight or flight* mode, I get it. But Ethan, you need to know, your worth is not tied to winning a winter guard show."

"I know."

"Okay, well, you say that, but that's not what I'm hearing," Samantha says. Her tone is somehow both gentle and firm at the same time. "Look, I understand the pressure you're under. And Mom and Dad's constant stories about their glory days don't make it any easier. Believe me, I am fully aware."

I laugh in agreement.

"But don't get so caught up in winning you don't take the time to actually enjoy your senior year. Don't make the same mistake I did," Samantha says.

My jaw drops. "What? Are you kidding me? You had everything. An awesome show, you were guard captain—"

"I was miserable," Samantha adds, cutting me off.

This genuinely blows my mind. "Guess I was so busy trying to keep up as a freshman, I never realized."

"Me either, not at the time," Samantha says. "But looking back, my obsession with getting another gold medal kind of made the year suck. My grades slipped. I never enjoyed performing, and I was kind of a militaristic bitch as a guard captain."

"Okay, *that* I did notice," I say and both of us laugh.

"Anyway, my point is," Samantha begins, taking charge again, "winning isn't everything and you have so much more going for you than that. I mean, you're still my annoyingly perfect little brother who killed his SATs and has a GPA I'd give my left eye for."

"Thanks," I mumble, and this time, I mean it. Then, in a thin voice, I add, "But I don't feel so perfect right now."

Samantha sighs. "No, but sometimes we need to fuck it up before we figure it out. What we do after, though, that's what matters most."

"Is that your official psychiatric evaluation?"

"As a matter of fact, it is, you brat," Samantha says, chuckling.

I run a finger through the condensation on the driver side window, drawing a frowning face in the center as I let her words sink in. "I really did fuck things up with Danny, didn't I? What am I going to do, Sam?"

"Well, I'd give it some space, let everyone calm down first, but you could start with an apology," she says.

"Yeah, but I kind of feel like he owes me one too. I mean, his guard was being really rude," I say.

Samantha sucks her teeth. "I think he gets a pass here. Not only did you ghost the guy—and I'm sorry, I love Andrew, but I've got to point this out—he's an asshole for making you guys warm up right next to East Valley. He totally did that shit on purpose, trying to rattle them before finals."

"You think so?"

"I know so. He's ruthless. He pulled the same stunt my junior year when Redfield High School got within six tenths of our score at another regional," Samantha says.

"Oh, my God. It was so awkward, Sam. I literally wanted to die."

"I'm sure. Nobody needs that kind of stress right before a performance," she says. "Sorry bro, you guys poked the bear and you got bit. I can't really say I blame them."

Guilt barrels into me like an eighteen-wheeler. "Hadn't thought about it like that," I murmur. "Now I feel even worse about what I said to Danny."

"So, tell him that. If you really want to make an honest attempt at patching things up with this guy, you're going to have to own your actions here."

"Where do I even begin? How? When?" Facing Danny seems nearly impossible now.

"You're going to have to figure that out. But when you're ready, you'll know," Samantha says. "Just don't let too much time pass before you try."

Chapter Seventeen

Danny

If I didn't know better, I'd swear the weather is making fun of me this morning. It's raining and bright at the same time, which, apparently, is called a "sunshower." *Thanks, Google.* It also happens to pretty much sum up my life right now. This past week has basically been one sunshower after another. Winning the West Regional, then losing Ethan was only the beginning.

On Sunday, Dad made my favorite breakfast of biscuits and gravy, but my stomach was one big stress-ball. I had zero appetite.

On Tuesday, I stayed up late studying for a history test and didn't realize I'd read the wrong chapter until I walked into class on Wednesday.

Thursday, Sanjay agreed to put aside his "loathing" of opening-day crowds long enough to see the latest Marvel movie with me and Conner, but, of course, tickets were sold out.

Then yesterday, I got an email saying my DNA results from 23andMe were ready, only to discover … absolutely nothing. Well, okay, not *nothing*. I did find out that I'm three percent French and ten percent Italian—I'm guessing those ancestors would have some interesting stories to tell—but on the whole Mom front, I totally struck out. Aside from the names of a few distant cousins, I got no useful information about my biological family. I'm beginning to think all this is a complete waste of time.

Which brings us to this moment—an altogether indecisive show day that doesn't know where it fits. Fucking perfect. I hate rain on show days. You can never get a good warmup outside, and it's nearly impossible to keep all your equipment dry.

Until a minute ago, I was watching cartoons on the couch, waiting for the guys to pick me up for rehearsal, but when I noticed that the metaphorical state of my existence was falling from the sky in real time, I got the brilliant idea I should embrace it—literally.

I'm now standing in the middle of my front yard, head back, mouth open, trying to catch raindrops and sunrays on my tongue like snowflakes.

Seemed like it made sense earlier—you know, become one with the sunshower and all. Now that I'm out here, though, I'm wondering if this might be a sign that I'm having a mental breakdown.

Fortunately, Conner's SUV pulls up, rescuing me from myself.

"You're late," I say as I get in and slide to the center of the back seat.

Riding shotgun, Sanjay gestures emphatically at the rain coming down outside his window. "Uh, because Mother Nature decided to be a whore this morning." He shoots an anime-level icy glare at Conner. "So, *this one* completely forgot that the gas pedal is the long one on the right."

Conner's expression is beyond exasperated. "For the hundredth time, dude, I don't speed when the weather sucks. Period. My parents would kill me if I got one scratch on this car, and I don't know about you, but I'm not exactly in a hurry for the three of us to have to start cramming into Danny's tiny-ass Beetle again—no offense, bro."

"All good," I say as Conner cautiously pulls into the road and accelerates.

Sanjay rolls his eyes, then turns to me. "And you. Why in the world were you standing in your yard?

You're half-soaked. Were you purposely trying to ruin your chances of having a good show-day wig?"

In Sanjay-speak, a wig doesn't just mean an actual *wig*. It can also mean your regular hair or hairstyle. No matter how many times I hear him say it, though, I always laugh because regardless of how he actually means it, I can't help picturing some grand, dragtastic hair sculpture inserted into the situation.

There's no way I'm even going to try and answer his question, so I respond by vigorously shaking my "wig," wet-dog style, inches from his face.

"What are you doing?" Sanjay squeals, recoiling, as he raises his hands to shield himself from the spray.

"Checking to see if water will melt evil bitches," I answer, giving him another spritz.

"I'm a good bitch! I'm a good bitch!" Sanjay exclaims, laughing. "It comes from a place of love, *of love*, you dick!"

I chill and the three of us crack up for what feels like a minute straight, which is sixty excellent seconds I'm not thinking heavy thoughts about Ethan—a new record.

"That's it," Sanjay declares, wiping water droplets from his arms and face. "You children get no help from me today. Your fairy wigmother is officially on strike."

In the rearview mirror, I watch Conner's forehead crease in confusion. "Wait, it's like, so early," he says. "Why are you worried about hair right now? We'll have plenty of time after practice to get ready for the show."

Giving me a sidelong glance, Sanjay mumbles under his breath, "See, this is why every straight boy needs queer friends." He then snaps his head forward and, as if addressing an audience, announces, "Okay, strike paused," before returning his focus to Conner. "Sweetie, starting the morning with a good wig is about so much more than good hair. It's a *feeling*, an attitude that affects your entire day."

He goes on, giving a detailed explanation of his philosophy about how "looking your best leads to feeling and performing your best." I'm grateful for the distraction. It gives me a chance to take over the music without having to fight the guys for it.

Once my phone is paired with the car stereo, I fire up my "Blue" playlist. (Three guesses what kind of songs are on there.) But before you accuse me of being melodramatic or assume I'm a complete simp, you should know that I'm a person who needs to wallow in my emotions before I can move on.

Listening to sad music when you're sad, it's like, yeah, it aches, but it's also strangely comforting to know someone else out there gets your pain so much they recorded a song about it. That, and feelings are sort of like muscles. Tire them out, and they're done for the day.

I'm sure I'm not the only person who's wired this way, right? I mean, sad music is popular for a reason. It's like, a whole industry.

We're almost through back-to-back Troye Sivan tracks when Sanjay stops mid-sentence and stares down the stereo display. "Oh, absolutely not." He frowns at me. "Still? It's been a week. This isn't healthy."

"I'm fine," I lie. "The music helps."

"Um, I'm talking about our health, not yours." Sanjay lets out an exaggerated exhale. "Danny, do us a favor. Ditch the depressing twink music and get an emotional support animal or something."

Conner makes a screwball face. "Yeah, I'm Team Sanjay on this one. You're bringing down the room, man. I don't get why you're still so hung up on this dude."

"I know, right?" Sanjay agrees, "If a guy did me dirty like that, I would've been all erase, replace, embrace new face."

If Sanjay's dating life were a movie, that would be his tagline. He has no shortage of hot hookups—at least, those are the stories he tells us, though, I'm sure he exaggerates. However, at the first sign things might go sideways or get too deep, he cuts it off and begins hunting for another.

Full transparency? I did try his approach. Sunday night, I blocked Ethan's number and all his socials, then went on QTIE and tried chatting with a few random guys. All it did was make me wish I were talking to Ethan even more, which double sucks, because after the way everything went down, I sort of want to hate him. But I can't get my heart to do it. He's, like, *in there*, a stain even the strongest Ariana Grande songs can't seem to get out.

"Tell me," Sanjay says, raising an eyebrow," has he even tried to contact you? Apologize?"

Doing my best to sound uninterested, I answer with, "I wouldn't know. I blocked him on everything."

"So, you do understand the assignment. Good." Sanjay smirks. "Him and his stuck-up guard can go fuck themselves. I mean, the nerve of that bitch, telling us we weren't *classy* enough after they were the ones booing us in the stands—and they called us trash."

An urge to defend Ethan rises in me. "I don't know. I've thought a lot about this, and I'm not so sure that was them."

Sanjay scrunches his lips to one side, giving me a look that screams, *really, bitch?* before he asks, "Who else would it have been?"

"Uh, literally anyone," I point out. "People talk shit at competitions all the time."

"Well, Catalina said she heard them," Sanjay says, as if that answers everything.

"Catalina says a lot of shit," I counter.

"True," Conner chimes in, "and she did kind of go psycho in the stands."

I gesture at Conner like, *thank you*, before I add, "Also, she was the one who called them assholes during warmup first."

Sanjay looks at us like we've been replaced by aliens. "You're joking, right? Who are you two right now?"

Conner shrugs. "Hey, man, I just call 'em like I see 'em."

I nod. "And all I'm doing is pointing out that we weren't exactly angels either."

Sanjay snorts. "Conner, were they or were they not giving off asshole vibes during warmup?"

"They definitely were," he concedes.

"And, Danny, no tea no shade, but the second we won prelims, Ethan basically lost your number and then read *you* when you called him on *his* bullshit. That's not boyfriend material, that's an entitled little prick. I know you want to get in his pants, but come on. When someone shows you who they really are, girl, believe them."

And that, right there, is the problem.

Do you ever meet someone and it's like—*bam*—instant connection? Not just that you like similar stuff or they seem cool. I'm talking about this feeling you get at the core of your core, this unexplainable sense that you *get them*, and they get you too.

That's what I felt with Ethan, every time. Talking in my car, holding hands at the top of Twin Peaks, making out in my room. I mean, how can you kiss someone that intensely and not feel something more?

So, yeah, I thought Ethan had shown me who he really was, and it sure as hell wasn't that asshole I competed against last week.

And the one thing that keeps me from believing I've just been deluding myself all this time is the way he looked at me right after he basically blew a hole in my heart. It was like he wished he could rewind time and take it back. I could see it in his eyes—or maybe I just saw what I wanted to see. Because if he truly felt that same kind of connection, how could he do what he did?

Of course, I'd die before trying to explain any of that to the guys, so I just say, "I don't know. I guess."

Sanjay slightly tilts his head to one side, flashes me a sympathetic look. Then, his expression hardens and his next words are way more serious. "Well, I don't have to guess, I *do* know. I know we're finally getting the credit we've deserved for years, and I'm tired of taking shit from privileged people thinking they can walk all over us. Recognize, respect, or get the fuck out of here."

Conner raises a fist in solidarity. "Preach, brother."

"Mmm hmm. Trust, honey, I am bringing the good word to the people," Sanjay says, his tone returning to its usual sassy frequency. "For example, yesterday, you know the message they included for us in the school's morning announcements, congratulating us on our win and wishing us luck this weekend?"

I nod.

"So, right after we got mentioned, Devan Washburn—you know, big butch basketball player Devan Washburn, who is oh-so-straight." Sanjay practically sings that last part. This is his subtle way of reminding us that he and Devan briefly hooked up in the bathroom at a party last year. "Get this. He looks at me and, loud enough for the whole class to hear, goes, 'Yeah, flaggots are so good at playing with poles,' and does this." Sanjay makes a jerking-off motion.

"That guy is such a douche nozzle," Conner

grumbles.

"Now, normally, I ignore his little homophobic comments—'cause, I know the real tea, and I can keep something on the DL that's supposed to be on the DL—but that pissed me off. I thought, *this fucker thinks just because he's white, hot, and supposedly straight, that he can say whatever he wants to me and get away with it? No ma'am!*" Sanjay sits up taller, juts his chin out. "So, without missing a beat, I go, 'I didn't hear any complaints from you last time.'"

"You did not," I say gleefully at the same time Conner says, "Oh, shit."

"Yes, I did, girl. And that shut him right the fuck up," Sanjay beams. "But, for real, I'm telling you, it is the dawn of a new day. I'm 100% done with people looking down on us. East Valley Winter Guard is going to get the respect we deserve, because we're fabulous." He's in full hype-mode now, voice rising in pitch, growing louder. "And we're going keep being fabulous when we *turn it out tonight!*"

Conner and I cheer in agreement.

Sanjay throws me a playful smirk. "But I don't see how we're going to get the fierceness flowing with Danny's *waah, waah, waah*, soundtrack."

"All right, all right." I chuckle, disconnecting my phone's Bluetooth. "By all means, have at it."

Sanjay links his Spotify, and soon the three of us are howling along with Doja Cat at top volume, letting every car we pass know that we are, in fact, boss bitches.

Three songs later, we roll into the student parking lot with so much energy, I'd bet we could take on all of Winter Guard International right here if we had to. Even the rain has packed up, and the sun looks like she's about to get her comeback-game on. But as we make our way across campus, something starts to feel a little *off,* and when we step foot in the quad, it's clear something is.

Two police officers are talking to Nikki outside the gym, where several guard members are nearby, intensely observing their conversation. We rush over to our teammates on the concrete steps, keeping our distance from Nikki and the cops.

"What's going on?" I whisper to Catalina.

"We're fucked," she says, anger rolling off her in waves. Her arms are folded, and her eyes have a glassy pink tint. She's obviously been crying, others have too. "Someone broke into the guard shed last night. They trashed everything."

Conner's eyes go wide. "For real?"

Catalina nods, jaw tense. "Nikki says we're going to figure something out, but I don't know how we're going to perform tonight. They stole a bunch of our equipment, spray-painted the shit out of the rest."

"Our rifles—" Sanjay breathes in sharply. "*My saber!*"

"All gone," Catalina says, straining to fight back fresh tears, then gestures in the general direction of the shed. "Go look."

The three of us hurry around to the back of the building and the bottom falls out of my stomach when I see our guard shed.

Two years ago, Nikki argued that we needed an additional place to store our props and equipment during the winter guard season. They'd outgrown the small closet in the band room long before I got here. Since there wasn't anything available that was big enough, she convinced the school board to let us build a big shed behind the gym. We all helped raise the money and it was kind of cool, finally having a small space on campus that solely belonged to us—not the marching band, not some sports team—just us.

But what was once a clean black and white structure with gold trim, is now covered in crude graffiti. The front doors have been smashed in. Splintered wood and torn strips of fabric litter the surrounding wet blacktop.

Inside, the damage is even worse. Shelves have been ripped off walls, supplies strewn about, and flags destroyed—their silks torn right down the middle. It looks like someone set a bomb off in here, then, like some deranged artist, signed their work. Bright orange graffiti is everywhere, mostly random stripes of paint with a few barely-legible gay slurs thrown in.

"Who would do something like this?" Conner asks, bewildered.

"Someone who's too stupid to know *faggot* is spelled with two Gs," Sanjay growls.

This wasn't just some random act. It was deliberate, hateful. They completely violated the one space at this school that held all our hopes and dreams for this season, world championships, *our show tonight.*

Air leaves my lungs in a rush as the full impact of what I'm seeing slams into me. *We're so screwed*, I think. My throat goes tight. Then, I remember all the times Nikki told us that the most important part of overcoming any challenge is deciding to face it.

You gotta step up and meet it, before you can beat it.

A desire to fight like I've never felt before ignites in my chest, spreading heat to every part of my body.

I whip out my phone, open Instagram Live, and start filming.

Chapter Eighteen

Ethan

He blocked me.
I cannot believe Danny freaking blocked me.

"Ethan, did you hear what I just said?" Andrew hollers from the top of the gym bleachers. I don't have to look at him to know he's scowling at me right now. I can feel the chill from his steel blue eyes locked on me. He's been in beast mode all morning, pouncing on us for the smallest mistakes.

"Of course I did."

I totally didn't, but I'm sure it was more-or-less the same correction he gave me the last four times we ran this choreography—I'm overshooting my spot on the floor and releasing the toss too early. As if I couldn't tell that's what I did. Give me a break.

We don't have a competition tonight, so Andrew is using today's rehearsal to make a few changes to our show. I don't think there's anyone here who didn't see that coming. We all knew we were going to have to do something after our placement at the West Regional.

That said, I did not expect him to rewrite a major saber feature and replace it with this insane shit he just crammed down our throats.

"Then apply the corrections you're given, and fix it. I'm getting a lot of scattered energy from you today. Get your head in the game," Andrew says sharply, then louder to the rest of the group he adds, "and that goes for all of you. Where's the focus? Where's the fire?"

I promise you, there's definitely a fire here, a big one. It's been burning in my chest ever since I finally worked up the courage to send Danny a message last night and found out he'd completely cut me off—*on everything.*

Text—blocked

TikTok—blocked

Snapchat—blocked

Instagram—blocked

I even tried sending him a DM on QTIE and was denied there too. What the fuck? He couldn't even wait a couple of days? Okay, so it was more like almost a week, but still, it took a lot for me to get there and for him to basically slam the door in my face makes me so ... *grragh*!

Then, as if all that wasn't enough, my parents decided this morning was the perfect time to tell me that they won't be able to come see me perform at WGI World Championships this year. They tried to give me some lame explanation about timetables and project deadlines, but I stopped paying attention at that point and tried to pretend like I didn't care.

Besides, I was getting this weird vibe, like they weren't being fully honest with me. I mean, seriously? They've never missed a WGI before and, sorry but facts are facts, they wouldn't be flaking if my sister was the one performing.

Whatever, it's only my senior year and the biggest winter guard competition on the planet. No biggie, right?

So, after being shit on by the universe, again, all I wanted was to come to practice and work off some of this stress, but can I? No, because apparently, I'm trapped in the rehearsal from hell.

"Reset, from the top," Andrew orders and I haven't even taken two steps before Heather calls my name, which is just perfect. Whatever. I glance in her general direction but keep moving.

"You know, part of the problem is the angle of

your path heading into your spot for the ending formation. You're getting too close to me and you're rushing the last eight counts," she says.

Honest to God, this girl makes me want to pluck a strand of her hair and attach it to a voodoo doll. I wouldn't go full evil queen or anything, just stick it with a few thousand pins is all.

Heather dropped her saber on that last run and now she's correcting me like she's the freaking show designer. It takes every ounce of restraint I have not to read her from cover to cover. Instead, I salute her and say, "Thanks, Heather," in a sickeningly happy tone.

"O-M-freaking-G. Best guard captain ever," Navi says sarcastically, but only loud enough for me to hear, when we settle into our spots. I'm so glad she's next to me on this feature. Her bestie energy is the only thing that's keeping me from completely losing my shit.

"Tell me about it," I mumble through clinched teeth.

"Set!" Andrew commands, and we hit our starting positions. "Check your spots—*Ethan!*"

Goddammit. What now?

I double check my position on the floor in relation to everyone else and realize I should move about an inch to the right. I do, but I can't keep my eyes from rolling as I reset.

"And drop the attitude," Andrew snaps. "If you had it right in the first place, I wouldn't have to correct you."

My jaw tightens. I am 100% not in the mood for this today. For fuck's sake, there are twenty-five of us in this saber feature and I know for a fact no one else is flawless right now either. Why isn't he calling them out?

Andrew cues up our music, counts us in, and I take a deep calming breath. When the downbeat drops, I spring into action with just enough "fuck you" energy directed at him to make myself feel better.

"I don't care. Get pissed. You're gonna do it right," Andrew sneers and he may as well have dumped gasoline over my head. My skin goes from on-fire to a full-on inferno. I swear I can see heat ripples in the air as I lean to the left, flourish my saber to the right.

"Pay attention to the tempo change here, *Ethan*. You're beginning to fall behind!" Andrew hollers, clapping the tempo over the top of the music like I'm some freshman riding the struggle bus.

I mean, first I was rushing, now I'm too slow. What do you want from me? I can feel my face turning every shade of red as I fight to stay on top of the saber work.

Of course, all this happens at the exact moment in our staging when I'm in line with Heather, who can't resist telling me I'm, "too close" as we begin to pass one another, even though I'm pretty sure she's the one who's in the wrong spot. But for some reason, Andrew is yelling at me again, not her.

And now I've had it—*officially!*

I make sure my next steps take me as far from our genius captain as possible while I speed into a hand change along the saber's blade above my head. I know I'm overcorrecting, but whatever. I'm *done*. Done with trying my best and getting yelled at. Done with this saber feature kicking my ass. Done with shitty scores, and bitchy captains, and boys who block you on every freaking account in the world, when all you want is a cha—

"Ethan! Watch—"

There's a flash of silver, a sharp pain across my forehead, then a brilliant explosion of light. I stumble back, knees wobbly, mind spinning, trying to work out where the printed stars on our vinyl floor tarp begin and the ones swirling around me end.

I lose my grip on my equipment, hear it clatter to the ground, and slowly piece together that I've been hit … with a saber … in the face.

A groan crawls up my windpipe.

"Are you okay?" Navi cries, as my vison begins to clear. Her panicked face floats into my field of view, a planet swimming in a spiral galaxy. "I'm so sorry. I didn't mean to … I-I didn't see you—"

"Cut! Everybody, cut!" Andrew shouts. He shuts off the music and my first thought is, *No! I've got to keep going.*

I shake my head to clear it and see two small crimson comets fall from somewhere in orbit, then splatter on the vinyl star field beneath my feet.

Navi gasps. "Oh, my God, *he's bleeding.*"

Suddenly, Andrew is at my side, ushering me off the floor, into the boys' bathroom at the other end of the gym. I lean against the nearest sink as he yanks two paper towels from the dispenser. He quickly folds them into a square.

"Hold this over the wound," he says, handing it to me.

I press the towel against the throbbing spot above my eyebrow. The contact is like a knife through my skull. I wince but keep applying pressure, despite the pain.

"How many fingers am I holding up?" Andrew asks, pointing three digits to the ceiling.

"Thirty," I blurt, giving him a sheepish grin. I probably shouldn't be joking with my deadly serious instructor when I'm literally bleeding from the head, but if I don't laugh, I'm gonna cry and I really, *really* don't want to cry.

"Well, in that case we may have to amputate," he

says with a wry smile and it's as if all the tension is sucked out of the room. Who knew Andrew could actually have a sense of humor during a crisis?

I let out an airless laugh and say, "Three," only it comes out heavy. It comes out like, "I'm sorry," the kind of sorry that sounds like I have so much to be sorry for. Which, let's be real, I do.

Andrew tells me to keep my head still, follow his fingers using only my eyes. He moves them from side to side, up, then down, his features locked into a serious expression as he studies my face.

"Eye movement seems to be okay," he says, "now, let's get a look at that spot where you got hit."

I pull the towel away, see the red stain that's soaked into the tan paper and glance at Andrew, waiting for his assessment.

He purses his lips as he examines my forehead, then nods approvingly. "Doesn't look too bad actually, just a small cut above your eyebrow there. Not too deep at all. You got *really* lucky. Could've been a lot worse."

He motions for me to hold the paper towel over my injury again and asks if I feel nauseated, dizzy, or lightheaded.

"No, I think I'm all right," I say. What I am feeling, though, is incredibly guilty. Poor Navi. She's probably freaking out right now, blaming herself for what was clearly my fault.

Damn, my sister was right. When I get pissed, I do overreact without thinking about the consequences. What a mess I've made—again.

"Sorry," I mumble.

Andrew nods, then sighs. I'm thinking he's about to give me a lecture, remind me that being a drama queen on the floor can lead to accidents like this. But instead, he pops open the first aid kit hanging on the wall and begins rummaging through it.

"The first winter guard I ever joined was this little Independent A Class group called Atlas. Ever heard of them?" he asks.

His question totally throws me off because, first of all, random, and also, I knew that he'd been in several World Class groups back in the day—I mean, everybody knows that. We've all seen the videos—but trying to picture a young Andrew Goman in a beginning-level guard does not compute. I never considered that he had a color guard origin story. Like most people, I think I just assumed he was born magically knowing how to spin and dance.

Andrew clocks my confused expression and chuckles. "No? Well, I'm not surprised. This was way before your time and Atlas was only around for a few years. Anyway, we were a decent little A-Class guard, but we could've been so much better."

He pulls a tube of Neosporin from the kit.

"You see, our instructor, Harvey Davis, was a firm believer that winter guard should be about having fun and shouldn't be too much work," Andrew says as he unscrews the cap from the tube and sets it on the countertop. "Because of this, everything we did was easy-breezy. If even one person was having a hard time with some choreography, he'd water it down, and we never threw any toss higher than a quad."

Andrew squeezes a blob of ointment on his finger and gestures for me to lift the paper towel. He gently dabs Neosporin over the burning spot above my eyebrow, dousing the heat with cool, soothing gel.

"The problem with that was we were never really challenged, never struggled, and so we didn't grow much at all. We quickly hit a point and just … plateaued."

He grabs a Band-Aid, peels the wrapper open. "I

173

remember going to WGI that year—where, naturally, we got nowhere near making finals—having a fine performance in prelims and being so disappointed. Not because of our score or placement—we got what we expected—but because I knew we had it in us to be so much more and we never even tried." Andrew looks me in the eye and there's something surprisingly vulnerable about his expression right now. "Let me tell you something, Ethan. That's the day I learned that when your end goal is simply being mediocre, deep down, even success feels like failure. And that regret, of knowing you didn't try your best when you had the chance, that's the worst feeling in the world."

Andrew gently secures the bandage over my injury and my head feels heavy, absorbing the weight of his words.

"So, then what happened?" I ask.

"I promised myself right then and there that I'd never half-ass anything important to me again. If it's worth putting in an effort, it's worth my *best* effort. That's how I've approached everything in life since then and that's what I've always tried to impart to all of you. And listen, I know I push y'all hard. Sometimes I worry I may push too hard—"

"You don't—"

He puts his palms out, gesturing for me to let him finish and I shut up. He continues.

"But when this is over, I don't want any of you to ever wonder, *what if my instructor would've done more? What if we all tried just a little harder, aimed a little higher? What could we have achieved then?* That's why I'm always telling y'all that we're aiming to make history, not simply go out there and win. Because when you know you've tried everything you can to be the absolute best you can be, you may be disappointed in the outcome of the situation but you'll never be disappointed in yourself. Do you get what I'm saying?"

I nod, realization dawning on me that he's talking about so much more than winter guard. "Yeah, I think so."

"Good," Andrew says, smiling as he shifts back into instructor mode. "Now, you're sure you're not feeling woozy or anything?"

"I'm sure," I say. "Head hurts a little, but I think I'll be fine to continue rehearsal."

Andrew considers this for a moment, then tells me he's going to let us go early for lunch instead. He makes me promise I'll check in with him after the break and tell him right away if I start feeling worse.

The second we step back into the gym, Navi rushes up to me, frantically apologizing through hugs and tears. I explain that I was the one who was the idiot, and though she doesn't seem completely convinced, she finally begins to calm down after the tenth time I tell her I'm the one who should be sorry and assure her "I'm fine."

Heather approaches me with a hug and an apology as well, which is seriously more bizarre than an episode of *Stranger Things*, but whatever. We both agree to let our earlier argument go and move on.

Then I notice a small group of guard members gathered in the stands. They're all huddled around Micaela, watching something on her phone.

She glances up, giving me an apprehensive look as Navi and I walk over.

"Hey, it's all good," I say, pointing to the Band-Aid above my eyebrow.

Micaela nods and I realize her expression isn't exactly one of concern, it's something more complicated. Her eyes cut over to Liam, then back to her phone screen—where pretty much everyone else's attention has remained this whole time—then finally back to me.

"What is it?" I ask.

Liam nudges Micaela and says, "Babe, you gotta show him."

"Show me what?" I ask, trying to sound chipper despite the sense of dread that's now creeping up my back.

Micaela sighs and waves me up the bleachers. When I plop down next to her, she hands me her phone and says, "This came up in my Instagram feed."

She taps the "replay" button on the screen. A video begins playing. I'm not sure what it is that I'm seeing at first, just a small messy space with graffiti-covered walls. Then the person filming turns the camera around and my heart leaps into my throat.

It's Danny.

"So, some assholes broke into our guard shed last night. They stole a few rifles and sabers, shredded a bunch of flags. They went to town in here. I mean, look at this mess," Danny practically growls in the video as the camera pans across the destruction. "We were supposed to have a show tonight but looks like that's not going to happen now."

A small ache starts in my chest, growing larger as I listen to Danny explain that he's not sure what they're going to do about the rest of the season. They don't have much usable equipment left and he doesn't know if they'll be able to replace what they need in time for world championships.

He ends the video asking anyone who might have any information about the break-in to come forward and help them "catch the assholes who did this."

"Dude, that sucks for them, but maybe it's good for us," Liam says. "If they're out of the picture then—"

Micaela makes a face at him that would probably turn anyone else to stone.

"Never mind," Liam mumbles.

"Being the world champions means being the best," Heather says, "not getting the gold because the best couldn't show up. Plus, what happened to them is just shitty. I wouldn't wish that on anybody."

Okay, I must have been hit harder than I thought, because I actually agree with Heather. Also, I can't believe what I'm about to suggest but this is about more than any competition. It's about being the best us we can be—the best me I can be. It's about doing the right thing, even if it's going to be more difficult than anything else I've ever done in my life.

I swallow hard and say, "I have an idea."

Chapter Nineteen

Danny

When Nikki discovered that our floor tarp was basically the one thing not damaged during the break-in, she got this determined look in her eye and called us all together.

"I don't know exactly how this day is going to end. But, by God, I swear to you I know how it doesn't. It *will not* end with us giving up," Nikki announced, voice full of defiance as she pointed to the smashed doors of the shed. "We may not have usable equipment right now, but we still have our bodies, a floor, and a lot of fight left in us. So, let's set up and rehearse what we can for now."

And that's exactly what we've been doing for the past two hours, perfecting staging on the floor, drilling dance choreography. We're all totally here for it too.

Believe me, any other rehearsal there'd be tons of talking and joking around between sets. Today, though, there's this silent intensity blasting out of everyone. It makes me feel so—I want to say "energized" but it's more than that, and honestly, moments like this are what make winter guard so cool.

You know how in a lot of sports someone will do something like score a touchdown or hit a homerun and everyone goes nuts because their team achieved something? And sure, I guess you can say that's technically true. It is a team thing. But also, technically, it wasn't really *the team* that made that basket or shot the winning goal. It was one person.

I'm not trying to knock other sports or anything, because when those things happen, they're awesome, and they occur in guard shows too. I mean, when someone on your team cracks a solo toss or your rifle line nails some crazy choreo, hell, yeah, it's a great feeling.

But then there are these other times when you're all doing the same thing to the same music, giving it the same intensity, and when you catch that toss or stick that landing all together, it's like—I don't know—how I imagine it would feel if every baseball player on a team could hit a grand slam all at once. Epic epicness, on a scale you could never experience by yourself.

When everything aligns like that, man, it doesn't just make you feel powerful, it makes you believe that, together with your team, you can do the impossible.

Despite the break-in, that's what this morning's rehearsal has felt like. At least it did until about two seconds ago, because something *beyond impossible* just walked into our gym. Ethan Decker. He's followed by four other members of the Landon High School Winter Guard. Between them, they're carrying three large duffel bags and have somber expressions on their faces.

The Earth's magnetic field flips—or maybe just my stomach.

"Hello, can I help you?" Nikki asks as they approach her.

"Uh, hi," Ethan says, keeping his eyes forward.

Somewhere behind me, Catalina asks, "What are *they* doing here?"

Other members of our guard have started murmuring similar questions, including Sanjay, who leans in close to me and says, "Oh, shit. Do you think they were the ones who wrecked—"

"No," I say, cutting him off, but I can't deny the same thought went through my head too.

"Um, sorry, we didn't mean to interrupt," Ethan says nervously. He swallows hard.

I watch his Adam's apple bob up and down. A

movie begins playing in my head, a memory, of us together in my room, my lips pressed against the smooth skin of his neck.

I shut the scene off and mentally slug my own brain. The traitor. How could it give in so easily?

"We, uh," Ethan continues, "we saw Danny's Instagram post ... about what happened and we wanted to help."

Ethan turns to face us for the first time since he walked in and I notice the Band-Aid above his eyebrow, the edges of a swollen area peeking around it.

My heart is a pocket-full of loose change spilling on the floor, scattering in all directions.

Ethan's eyes meet mine and the sudden urge to run to him, protect him, is so strong my leg muscles twitch. But then his cheeks flush and he turns away. I come to my senses, remind myself that it's my heart that needs protection from him.

"We don't need your help," Catalina grumbles.

"Cat, don't be rude," Nikki scolds.

One of the other Landon members steps up. "It's okay," she says. "We get it." She glances at us and smiles warmly. "Hi all, I'm Navi and this is Ethan, Micaela, Liam, and our captain, Heather." She gestures to each person as she says their name. "We're from Landon." A small nervous laugh slips out of her. "You probably already know that, though. Anyway, things got a bit ... tense between our guards last week and, right up front, we want to squash that." She looks at Micaela, who seems a little reluctant at first, but then steps forward.

"For the record, after awards last week, I didn't say anything about you guys. I don't know who did, but it wasn't any of us," Micaela says. "I'm a firm believer that the competition should be on the floor, not in the stands." Her tone is a lot colder than Navi's and that last part had a bit of an edge to it. In all honesty, though, if Cat flipped out on me like she did on that girl, I probably wouldn't be able to let it go either.

"Which is why we're here," Heather says. "When Micaela showed us the video of what happened to your equipment, we all agreed that was way effed up." She bends down and unzips one of the large bags they carried in with them, revealing the contents inside. "We brought sixty flags—thirty yellow silks and thirty blue ones. They're just basic practice flags but you can use them for as long as you need."

"We brought extra rifles and sabers too," Ethan says, pointing to another bag. "We didn't know how many you might need, so we scraped together everything we could spare." He looks directly at me. "Not sure if this is enough, but we wanted to make things right if we could." He swallows, mouths a silent, "Sorry."

I'm not sure if he means "sorry for this shitty thing that happened to your guard" or "sorry for being so shitty to you," but I do know I can't maintain eye contact with him right now, not while I'm trying to keep the shape of my face from changing.

"And you're sure Andrew is okay with this?" Nikki asks.

"Absolutely," Heather says. "He was all for it when we told him what we were thinking."

"Well, we all agreed," Navi says, beaming with pride as she points finger guns at Ethan. "But this guy here is the one who suggested the idea."

Now what the hell am I supposed to do with that?

Did Ethan ditch me and act like a sore-ass loser at the show? Yes. Is he the same dude who basically ripped my heart out and stomped on it in front of the world? Totally. But he's here, now, doing all *this*, and I can't pretend like I'm not a little moved by it.

Even the way he's standing—slouched posture with his hands buried in his pockets, face turning a darker shade of pink—he's all guilty puppy. I mean, come on, how can I not find that super adorable?

Nikki smiles. "Thank you. This is so—" her phone pings with a text and she pauses to check it. "Oh," she gasps. Her hand flies to her mouth. Then her eyes instantly fill and little streams begin flowing down her cheeks.

I feel the blood drain from my face. This can't be good. I've never seen Nikki cry before.

She pulls her hand away from her mouth and begins fanning herself. "I'm sorry. That is so unprofessional of me," she says, making an obvious effort to regain her composure. "Sorry, I'm just a little overwhelmed here." She clears her throat and announces, "That message was from the Davis High School Winter Guard director. She says they've set up a GoFundMe for us and she's offering to let us borrow equipment too."

The gym begins buzzing with excited voices, smatterings of applause, and a few random high fives between my teammates. I exhale, relieved. If we'd gotten more bad news in front of Ethan, I think I would've literally died.

"Thank you so much," Nikki says, her eyes scanning across each member of the Landon guard. "Sincerely, the fact that you came all this way, when I'm sure you have a rehearsal of your own to worry about. I am blown away and *so proud* to be a part of the color guard community this morning."

She goes down the line, hugging every one of them, and as I watch her embrace Ethan, I so badly wish it were me who was feeling the heat of his body, breathing in the scent of him.

Okay, it doesn't matter how hot he is, I have got

to stop that. I'm no pushover and what did Ethan expect anyway? That he could treat me the way he did, then do this one nice thing and I'd be all over him like, "Oh, wow, you're my own personal superhero, thank you, all's forgiven." That may work just fine in movies with happy endings, but this is reality. In real life, people do real damage to real hearts and it's not so easy to forgive.

Then again, if people only forgave each other when it was easy, the world would be a way more fucked up place, right? I don't know.

I'm so distracted by the tug-of-war raging in my mind, it takes a few seconds before it registers that members of my team have begun thanking the Landon guard too, approaching them with handshakes and hugs of their own. Among them are Conner and (of all people) freakin' Sanjay, who envelops Ethan with the biggest bear hug.

"Uh, what was that?" I ask when Sanjay plops back down next to me.

"Making a deposit in the bank of karma," he says like it's the most obvious thing in the world. "I ain't about to tempt that bitch right now."

"What happened to, 'him and his stuck-up guard can go fuck themselves?'" I ask.

Sanjay gives me a dismissive wave. "Girl, that was so ten minutes ago. I'm over it."

Most people might think a one-eighty like that is the sign of a crazy person, and they may be right, but it's also completely normal for Sanjay. I've gotten into some Avengers-level arguments with him before, even a couple where we didn't talk for days after. Then, out of the blue, he'll text me like nothing ever happened.

Even those times when I've been a total asshole and tried to apologize for something, he always responds with, "Girl, that was so ten minutes ago. I'm over it," and that's the end of that. Weird, I know, but over the past two years I've come to accept that's just one of his many quirks, and at times like this, I wish it was one of mine too.

After an awkward goodbye, the Landon guard wishes us luck and as they walk out of the gym, I catch Ethan glance back at me just before the doors close.

Panic flashes cold across my skin. What am I doing? Am I really going to let him leave without saying anything? Am I really going to be *that guy*?

Nikki tells us to take five and I turn to find Conner frowning at me like he can read my mind. He gestures at the door like, "Go," and I'm a bullet firing out it.

"Ethan, wait," I call after him.

He stops short, turns around, then asks his friends to give him a minute. They continue on and now Ethan and I are standing face to face, only a few feet apart, all alone for the first time in what seems like forever.

"Uh, hi," I begin and stop, pulse thrumming, suddenly not quite sure what to say.

"Hi," Ethan says.

Pointing to the Band-Aid above his eyebrow, I make a pained face and say the first lame thing that pops into my head. "That doesn't look so good."

"Oh, that," Ethan says, complexion turning a deeper pink hue. "I'm fine. Just got attacked by a wild saber is all. You know how it is."

"Yeah, vicious little things," I say, trying to bite back the smile forming on my lips. Those damn green eyes of his, adorable freckles, pouting lips, I can feel the spell they're casting over me, the hypnotic effect they're having on my mind and body. I shove the next words out before I lose my nerve. "So, uh ... is that true, what your friend said? That bringing us all that equipment was your idea?"

Ethan nods.

"That's really cool of you," I say. "Thanks."

He gives me a crooked smile. "Well, since you blocked me on everything, I had to find some way to get your attention."

"Oh, yeah, right," I mumble. "Sorry about that."

"Please, I'm the one who should apologize," Ethan says softly. He takes a deep breath, squares his shoulders. "Danny, I am so sorry. I didn't mean to ghost you like that at the regional, really. Things just got so crazy so fast. And I was going to text you, I swear I was. I just needed a minute to get my shit together. Then one minute became ten, then an hour, then three hours, and the longer it was, the less I knew what to say."

The words tumble out of him in such a rush they sound like one continuous sentence.

"You could've just told me you were busy with rehearsal. I would've understood, you know." Wow, that came out sharp.

"It's not that simple."

"Uh, yeah, it is. Open phone. Send text. Done," I say, not even caring that I've fully slid into the sarcastic zone.

"It's more complicated than that," Ethan says, irritation creeping into his voice.

"Why, because we won?"

"No, because we lost," Ethan snaps. "And I didn't want you to see me like that."

"Like what?"

"Like a loser, all right?! I didn't want you to think I was a loser."

"Why would…" I shut up, as it slowly dawns on me.

I've had him on a pedestal for so long it never

occurred to me that Ethan could be insecure too, that he would actually worry about what *I* think of *him*. For the first time, I think I get it, really get it. Being a world champion isn't just an achievement for Ethan, it's part of his identity—an identity he feels he has to live up to.

"You know, Ethan, I didn't want to go out with you because you were on the Landon Winter Guard," I say.

"Okay, good to know. So, why did you want to go out with me?"

"Because you're *you*. Because I like you, a lot. I thought that was obvious?" I say, nervously. "Did you really think that would change just because of some dumb regional?"

"I don't know," Ethan says. His voice is surprisingly high-pitched. "It's not like I thought it all out or anything. I just sort of panicked. Then the next thing I knew we were warming up for finals right next to you, which totally sucked out loud—"

"Wait, that wasn't on purpose?"

"It's not like we had a choice. We went where Andrew told us to go. Trust me, no one in our guard wanted to be there. We were trying to focus on us. Then you guys started being all…" His voice trails off. He looks away and shakes his head.

"Being all what?" I ask.

Ethan exhales. "Nothing. Forget about it."

"No, tell me. I want to know."

"Obnoxious. Okay? You guys were being super obnoxious."

I nod in agreement, giving him a guilty grin. "We totally were."

"So, yeah, that pissed us off, but you've gotta believe me, we didn't say shit about you guys—not until what's-her-name went off on Micaela. Then," Ethan shrugs, "you know the rest." He swallows hard. "Look, what I said to you that night, I didn't mean it. I've been trying to think of how to tell you that for a while, I just didn't know how."

Gesturing at the gym I say, "Well, this is *one* way to do it."

We laugh and it's as if the sun chose this exact moment to shine brighter through the drifting clouds above. The rays feel good on my skin, but compared to the heat of Ethan's smile right now? No competition.

"Very dramatic," I add in a silly-serious voice, desperate to hear him laugh again.

Success.

"I am a performer," Ethan says. "Not sure if you knew that."

"Sounds vaguely familiar," I say, stroking my chin. I can't stop grinning.

"In all seriousness, though," Ethan begins. His smile fades. "What happened to you guys is insane. I hope the equipment helps."

"Thanks," I say.

"Any idea who might've done this?"

I shake my head. "Vandalism isn't exactly a rare thing here at East Valley. Our instructor filed a report with the cops, but who knows if they'll do anything."

"Yo, Danny," Conner says, poking his head outside the gym. "Rehearsal's back on."

"Be right there," I holler back, then return my attention to Ethan. "I gotta go."

"Same," Ethan says. "We're probably going to be so late getting back."

"Thanks again, for everything," I say as sincerely as I can and I feel like we should seal this moment with a hug or something but I'm not sure we're there yet. Maybe a handshake? No. That would be so cringe.

"Danny!" Conner calls again.

"Coming," I say, grateful his interruption gives me an easy out. I offer Ethan a lame little wave as I step back. "So, see you around?"

Ethan waves back and grins. "Definitely."

JASE PEEPLES

Chapter Twenty

Ethan

"Ethan, chill," Navi says sweetly, placing a hand on my knee. My leg has been jackhammering up and down. I can't get my foot to stop tapping. It's like my brain and body are total strangers. `

We're at the Cupertino Winter Guard Invitational and, in my head, I'm excited to be here. My heart is another story—it's bouncing off my ribs like I just chugged a Red Bull. I've got sweaty palms and cottonmouth, too. It's highly possible I'm nervous, which makes me wonder if I somehow ended up in an alternate universe.

I mean, it's not like I've never been nervous at a winter guard show before, but only when I'm about to perform, not when I'm sitting in the stands waiting for someone else to take the floor in competition.

It's 8:22 and, according to the schedule, East Valley Winter Guard is going to walk through the performer's entrance any second—Danny is going to walk through that door any second.

My opposite foot starts tapping. This time, Micaela presses a firm palm on my thigh.

"Don't make me tie you to the bleachers," she teases, giving me a sideways smile.

"Sorry, I know. I just want them to have a good show," I say, like anyone here believes that's really the reason I'm so jittery.

"They went through a lot just to be able to perform tonight. I'm sure they're going to be great," Heather says, who, by the way, has been way cooler today than I ever thought possible.

After our rehearsal, when I suggested we come watch East Valley perform tonight, I figured Navi, Micaela, and Liam would be down to go, but never, not in a million years could I have predicted that Heather would ask to join us. And, never in a billion years would I have imagined that I'd be giving her the short version of the Ethan/Danny saga on the way here. And never, ever in a million-billion years would I have guessed Heather would call me "so nice" for wanting to surprise Danny like this.

But, hey, apparently, that's the universe we live in now, so I'm rolling with it. I just hope it's one where Danny thinks me showing up here is awesome too—or will he file a restraining order?

The guard that just performed finishes clearing the floor and then, finally, East Valley enters. The crowd begins cheering before they're even introduced and when the announcer says, "Please welcome our next unit in competition…" the gym erupts with thunderous applause. The second my eyes locate Danny, though, it feels like every one of my molecules is roaring ten times louder.

My body instantly notices how good he looks in his uniform too, internal temperature jumping each time his bare biceps flex as he sets his equipment across the front sideline. Seriously, whoever designed that uniform, *thank you.*

The crowd begins to quiet down and suddenly my mouth decides it's got a mind of its own.

"Go Danny!" I shout.

His eyes immediately catch mine. Now I totally want to crawl under the bleachers and hide. Why did I say anything? What if knowing I'm in the stands makes him nervous? What if he doesn't want me here? What if—

Danny's face breaks into the most amazing smile.

All the energy from the western power grid feels like its surging through me and I electrocute and die only to be resurrected a second later, because this time, nothing, not even death can keep me from being right here, right now.

"Presenting their program, *The Ultimate Fight*," the announcer's voice booms over the speakers above, "the California Color Guard Circuit is proud to present East Valley High School."

The deafening cheering isn't a surprise, but the vibe in the room sort of is. I know what it's like when you can feel the audience's love on the floor. This, though, it's like the support has been cranked up to eleven. I get the sense that everyone in this gym heard about East Valley getting vandalized, and it's got them fired up in the best way.

The guard hits their starting positions inside a large black octagon at the center of their stark white floor tarp. Half the performers are in a tight block formation on the left while the others are mirroring them on the right—fighters ready to square off in the ring.

Their music begins, trumpets playing a familiar bold melody. I think it's the theme song from *Creed* or, no, it's *Rocky*, one of my Dad's favorite old movies. For a full sixteen counts, the guard stands there, unmoving, in a powerful stance as the horns blare on—the anticipation in this gym is off the chart.

Then a voice booms over the top of their music, but it's not the competition's announcer. This one is part of their soundtrack, part of their show.

"Ladies and gentlemen, this is the main event of the evening!" the voice howls in that way fight announcers do, where they hold the vowels in every other word like long notes.

Ding!

A bell rings and the music shifts to a dance remix

of the *Rocky* theme song as East Valley explodes into action. The opposing groups on each side of the floor begin moving toward one another, performing choreography that resembles martial arts moves.

Things intensify when the groups meet in the middle of the octagon, trading sweeping fan kicks and double punches. Of course, I can't take my eyes off Danny. There's this aggressive, yet controlled, masculine edge to his every movement. He seriously looks like a badass action hero out there, which is so not my thing, but in Danny's case, it's super-hot.

Out of nowhere, ten rifles are tossed high into the air, completing seven rotations before—ding! That same bell rings on the beat of their catch. The entire gym freaking loses it and I'm right there too, screaming like I'm at a Shawn Mendes concert.

Their music changes again. Rap lyrics blast as flags and sabers join the rifles on the floor and it's all just so damn cool, the mix of music, the sound effects, the fight choreography, all of it.

For the next six minutes, I forget about the drama of the past few weeks, all my worries and what ifs, and simply watch Danny and his team blow the roof off this little gym, again and again.

Then, just when I think they can't possibly top themselves, they end their show with an ensemble flag feature that triggers a rabid standing ovation from the entire audience. I'd bet every person in here five dollars that no one is standing taller or cheering louder than I am for Danny, though.

"Well, damn, East Valley. Tell me you're fierce without *telling me* you're fierce," Micaela says, clapping as the guard begins to clear the floor.

Leaning in closer to me, Navi says, "Can you say one hundred percent fire? That was sick!"

"Totally. I am so happy for them," I reply, and it's true. I am happy for Danny, but what I'm feeling is so much bigger than that, lighter too. It's like my bloodstream has become carbonated. There's been this cycle of happy bubbles flowing from my middle, bursting under every inch of my skin ever since he smiled at me.

"They were *so fun*," Heather says.

Whoa. She's right. I've been caught up in scores and legacies and competition for so long I'd almost forgotten how much fun all this can be. Holy shit. I'm actually having *fun* at a winter guard competition—and we're not even competing!

Watching Danny and his team throw down like they did, especially after what they went through today, I think it woke something up in me, in all of us, because all through the awards ceremony, we're like little kids, laughing and going overboard applauding for A and Open Class guards we don't even know when they're handed trophies.

There are only two other Scholastic World Class guards competing here tonight, but they're not on East Valley's level, so when they take third and second place, no one is surprised.

"And in first place …" the show announcer begins.

My pulse quickens. I'm super anxious to find out their score. I'm fully expecting a competitive 84-something or maybe even a slightly high 85. I do not expect the "89.1" that literally knocks the wind out of me.

I swap wide-eyed WTF looks with Navi and Micaela. Their jaws are hanging just as low as mine. We're keeping up with the rest of the audience, but our earlier enthusiasm is gone.

"Uh, that seems, like, really high," Liam says.

"Because it is," Micaela mumbles.

We sit there, shocked, as the stands begin to empty and a new crowd forms on the floor.

"Hey, come on you guys," Navi chirps, cheerleader energy at a hundred and ten. "I'm not worried one bit. East Valley got a high score at a *local circuit show*. Awesome. Good for them. They rocked. It doesn't change their national ranking."

"Right," Heather quickly agrees. "Only scores from official WGI regionals count."

"Exactly," Navi says. "I'm sure if we were competing here tonight, the judges would've given us a crazy high number too."

Micaela nods in agreement, but her frown stays firm as she begins scrolling on her phone.

My lungs finally remember how to work, and I take a calming breath.

"And we all know," Navi continues, "you can't really compare—"

"SHIT!" Micaela exclaims, large eyes locked on her phone screen. "Shit, shit, *shit*!"

"What is it?" I ask.

"Scores from the Miami regional. Look what Hillside High School got." Micaela thrusts her phone toward me, and I can't believe the numbers that practically leap off her screen.

"Wait, what, 90.3? They gave them a 90.3?! But that's ..." I can't even finish my sentence. The sensation inside me feels like sinking.

Navi opens her mouth like she's going to say something positive again, then closes it and shakes her head.

"*Fuck*," Liam groans.

"I know," Micaela says, sounding as defeated as I think everyone is feeling right now.

"Stop it. Just stop it, all of you," Heather says

sharply. "Hillside is only ranked first for now, they didn't win world championships, so don't start talking like we've already lost. We wanted strong competition, right? Well, guess what? Now we've got it from across the country—literally. All this means is that we've got work to do."

And just like that, she's on my nerves again, everyone's actually. I can tell by the way Micaela's eyes cut across at a diagonal and still haven't come back down, along with Navi's tight-lipped smile.

It's not that Heather isn't right, but does she always have to be such an authoritative bitch about stuff? Ugh, I would've been a way better captain.

"Okay then," I say, standing up. "I'm going to find Danny."

"Good idea," Navi says. Her tone is extra sweet. The look on her face, though, is more like, "Run! Save yourself! Go!"

I make my way down the bleachers, into the pool of people, where I find Danny posing for a picture with two girls from another guard. He looks so happy, grin stretching ear to ear, brown eyes practically glowing.

He's beautiful.

I've felt that way since the first second I saw him, but the thought vibrates through me at a different frequency this time, hits a deeper note. I don't know what that means exactly. It's an achy, joyful, strange sensation. I think I like it.

When Danny sees me, his whole face seems to light up, and it feels like mine does too. He bullets through the crowd, throws his arms around my waist, linking his hands at my lower back and pulls me close. The feel of his body pressed against mine sends an electric jolt straight to my groin.

The next thing I know, he's laughing, spinning

me around. I never knew how much you could miss a person's touch.

Danny sets me down, releasing me quickly. His expression, I can tell this surprised him, the way he lost himself, hugged me without even thinking about it.

"Sorry, I just," he shakes his head, "I can't believe you came. You're here!"

My eyes prickle with tears. I was such a dick to him, and still, here he is, after everything, giving me the most genuine smile in the history of smiles. I hate that I have to compete against this guy, hate that, even now, part of me is wondering how our teams would've stacked up if we'd performed here tonight.

I bury the thought in the back of my brain. That's a thing that's going to happen. We're going to face off in a few weeks at WGI. I know, I know, but ... later. Right now, I don't want to think about that, or Hillside High School, or the fact that we're now ranked in third place. *Third freaking place.* Whatever.

There's so much more I want to say to Danny, so much I feel, but there's no way I'd ever be able put any of that into words, so I just try to match his happy expression and tell him how I feel with my eyes as I say, "I'm here."

Chapter Twenty-One

Danny

Just when I thought today couldn't get any crazier, Ethan asked me to hang with him and his friends after the show, and what was I supposed to say? *No?*

Yeah, right.

Luckily, my boys were willing to tag along—hanging with Ethan's whole crew by myself would've been so awkward. We met up at this sweet 1950s diner, and now we're sitting around the same table like we weren't trying to go all *Hunger Games* on each other last week.

"Oh, hell no. They got a WHAT?" Sanjay asks.

And the crazy just keeps coming.

Scores for the Miami, Austin, and now the Chicago regional have all been posted to the WGI website—it's so not good.

"A 90.2," Michaela says, glaring at her phone screen. "Kings High School got a ninety-point-fucking-two at the Chicago regional."

"So that makes two guards breaking 90?" Liam asks.

"Three," Micaela corrects, clearly disgusted. "Hillside High School in Florida with a 90.3, then Kings with a 90.2, and Northlake in Texas with a 90.0."

Sanjay throws his hands in the air, then dramatically drops them to his sides and slumps in his chair. "Great. Now we're ranked *fourth* overall."

"Which puts us in *fifth*," Ethan says with a wince. "I'm so glad Heather went home because I *could not* with another one of her lectures right now."

Seeing him so disappointed makes my next

heartbeat feel heavier.

"Ugh, you guys, I'm seriously going to need a double fudge sundae to deal with this, but hello, massive guilt if I eat it all by myself. Anyone willing to help a girl out?" Navi asks.

Conner's eyes widen. "I would..." he says quickly, then stops. His gaze flickers down and bounces around the table as he continues, "...be willing ... to do that. I mean, uh, if you want."

Yeah, I thought I caught him checking her out earlier.

"You're so sweet. That would be amazing. Thank you," Navi says as her frown flips.

Color spreads in a heat map across Conner's face. "Sure thing. No problem," he says, nodding like a bobble head.

"Smooth. Real smooth," Sanjay mumbles loudly.

"Shut up," Conner grumbles, throwing a tiny balled-up straw wrapper that rebounds off Sanjay's chin.

I butt in to rescue Conner, steering attention away from his clumsy attempts at flirting, back to Sanjay and the main topic. "Seriously, double shut up. What's with all the freaking out? Compared to last year, we're doing awesome. Fourth is great."

"Yeah, man," Conner says. "We weren't expecting to win anyway, just make top five."

"Exactly. It's all good." I shrug, trying to come off super chill because complaining about our placement in front of the Landon guard kind of feels like we're rubbing it in their faces.

Ethan and I just got started on this reboot—at least I hope this is a reboot—and I don't want Sanjay's dumb ass ruining it.

"Speak for yourselves," Sanjay says. "I fully intend to add *WGI World Champion* to my Instagram bio when this season ends."

"Uh, I'm sorry, what was that?" Micaela asks, squinting at Sanjay.

Great. Just fucking great. I'm going to kill him.

Micaela holds up her hands, displaying her royal blue fingernails for us all to see. "Then you better come correct, bitch, 'cause you're gonna to have to snatch that medal from these sharp-ass claws," she says.

Sanjay's mouth falls open and his eyes go wide. For once he doesn't have some smart reply ready to fire back. After a few excruciating seconds, a playful smile cracks Micaela's lips and something between a laugh and an exhale comes out of me, along with everyone else.

"This. Bitch. Is. *Fierce*," Sanjay squeals, clapping with each word. "Serving she-did-not-come-to-play realness. Yes, ma'am! And you better *get it* with them flawless nails, too, bitch. Yaass!"

"Who, me?" Micaela says, feigning surprise before striking several poses, photoshoot style. Everyone cracks up and the depressing fog that's been hanging over our table lifts a little.

Beaming, Ethan turns to look at me. I can feel the edges of my mouth tugging upward. He seems as happy as I am that our friends are getting along so well and I love it. It's weird, how the smallest hint of what he's feeling can affect me. He raises his eyebrows, bumps my leg with his. I bite my lower lip, bump him back.

His eyes are like two little magnets, tugging at me, pulling me in. God, I would so kiss him right now if we were alone. Instead, I tap his thigh with my hand. When he moves to tap me back, I hook his pinky finger with mine and make a funny face as I give him a tiny squeeze.

Ethan laughs the most adorable little laugh and whispers, "Dork," as he bumps my shoulder with his, but he doesn't try to pull his pinky away, and neither do I.

"But for real, you guys, am I the only one who cannot believe Hillside High School, out of everyone, is ranked first right now?" Navi says.

"Wait, are they the ones doing that Yoga show?" Sanjay asks.

"Yes," Micaela groans.

Conner lights up. "Dude, I just saw that video and I was like, *what the fuck*? Their show is so dumb."

"I know, right?" Navi says.

Sanjay scrunches up his nose. "And that flag choreography. Beyond basic. Yeah, it's a no for me."

"Thank you!" Micaela exclaims. "I said the same thing."

Ethan lets out a weary exhale. "Okay, guys, can we *please* talk about something else?"

From the shocked/amused looks his friends are giving him, I'm going to guess Ethan—the king of color guard—has never said anything like that before.

"Sorry," he softens. "It's just kind of depressing and there's nothing we can do about it right now, so, yeah. New subject, please."

Micaela arches an eyebrow. "Sure, we can do that," she says methodically, turning to Navi and Sanjay. "Right, ladies?"

Three pairs of eyes cut over to us, then back to each other. I'm not sure what kind of telepathic communication they just shared, but the same mischievous grin they're all giving us is making my insides ice up.

"Oh, yes," Navi muses.

"Absolutely," Sanjay adds, sounding like a character straight out of *Bridgerton*

"Seems to me there's some rather suspicious activity happening at that end of the table," Micaela says as she swirls a fingernail through the air at me and Ethan. Everyone is staring at us now.

"Lots of googly eyes going on over there," Navi agrees.

"Some definite under-the-table action too," Sanjay says in a tone that implies something way dirtier.

Navi and Micaela inhale sharply, pretending to be scandalized. Liam and Conner laugh.

Our wrapped fingers fly apart and I say, "We are not," at the same time Ethan says, "What? No."

In my peripheral, I can see Ethan's face has turned nearly as red as his hair, and from the way my cheeks are burning, I'm going to guess mine is about three shades darker.

"Aww, they're blushing," Navi says, voice an octave higher.

"Yup, told you." Sanjay gestures at us. "*Guilty.*"

"Shut it," I say, but I can't keep from laughing.

Navi waves a dismissive hand in our direction. "Oh, please. You two don't get to be that cute and not have us make fun of you. It's, like, a universal law."

"Besides, after all the sappy breakup music your mopey ass forced me to listen to this week, I think I earned it," Sanjay says.

I glare at him so hard. "Dude," I warn. My face is on fire.

Micaela points to Ethan. "Oh, let me tell you, it's been a nonstop Sam Smith fest at that one's house for days."

"Micaela!" Ethan squeaks.

Wait. Ethan was legit listening to Sam Smith? For days? Because of me? Something compresses in my core.

"Okay, well, on that note," Ethan says, standing up. "I'm going to use the bathroom … or something. I'll be back."

As he rushes off, Micaela starts singing, I'm talking full-out singing, "Too Good at Goodbyes" and it takes all of five notes before Sanjay and Navi join in—way off key.

I'm not hanging around for this either.

"Yeah, I'm gonna … be back too," I say, and I can hear everyone crack up behind me as I hurry after Ethan.

At the end of the restaurant, I expect Ethan to take a left toward the bathrooms, but he takes a right out the front door instead.

Wait, what? Is he ghosting me again? The thought is like a boot on my chest, stopping me in my tracks.

My phone buzzes in my pocket. I fish it out and my heartbeat spikes when I see I have an unread text message from Ethan.

Meet me outside?

Chapter Twenty-Two

Ethan

Danny pushes through the diner's swinging glass doors, joining me under the pink and turquoise striped awning outside. Before either one of us can say anything, we simultaneously let out nervous laughs.

"That was, uh…" Danny begins, shaking his head.

"…so embarrassing," I finish, shaking my head too. I'm certain my cheeks are redder than red and I've got a ridiculously big smile on my face, but there's nothing I can do about any of that.

"Just a bit," Danny agrees, sliding his hands into the front pockets of his jeans. "Maybe it wasn't such a good idea to get those three together?"

"Trust me, unleashing the power of a new evil coven on the world is not exactly what I had in mind when I asked you here," I say.

Danny hums, nodding slowly as he mulls it over. "Evil coven, huh?"

Aargh, come on Ethan. That was the dorkiest, Harry-Potter-nerd-boy thing you could've said. "Yeah, no, yeah … never mind, that was … kind of stupid."

"No, no. It's not," Danny insists. "I was thinking it was accurate AF, actually."

"Yeah?"

Danny looks around, all suspicious like, then motions me to come closer like he's got a big secret to share. I lean in—the air between us is instantly charged, making the hair on my arms stand at attention.

Danny whispers, "No lie, I was legit scared for my soul back there." His warm breath tickles the spot on my neck just below my earlobe. I shiver and what I'm pretty sure started off as a laugh comes out as a giggle, which is so not hot. Great.

"Yeah," I say, because apparently, that's all I know how to say now—and why did it have to sound so dreamy? I would swear under oath that his smile is making me stupid. I focus on the Coca-Cola neon sign in the window behind him, take a slow breath, and let it out at half speed.

"So…" Danny says.

"So…" I reply.

Awkward. This is the part I hate, that point in a conversation where you've run out of easy things to say and there's only more serious stuff left, but you're not really sure how to start.

Finally, Danny clears his throat and says, "So … Sam Smith, really?"

I inhale sharply and he busts up. "Don't even," I say, playfully shoving his shoulder as I laugh too. "And what kind of songs were you streaming again?"

"Uh, that's classified information."

"Is it, though? Because I could've sworn I heard your friend say *breakup music*."

Danny shakes his head, holding back a smile. "He's crazy. That would have to mean we had something to break up, which we didn't."

My chest deflates a little and I try to keep the muscles in my face from drooping as I say, "Right."

Danny's eyes go wide. "Well, I mean … not that we … it's just … you know."

"Yeah, no, totally … we never…"

"…officially, we didn't…"

"Right, right."

Oh, my God. We sound like robots short-circuiting. Feels like it too. I can't stop moving around and I'm all itchy everywhere. Why can't this stuff ever be easy?

"Not that we couldn't have been ... if we wanted," Danny says. His tone sounds more cautious than panicked now. "I mean, I would've been cool with that."

Wait. What? Is he saying what I think he's saying? That he wanted us to be a couple in real life? *Boyfriends*. The thought that I screwed this up, lost something I wanted so badly, pushes like a knife between my ribs.

"Listen, Danny—"

"Hey, no worries," he says quickly, cutting me off. "I get it. You weren't looking for that kind of thing."

"Are you kidding me? Danny, I totally would've." I grimace, scratch at the back of my neck. "I mean, if I hadn't fucked things up ... we, maybe ... I don't know. I'm just sorry. I am so, so, so sorry—"

"Whoa, whoa," Danny interrupts, placing his palms on my shoulders. His voice is like a calm breeze. "We don't have to go there again. We can just," he shrugs, "act like it never happened. Retcon our entire history. You know, reboot."

Hope balloons at my center, and I'd probably float away if Danny's hands weren't anchoring me to the Earth.

"Yeah?" I ask.

"Definitely."

Before I can fully process what all this means, his mouth is on mine and every synapse in my brain melts into goo. On instinct, my hands slide around his sides, travel over the mountain range of muscle up his back, and when our lips part, I pull him into another kiss because this isn't a want, it's a *need*.

"We should've ... done that way earlier," Danny gasps after we finally come up for air.

"Totally," I pant.

"So, you said you *would've* before, but what about now?" Danny asks. His voice sounds weirdly strained.

I lift my chin to look at him. His expression is a hundred percent troublemaker. He's hinting about way more than a kiss. I think he's talking about us, together. As in *together*, together. An uncomfortable laugh tears out of me. I shift my gaze to the safety of the neon sign again and nod.

"I'm sorry, I didn't catch that," Danny teases.

Squirming, I say, "You know."

Danny coils his arms around me and I'm happy to be imprisoned by his fingers interlocking above my waist. "Nope. Don't think I do," he says. "You might need to spell it out for me."

I bite my lip, tilt my head back, and groan. "Are you really gonna make me say it?"

Danny's grin is wicked. "Oh, yeah."

I close my eyes, take a deep breath and let it rip. "Fine. Yes. It would be cool if, you know, you plus me could, like, equal a boyfriend thing."

His forehead wrinkles in confusion. "Umm, I'm really bad at math, so—

"Oh, my god!" I exclaim. "Danny, would you be my boyfriend?"

He cracks up, then does this annoyingly cute thing where he tilts his head from side to side as if he's considering it.

"Never mind. I take it back," I say and as I start to pull away, Danny wraps me in, bringing us chest to chest, faces so close our noses nearly touch.

"Ethan." He says my name like it's music. His eyes, they're sparkling, practically dancing. "I would love for you and me to equal a boyfriend thing."

Our lips touch again, my insides erupt like a

fountain. A gigantic fountain. A Las Vegas-sized fountain, with music and colored lights and a hundred jets of water shooting ten stories into the sky, because—I'm. Kissing. My. *Boyfriend*. And it's the most incredible thing ever.

"Okay, boys, put it back in your pants," Micaela teases. She's flanked by Liam and Conner and, holy shit, did they teleport or something? I didn't even hear the restaurant door open.

"Stalkers," I groan, "why are you following us?"

"Sorry to interrupt your little make-out sesh, *but*," Micaela says, gesturing to Conner, who, now that I notice, seems a little bewildered. "He just found out something you're gonna want to hear."

Chapter Twenty-Three

Danny

The look on Dad's scrunched-up face as I walk into the living room tells me exactly what he thinks of my outfit.

"No?" I ask, shifting my balance from my right hip to my left, doing my best to pose like male models do at the end of a runway.

"The lighter beige chinos are a yes, but the black and orange shirt feels less spring and more fall to me," Dad says, all diplomatic.

"Yeah, it's a little Halloweenie—and snug," Pop adds with a disapproving frown. "Did that shirt shrink? It's a bit much in the chesticles area there."

I drop my chin at him. "No, Pop, and don't say *chesticles*, like, ever." Um? I know he's trying to be silly, but this is not the time.

Pop throws his hands up in surrender and chuckles.

"Maybe try a calmer color?" Dad advises, giving me an encouraging smile. He knows how important this afternoon is to me. They both do. As we speak, Ethan is on his way here to pick me up for our first official date as boyfriends.

Boyfriends.

It's been almost three weeks and I still get super pumped every time I think about it—me and Ethan Decker are for real, legit, together. By the way, that drumbeat you hear is my heart pounding against my chest—double-time.

With a dramatic sigh, I leave the room and say, "Fine, I'll try something else," then from down the hall I add, "even tighter this time," over my shoulder, just to mess with Pop.

He gives me a sarcastic, "Good idea," at the same time Dad hollers, "Fourth outfit change will be the charm. I can feel it."

Okay, the straight-up truth is, I specifically picked out this shirt because I liked the way it showed off my arms and chest. From the second Ethan sees me today, I sort of want to encourage certain thoughts and actions if you know what I mean.

At this point, I'm pretty sure I am literally going to die if I don't get to kiss him soon, because even though we've been together for nearly three weeks and we call and text every day, you know what we haven't been able to do? Hang out in real life. Not that we haven't wanted to, but our schedules…

Last weekend our guard traveled down to San Diego to compete at our last regional of the season, and the week before that, Ethan's group had one in Las Vegas.

Upside—we're now ranked third and second respectively going into world championships. Downside—you do not know torture until you have a hot boyfriend and the closest you're able to get are shirtless photos on your phone during some private time.

Seriously, if I had known that night at the diner that we wouldn't be getting to see each other for a little while, I would've made sure we found a more secluded spot, so I could get my kisses in while I could. But—sucks for me—that's not how it went down.

Once Conner and the others told us they found out it was Devin Washburn and two other shits from our basketball team who trashed our guard shed, things got distracting, to say the least.

I still can't believe those guys were dumb enough

to actually upload a TikTok of themselves sword fighting *with our sabers* to Devin's account. I mean, sure, post video evidence of you with our stolen equipment on the internet for all to see. Who's gonna know?

By Monday, it was all over school. Our principal even made this big announcement about how "destruction of school property is a serious crime" and that "anyone caught would be prosecuted to the fullest extent of the law."

I hope they're all expelled. Assholes. They almost screwed us out of our best season ever, and for what? Sanjay thinks that when he called Devin out in class for his antigay crap and hinted about their real-life hookup, that's what set him off. Which, even if it's true, I'm sorry, no, you don't get to use your internal homophobia as an excuse to do fucked-up shit. If anyone knows that, it's me. What Devin did is not Sanjay's fault. It's his. Full stop.

So, after all that drama, you bet your ass I've earned a date with my boyfriend, and goddammit, I'm going to look as hot as I possibly can for it.

I take Dad's advice, throw on an olive-green shirt, and leave an extra button undone. It's more subtle, but yeah, I'm kind of feeling my reflection right now.

My phone buzzes on my nightstand. I pick it up, expecting a text, but it's an email notification. The subject reads, "Your AncestryDNA results are in."

My pulse jumps, my brain instantly going into defense mode, reminding me not to get my hopes up after the suckage that was my 23andMe results. Logically, I know this is likely going to be more of the same, but I can't ignore it.

"How's it going in there?" Dad hollers from the living room.

"I'm still deciding. Give me a minute," I holler

back, closing my bedroom door.

I sit at my desk, open my laptop, and log into the Ancestry website. I scroll past the prompt asking me to *Start a Family Tree*, past my *Ethnicity Estimate*, then click on *View All DNA Matches*. The page loads, and all my organs feel like they're sliding out of my body.

There, under a section titled *Parent/Child,* is an account. More specifically, an account with the initials A.D. that has 50% shared DNA—my mother.

Endorphins flood my bloodstream. In the space of a few seconds I go from flying high to crash landing. Other than confirming this account is 100% a parent-child connection to me, there's no additional information, no close family associations, no anything. There isn't even a way to send her a message. The account is mostly private, locked.

I've learned nothing—less than nothing. I mean, A.D.? What does the D stand for? Is that Ana's middle initial? Did she change her last name from Ramos to something else? I have no idea.

Heat rushes into my cheeks, builds behind my eyes. I slump over my desk, burrow into the crook of my elbow as my face cracks, and I burst. Did I really think this would be so easy? That I'd do this dumb test and learn everything I ever wanted? Why? Because I found some anonymous asshole on Reddit who said they did? I'm so stupid, so very, very stupid. I'm never going to find her.

"Hey, do you want some help narrowing down choices?" Dad hollers from the other side of my bedroom door.

I jolt upright and quickly close my laptop screen. Without thinking, I answer, "No," but it comes out gravelly and strained.

Dammit.

"Is everything okay?" Dad asks, voice full of concern.

"I'm fine," I reply in a tone nobody could ever believe.

"You don't *sound* fine."

Great. Just great. I've set off his bullshit detector.

Dad knocks, lightly at first, then louder. "Danny? *Danny*? Answer me." When I don't, he opens my bedroom door.

"Don't—" I protest, but it's too late. Panicking, I start to stand up, then sit back down, and freeze. I don't turn around, don't breathe, don't do anything except try to hold back the tidal wave cresting inside me.

"Danny?" He says my name so softly, but that's all it takes for my defenses to crumble. A sob breaks free, and I hide my face in my hands.

Dad instantly shifts into freak-out mode, calling for Pop, hovering over me, asking if I'm sick or hurt.

I shake my head, *no*. The tears won't stop. My throat feels like it's full of wet sand. I don't understand why this is hitting me so hard.

"Well, what is it?" Dad presses, impatience creeping into the edges of his voice.

"Nothing," I croak, hating how pathetic I sound.

"Don't tell me *nothing*. This is obviously not nothing." His sharp parental-tone is at 100 now. "Danny, what in the world is going on?"

A few years ago, I would've armored up and gone to war with him. Even a week ago, I would've made up an excuse and stuck to it, no matter how ridiculous it sounded. But now I don't do any of that. For some reason, I do the thing I never thought I would. I open my laptop and gesture to the screen.

Dad's eyes cut from me to my computer, where they stop long enough to soak up the information on the monitor, then swell with understanding. "Oh, son," he says in a sad, flat pitch I've never heard come out of him.

"What's going on in here?" Pop asks, appearing in my doorway.

"Clayton," Dad begins, then gestures to my laptop.

Pop approaches, brows furrowed as he scrutinizes the words on the screen. "Is this—" he starts, then realization seems to set in and all his features fall. He exhales. "Oh, boy."

They both seem so disappointed. I didn't picture telling them like this. Truthfully, I didn't picture telling them at all.

"I'm sorry," I blurt, swiping at my eyes.

"Daniel, look at me," Pop says and he never uses my full name, so I do. "You have nothing to be sorry for. Understand?"

I nod, but I can't maintain eye contact with him because it's a lie. I think of all the times I wielded Ana's existence like a weapon against them and feel like I've been punched in the gut. A desperate need for them to understand comes over me.

"This isn't ... it's not ... I ... I..." I don't have the words. Why can't I find the right words?

"Hey, hey," Dad says, gently rubbing my back. "It's okay. You don't have to explain."

I feel like he's babying me, and I hate it. I'm not a fragile little boy.

"Yes, I do," I bristle, shrugging him off. "I just ... I need to find her, okay? *For me*."

Dad backs off, exhales. "Danny, why didn't you tell us you were feeling this way?"

I shrug.

"How long have you been at this?" Pop asks.

"A few months, maybe," I say. "But it doesn't

matter. Nothing matters. I'm never going to find her." A hot itchy sensation flares up between my shoulder blades. "This was a total waste of time. I don't know why I bothered with this stupid test. I don't even know who the fuck A.D. is. I didn't learn anything!"

Fed up with the proof of my failure being projected at me in 4K, I slam my laptop closed. I fully expect one of my fathers to get onto me for being so rough with my computer or to tell me to watch my mouth, but they're just staring at each other, having one of their silent conversations.

After an eternity, Pop tilts his head, jaw working over something that seems unpleasant as Dad squeezes his eyelids shut like he's preparing for a head-on collision.

"He needs to know, Glenn," Pop says.

Dad's expression relaxes and he lets out a resigned sigh. "I know."

Dread creeps up my spine. I suppress a shudder. "Know what?"

"Durrell," Pop says flatly.

"Huh?"

He looks right at me. "Your mother's name is Ana Durrell now. She married about five years ago, we think."

Everything, everywhere in me goes numb, like my soul has been knocked out of my body and I'm just a human shell. Pop is saying something else, but it's hard to hear, hard to think. Out my window, I notice a car driving by our house and wonder where it's headed.

Someone asks Pop, "How do you know that?" The sound sucks my spirit back into my body, and I realize the question came from me.

"For a time, she was ... corresponding with us," Pop says.

"Corresponding?" The fuck does that mean?

As if on cue, Dad reenters my room—I didn't even notice he'd left until now—carrying an envelope.

"We stayed in touch with Ana for several years. I wrote her a letter every January, after the holidays, updating her on how you were doing. She stopped responding after your fifth birthday, but I continued sending her updates every now and then," Dad explains.

Pop jumps in, adding, "We thought it was important to keep that door open in case there was a chance you two could have some kind of relationship in the future."

Dad nods in agreement, exhales slowly, and continues. "Then about six years ago, she sent this." He offers me the envelope, and I take it.

The first thing I notice is how pretty her bubbly handwriting is, the opposite of mine, but still, knowing this letter came from her and is now in my hands feels weirdly like I'm connecting with her in some way. Then I read the return address and do a full-on double take—this letter was sent from Santa Cruz, California.

My heart leaps into my throat. All these years, I've wondered where in the world she could be, and this entire time, my dads knew she was less than fifty miles away.

Heat travels up the sides of my neck. "How could you keep this from me?" I whisper and I don't know how it's not a shout.

Dad shakes his head. "Danny, we were trying to protect you—"

"By lying to me?" I ask, voice a hundred octaves higher. "Thanks so much for that."

"That's not fair, Danny," Dad says.

"Fair?" An angry laugh punches past my lips. "Like any of this is fair to me!"

"Maybe you should read what she wrote before

you say another word, Daniel." I'm not sure what to make of Pop's strange tone. It sounds a lot like the one he uses to warn me when he thinks I'm about to cross a line during an argument, but there's something else I don't recognize there.

"Whatever," I mumble, because I need to have the last word right now. I need a win. Fortunately, Pop lets me take it and doesn't say anything.

I open the envelope, pull out the letter. My hands shake a little as I unfold the single sheet of lined paper and begin to read.

Dear Glenn and Clayton,

I am happy to know that Danny has a good family and is doing well, but I do not wish to stay in contact any longer. I don't mean to sound cold-hearted. I have begun a family of my own. I need to close this chapter of my life and move on.

I don't wish to get into personal details about me or my family. Please understand that I want them left out of this completely. I don't mean to sound unkind, but please respect my wishes as there are others to consider. I do wish you and your family all the best.

Regards and goodbye,

Ana Durrell

It's bizarre, how you can feel nothing at a moment when you know you should feel something, but my mind is completely blank. I fold the letter up and slip it back into the envelope, then everything slams into me all at once, ripping open a black hole of worthlessness. Tears blind my eyes. I can't stand the thin, strange noise coming from the back of my throat as I cry.

"I know, I know," Dad says softly.

"It's okay, Danny. We understand," Pop adds. He places a hand on my shoulder and all my cold grief is replaced with searing anger. I jump out of my seat.

"Don't touch me!" I explode. "You don't understand, *liars*! I will never forgive you for this, ever! I hate you!"

In my eighteen years, I've seen them react in different ways to a lot of different things, but I've never seen them like this before, with big fearful eyes and faces drained of color. I know I'm scaring them, and I don't care. Keeping this essential truth from me, that hurts more than anything else ever has.

I push past them, bullet out of my room. Pop calls after me, but I keep going, down the hall, out the front door. I don't stop running.

Chapter Twenty-Four

Ethan

As soon as I park in front of Danny's house, he's rushing out to me before I've even shut off the engine. I smile, start to wave, he couldn't wait to see me. But then I realize that he's not actually running in my direction. He's already across the lawn and halfway down the block.

It takes a few seconds for my brain to process what my eyes are seeing—my boyfriend, fleeing from his house like it's a burning building, looking really upset.

"Danny?" I call out as I fling open the car door and undo my seatbelt.

If he heard me, he's not stopping.

"Danny, wait!" I shout louder, chasing after him.

My mind starts scrolling through possible scenarios that could have led to this. I think of all the scary movies I've watched where people run from a house after discovering some horrific scene inside. I force my feet to move faster.

Danny is at the end of the block now. I shout his name again and this time, he stops. He doesn't turn to face me, though. Instead, he leans his back against a large maple tree and slides to the ground.

"Holy shit! What ... happened? Are you ... okay?" I ask between breaths when I finally catch up to him.

Danny shakes his head without looking up at me. Tears roll down his face, one side and then the other. I open my mouth to say something, but nothing comes. I don't really know what to ask or do right now. All I know is, seeing him like this—curled up next to a tree, crying his eyes out—hurts. I want to hug him but I'm not sure that's the best idea right now, so I sit down next to him and wait for a signal.

Danny wipes at his eyes with the back of his hand, his expression changing from sad to stoic. He sniffs. "So, I sort of found my mom." His voice is almost monotone. "My dads always told me they didn't know where she was or how to contact her. Lies. All lies."

I can feel my eyelids opening wider, jaw slowly lowering like the drawbridge of a castle.

"They were hiding this from me," Danny says, handing over an envelope. "Go ahead. Read it."

I'm not exactly comfortable with this, but the pleading look Danny's giving me makes it impossible not to do what he asks. So, I read, and the oddest feeling begins in my chest. It's a crinkling, crushing sensation that intensifies with each line, like someone is slowly stomping an aluminum can just above my sternum. I think it's my heart breaking for him.

"Whoa," I say when I reach the end, which is so lame. Given all the dramatic series I've binged over the years, you'd think I'd have something better to add in this sort of situation, but no. Real life isn't like an episode of *Never Have I Ever* or even *Riverdale*. There's no profound monologue on the tip of my tongue. I've got no words of wisdom to offer. All I can do is listen, feeling completely useless, as Danny fills me in about the argument he had with his parents.

"They had no right to hide this from me," he says when he's finished. "She's my mother. *My mother*." His tone becomes more heated as words fly out of him with increasing speed. "I mean, what if they pissed her off, writing her all those letters? They're so annoying, always pushing, pushing, pushing. What if they're the reason she sent *this*?" Danny holds up the letter, giving it an angry shake.

I wish I had answers for him—or at least the ability to give him some support, but I've got nothing.

"I should've been allowed to contact her, but nope, they thought it would be a better idea to look me in the eye and bullshit—for years, they pretended like they didn't know where she was, and I'm supposed to just be cool with that now that I know the truth? How can I ever trust anything they ever tell me again?"

Danny stands up so quickly it startles me.

"No. No. You know what? I don't accept this. I *won't* accept this," Danny says, pacing back and forth, the sidewalk shimmering under his bright white shoes in the afternoon sun. "I'm done letting other people decide what parts of my own life I get to know. I've got her address now. Why don't I just go?"

I'm not sure if he's asking me or just thinking out loud, but for the first time since I caught up to him, I'm finally able to form words again. "I don't know. Are you sure that's a good idea? I mean, she..." I trail off, because I can't bring myself to point out the most fucked up part of that letter—she said she doesn't want to have anything to do with him. Mercifully, something else pops into my head. "She probably moved. I'll bet she doesn't even live there anymore."

Danny stops, seems to consider this for a few seconds, then starts pacing again. "I have to find out. I have to know or it's going to drive me crazy." His forehead creases, lips condense into a tight line. "I'm gonna do it. Right now."

Everything in me is screaming this is a bad decision. I jump to my feet. "What? Now? Danny, maybe take a minute first. What if she freaks out and—"

"I *need* to meet her, Ethan," Danny says, eyes locking on mine. His rigid posture and determined expression make it obvious there's no talking him out of this. Then he softens and adds, "Before I lose my nerve."

And there's that crushed can feeling in my chest again.

I swallow hard and nod. Really, what more could I possibly say?

Danny takes a deep breath, inches closer to me. "I've got a crazy favor to ask," he says, eyes drifting down to the sidewalk. "You don't have to do it if you don't want to."

I'm a little worried about what comes next, but I already know there's no way I could say no to his pleading face right now.

"That's okay. What is it?" I ask.

"Would you go with me?"

Chapter Twenty-Five

Danny

The surprising thing about going to meet one of your birth parents for the first time isn't that you're an emotional mess along the way. It's that there are also entire minutes where the universe goes still and you're at peace with your place in it.

That is, until you pass another car on the freeway with kids in the backseat and a woman behind the wheel, likely their mother. That's when you're reminded of everything you never knew, and those feelings start swirling inside again, threatening to suck you down into the darkest depths of yourself.

"Okay if I turn on the radio?" Ethan asks when we hit stop-and-go traffic on Highway 17. It's the first thing either one of us has said since we took off about thirty minutes ago.

"It's your car. You're the boss here," I say, forcing it to come out upbeat and tagging on a smile at the end. It's not genuine, but I'm trying. My fucked-up life has already hijacked our date. I don't want to make this any more awkward for him by being a whiny little bitch.

Ethan gives me an unsure grin back. He taps the power button and the DJ tells us to keep it locked on Wild 94.9, the Bay Area's number 1 hit music station, just before Sam Smith's smooth vocals slide through the speakers.

Ethan sits up straight. His face goes from a grimace to this teasing *don't you say it* expression. I try to hold back, but then Sam hits a super high note, and the smallest hint of curving begins in the corners of Ethan's mouth. I can't help it. I crack the hell up, then Ethan does too, and it's as if a knob gets turned in my chest, opening a valve, releasing all the tension trapped in there. We laugh and laugh until the car behind us honks, obviously impatient for us to close the gap between Ethan's Prius and a white Lexus now stopped ten feet ahead.

"I'm never going to live that down, am I?" Ethan asks, switching to another station as we begin to roll forward.

"Probably not," I say and this time the smile I give him is real.

Beaming, Ethan shrugs. It's such a small movement, but it feels so much bigger than that. It feels like *acceptance*—not just about the playful teasing, either. I'm talking about acceptance of me, us, all this crazy. It feels like … well, more than I can say.

Maybe that's why I asked him to come with me. It's not something I thought about, it just seemed natural. Is that how you know you've legit fallen for someone? When you can't picture going through even the scary shit without them?

I don't know. Maybe. But I do know that I'm so grateful he's here. I mean, how many guys would be willing to drop everything to help you chase down what may be nothing? Not many. Ethan did, though. Without hesitation. That's gotta mean something, right?

A rush of guilt goes through me when I realize that I haven't even thanked him yet. I clear my throat. "Hey, Ethan, I just wanted to say I appreciate all this."

"Yeah, of course, it's no problem at all," he says.

"Seriously, I really do. You driving and—"

"Don't even worry about it," he insists.

I get the sense I'm making him uncomfortable, so I let it go and just nod.

He turns to look out the driver's side window for

a minute. When he turns back, he keeps his gaze forward, his lips pinched to one side. His eyebrows rise and fall with his next breath, and I can tell he's wrestling with something he wants to say.

"What?" I ask.

Ethan opens his mouth, then stays silent for a beat. Finally, he exhales and says, "Listen, Danny, I wanted to tell you that I—"

My phone begins buzzing with an incoming call from Dad, cutting into our conversation like a chainsaw.

"Shit," I mumble, staring at the screen. I'm sure they're freaking out, wondering where I'm at, what I'm doing.

"Do you want to answer it?" Ethan asks.

"No," I say, feeling a small sense of satisfaction watching the call go to voicemail. Let them worry. I am fresh out of fucks to give. "As a matter of fact," I say, then power off my phone, shove it into my pocket, and return my full attention to Ethan. "Sorry, you were saying you had something you wanted to tell me?"

"Oh, uh, yeah … just that…" Ethan pauses, taking his foot off the brake long enough for us to roll forward a few feet, then come to a full stop again. "Um, I was going to say that I, uh, that I'm totally cool with driving, really. Happy to do it."

Okay, I am one hundred percent sure that's not what he was going to say. Was he going to tell me how insane he thinks what I'm about to do is? If that's the case, I really don't want to hear it, but I don't think that was it. I got the sense he was trying to say something more … personal.

Ugh, part of me wants to pull it out of him, but it kind of feels like the calm we were enjoying in the middle of this shitstorm has totally passed. (Excellent timing, Dad. No, really, thanks so much. Now I've got another reason to be furious at you.) I'm not going to push him right now.

"Awesome, thanks," I say softly, even though the muscles in my jaw are tensing up again. I rest my head against the passenger window. The cool glass feels good against the side of my warm face.

Soon traffic begins moving again, but the conversation between me and Ethan has ground to a halt, which is probably for the best right now. It gives me the chance to focus all my attention on calming the angry beast inside of me who keeps threatening to break out of his cage.

When I meet my mom, I want her to see me as a mature, cool dude she can be proud of. Not some emotionally unstable loser who makes her feel like she dodged the world's biggest bullet when she put me up for adoption.

The remainder of our drive helps with my crazy anxiety. I've always thought it was one of the most beautiful in northern California, the way the highway winds up into the Santa Cruz mountains, through miles of Redwood trees that stretch to the sky.

But my chill vibe begins heating back up as soon as we take the Chestnut Street exit, then my heartrate doubles a few blocks later when Ethan's Waze app tells us we've arrived at our destination. He finds a parking spot on the street two houses down and shuts off the engine. I have to remind myself to breathe. It's no biggie, just something I've been waiting eighteen years for, that's all.

"Are you sure you still want to do this?" Ethan asks, the space between his eyebrows crinkling with concern.

Maybe that's what he was going to ask me earlier. He doesn't get why we're really here, how deep this goes for me, and let's be real, how could he? Ethan lucked out with a perfect family. He's always known who he is and where he comes from. People have no idea how those questions can get at you throughout your life—or what the millions more that come with knowing you were rejected before you were even born can do to you. It's not good. Trust me. You'd do anything, *anything* to find answers. Because all the shit you don't know is what hurts the most.

But how do you explain all that to someone? I don't think I could if I tried.

"I'm sure," I say, sitting up taller, trying to project a level of confidence I absolutely do not have as we get out of the car—the biggest performance of my life.

The address isn't all that different from the rest in the neighborhood. It's just another small bungalow-style house, but the bright blue color and blooming rose garden make it feel like more of a home.

I step onto the porch and wonder what it would've been like to grow up in this city by the beach, to live in this place, play in this yard—with her. How different would that life be? Would I be happy? Would I still be me? In that world, would she love me so much she could never imagine a life without her son? Will she even like who I am in this one?

My knees begin shaking and I have the sudden urge to run in the opposite direction. I turn to Ethan, who's hanging two steps behind. Not so far that it's weird, but like he's trying to respect my space. He gives me an encouraging *you got this* nod and it's exactly the boost I needed to see this through.

I take a deep breath and ring the doorbell.

Universes die and are reborn during the endless seconds that follow. Then I hear footsteps, fast and heavy, inside. The door swings open, sucking all the air out of my lungs. A little girl, who couldn't be older than five or six, is in the doorway, grinning up at me. She's wearing a Disney Princess dress—Elsa from *Frozen*, I think.

"Hello." She giggles, making the black pigtails on the sides of her head bounce. "Who are you?"

"Hi, I'm ..."

The little girl scrunches up her nose and I recognize its rounded shape, her squinting brown eyes. They're a smaller version of mine. The realization is an electric surge that fries my nervous system, zapping my legs. Somehow, I'm still standing when my brain finally manages to reboot.

I struggle to find my voice and finally spit out, "Is, um, is Ana home?"

"Uh huh, Mommy is watching *Frozen*. I like *Frozen*," the little girl says.

"I can tell," I say, forcing a small laugh.

She looks up at the ceiling, begins swaying from side to side. "Um, hey, you know that part when Elsa sings, *Let it* go—"

"Maddie, you know you're not supposed to answer the door by yourself," an airy voice says from inside, and then it's as if she appears out of nowhere, right in front of me. Her wavy black hair is longer, with streaks of silver near her temples. There are light wrinkles across her forehead and in the corners of her eyes, but she still has the same radiant smile as the woman in the one and only picture I have of her. It's my mother, Ana.

Sweat is soaking my armpits and my heart is trying to head-butt its way out of my ribcage.

"Go watch your movie," Ana says, ushering the little girl back into the house before turning to me. She shakes her head. "Sorry about that. Little stinker gets faster every day, seems like. Can I help you?"

"Um, yeah, you, u-uh, I-I'm, uh," I sputter, sounding like a car engine trying to start on a cold morning. I inhale and salt air fills my nostrils and my voice turns over. "Hi, I'm Danny."

Ana looks confused, smiling at me like I've just told her a joke she doesn't get. Her eyes dart over to Ethan, then back to me. I try again.

"I'm, uh, I'm ... your son."

Nothing, for one, two, three, four, five, *six* excruciating seconds, and then something I never expected—my mother laughs. It's nearly silent and forced but its sharp edges are like thorns, filling the space between us. I take a step back.

"No, that's..." she begins, and I think she's going to deny it.

"I'm pretty sure you're my biological mother," I say, straining to get the words out.

The smiling mask on her face slides away, revealing an unrecognizable expression underneath. "What do you want?" she asks.

What do I want? I don't even know how to answer that.

"Nothing," I say, my tongue sticking to the roof of my dry mouth, making me sound strange. "I just, I—"

"Why would you ... I mean, you can't..." Ana stops, glances over at the wall, the wrinkles on her forehead compacting into a tight ball, concentrating like she's trying to work out a math problem in her head. Her breathing becomes heavy and she places a hand on her chest.

Holy shit. Is she having a heart attack?

"Are you okay?" I ask.

"My God, you can't do this to people ... just show up at their door," Ana says, getting ahold of herself.

"But you're my mom and I—"

"No," Ana says sternly, looking me directly in the eye. "I may have…" she stops, looks over her shoulder like she's checking to see if anyone is around, then turns back, lowering her voice to a whisper. "I may have given birth to you, but I was never your mother."

Something plummets into my stomach, where it sinks, and drowns. I'm pretty sure it was my heart.

"I'm sorry, but you have to go. Please don't come back here again," Ana says, and then she's gone, leaving me with a door in my face, and the metallic click of a lock ringing in my ears.

Chapter Twenty-Six

Ethan

"Well, at least now you know, right?" I say as we leave the city limits.

Danny doesn't say a word. He's been like this since we got back in the car—staring ahead at nothing, a blank expression on his face. I think he's in shock, which I totally get, but I'm really starting to freak out here. What if he had a mental break or something?

Desperate to help him find some kind of silver lining, I say, "You never know, maybe, with a little time, she'll come around and—"

"No," Danny snaps, and I jump. "That's never going to happen."

"All right," I say, soft and slow, as if backing away from a growling dog with its teeth out.

"She doesn't give two shits about me. She doesn't care. She never did and never will," Danny snarls. "You saw her. She was freakin' terrified of me—like I'm some kind of monster."

"Well … yeah, but," I stutter, then shut up, thinking it's better if I don't finish that sentence right now.

"But?" Danny asks.

"Nothing." Me and my big mouth. I'm saying all the wrong things here.

"Don't do that shit to me again, start to tell me something and then change the subject. I am so sick of everybody lying to me," Danny says sharply.

I try to remind myself that he's not mad at me, it's the situation. He's dealing with a lot, which is why I didn't tell him what I almost let out on our way down here either.

"Come on, Danny," I plead, trying to deescalate things. "I'm not lying. Haven't you ever started to say something and then changed your mind?"

Danny frowns. "Not when it's important, no."

"It's so not important."

"Just say it, Ethan. Jesus."

He's not going to let this go. I don't want him getting any more pissed at me, but he wants honesty, so, fine, here goes.

"Okay, what I was going to say was, you did, kind of, surprise her is all," I begin, trying not to sound judgy. "I mean, showing up at her house was … maybe not the best thing you could've started with?"

He turns to look outside the passenger window, but in my peripheral, I can see his reflection, fuming and miserable in the glass.

"Well, sorry we can't all be as *perfect* as you," Danny says bitterly.

"Huh? What's that supposed to mean?"

"It means life is a little more challenging for some of us."

"I didn't know it was a competition," I say, heat drifting up my neck like steam, "and my life is plenty challenging, thank you very much."

"Oh, please. You have no idea how good you have it, going to your perfect school, performing in your perfect color guard, living with your perfect family."

"What the fuck, Danny?" I fire back. I was trying to be understanding but I'm not going to just sit here and be his punching bag. "You think my family is so perfect? Why, because my mom and dad are my biological parents? Yeah. Sure. That totally makes sense. News flash. They're so wrapped up in their jobs, they barely even notice me anymore, but whatever. Don't let the facts get in the way. We share the same DNA, so, yes, you're right, everything is awesome."

Danny exhales loudly, but nothing follows, so I keep going.

"You know, in a lot of ways, I wish my parents were more like *your dads*. At least they seem to care about more than what you scored at the last regional."

"Yeah, they care so much they've lied to me my whole life," Danny hits back.

"About that?" I gesture to the city behind us. "Yes!" A rush of adrenaline hits my bloodstream and my mouth takes off running. "Anyone who read that letter could see it was *so obvious* you meeting your mom like that was never going to end up any other way than *not great*. Why would you put yourself in that situation?"

"You wouldn't understand," Danny growls.

"You're right, Danny." I know I should stop, just shut up, but this train has left the station. I can't get off. "I don't understand how you can be so dense about this, but now I get why your dads maybe didn't want to tell you. They were trying to protect you. How dare they?"

"So now you're taking their side? Great, thanks for that."

"I'm on your side, Danny! Everyone is on your side, and it's been so shitty to have to—"

"Oh, I am so sorry this has been hard for *you*."

"Of course it is! *I love you* and seeing you hurt sucks!"

I can see the moment that word crashes into Danny, the pileup of emotions it causes on his face. Surprise, confusion, fear maybe. I don't know. There are so many I can't tell what he's thinking.

I'm still doing almost eighty down the highway, but my insides feel like they've been wrapped around a tree. I knew I wanted to tell him today. I practiced a hundred different ways how I might put it out there, like, casually after he'd tell me a joke that made me laugh, or sweetly whisper it in his ear between kisses. I never imagined it would just slip out like this, at the worst possible time, in the middle of a fight.

Danny's skin is almost glowing red. He opens his mouth, lips forming different shapes, like he's trying to get something out but doesn't know how to start. Finally, he says, "Oh, uh, Ethan, I-I don't, uh…" he swallows hard and hides his face in his hands.

Oh, God. Is he trying to tell me he doesn't feel the same way? If he is, I don't want to hear it. I don't want to know. Panic spikes in me, end to end, and a frantic need to fill the silence takes over.

"Listen, Danny, I know today didn't go the way you wanted, but if you ask me, you're the one who doesn't know how good you have it. There are so many people in your life who care a lot about you, and it's got nothing to do with biology," I say, fighting back the cry forming in my throat. "It's because of who you are. You are kind, and thoughtful, and so brave, and if that woman is going to throw away her chance to know that wonderful person, you need to throw her away. She doesn't deserve you. I mean, your family, friends, all of us, we—"

"Stop," Danny croaks, lifting his head. Tears begin falling from his eyes, and the pained expression on his face stabs my heart. "I can't."

What have I done?

"Danny, I'm sorr—"

He holds up his flat palms against the air, like he's trying to push me away, push away the whole world, and asks, "Can you just take me back home, please?"

Chapter Twenty-Seven

Danny

When someone tells you they love you, it's supposed to make you feel unstoppable, or like you're levitating, or a million other clichés pop stars sing about. So, I don't know why I shut down when Ethan said it.

Actually, that's a lie, and haven't I told myself enough of those today?

It's the rest of what he said that sent me down a shame-spiral. I want to be pissed off at him for it, but I'm pissed that I can't be pissed because maybe he's sort of right.

"Listen, Danny, I ..." Ethan begins when we roll up to my house.

I can't. Whatever else he's going to say, I seriously can't right now. All I want is to curl into a ball and disappear.

"Thanks for the ride," I mumble, practically jumping out of his car. I don't look back. Not even when Ethan sighs and it sounds like he's breathing fire. Not even when he growls, "Fine, be that way then." Not even when his tires screech as he drives off into the night.

It's probably for the best, I tell myself. Ethan knows what a mess I am now. I'm sure he was going to figure out sooner or later that getting involved with me is a mistake because that's all I make. That's what I am.

The thought of facing my dads is like a stone in my belly, getting heavier with each miserable step up our driveway. I'm fishing my house keys out of my pocket, praying I'll be able to sneak into my room undetected, when my parents open the front door. I flinch.

"Thank God," Pop mutters under his breath. They

must've been watching out the window, noticed the second Ethan's car pulled up.

"We've been worried sick," Dad says, looking me over. "It's been hours. You weren't answering our calls. We thought—" His voice cracks, and he clamps a hand over his mouth.

"It's all right, Glenn. He's back. He's safe. That's all that matters," Pop says. When he wraps a reassuring arm around Dad's shoulders, I notice the jagged edges of his fingernails. He's been biting them again. He only does that when he's really stressed.

The stone in my belly has become a boulder, threatening to crush every bone in my legs under its massive weight.

Pop turns to me, and asks, "Are you okay, son?"

I shrug, look down. I'm a lot of things right now, but none of them are okay. "I don't know," is what I mean to say, but as I raise my head and make eye contact, my vision goes blurry and the only words that come out are, "Poppa, Daddy…"

It's been years since I called either one of them that, and I can't say exactly why I do now. Maybe when you fuck up as badly as I have, it doesn't matter how old you are, a part of you is still that little kid who just wants your parents to hold you and tell you everything will be okay.

The edges of Pop's eyebrows droop as he mouths a silent, pained, *Oh*. Then he opens his arms wide, like he just knows what I need, like he can read my mind, and the boulder in my belly rolls away.

Suddenly, it's as if I'm five years old again, falling into his embrace. He holds me tight, let's me wail against his shoulder, and repeats, "It's gonna be all right," while Dad gently strokes my hair.

When I've gotten the worst of it out of me, after

my crying morphs into short sniffles and shaky breaths, Dad says, "Hey, how about we go in the living room and I'll fix us some tea?"

I nod, and minutes later, we're all sitting on the couch, sipping steaming mugs of chamomile. The silence that follows is kind of comfortable, actually. I'm sure I could spend the rest of the day like this, not talking. But I decide to keep it real, rip the Band-Aid off and get everything out in the open.

I tell them about driving to Ana's house with Ethan, and how I was gutted when a little girl who looked like me answered the door.

"It sucks. I have a sister out there I'll never know, and at the same time—this is so dumb—but I'm kind of jealous of her, too," I say. "Why was she good enough to keep, but I wasn't?"

"Danny, you can't think about it like that," Pop says.

I nod like I agree, but I'm sure that's a question I'll always wonder about.

"What double sucks, though, is that I was so sure Ana would feel something if she just *saw me*, that we'd have some sort of connection, you know? But, yeah," I add, pointing a finger gun at my temple and mime firing it, "so delusional. All she did was confirm that I was a big, freakin' mistake."

"Oh, my God. No. *No*. You cannot do this to yourself. You are the furthest thing from a mistake," Dad says and his tone is somewhere between offended and horrified. He glances at Pop and something passes between them I can't read.

Pop gently blows at the white puffs rising from his tea, takes a small sip, then sets his cup down on the coffee table. I fully expect he's about to follow up Dad's comment to me with more of the same. Not sure how much more of that I can take.

"When your dad and I decided that we wanted to grow our family, we were convinced surrogacy was the right fit for us," Pop begins. "The process took forever, and it was insanely expensive, but when we got the news that our second attempt had resulted in a successful pregnancy, well, it was all worth it."

What? I sit up straight. They never told me this.

Pop clears his throat and continues. "We kept it quiet at first. We knew anything could happen at any time, so we tried not to get too excited. But after three months, that became impossible. We told our family and close friends. Everyone was so happy for us."

Pop looks at Dad and smiles, but it feels more sad than happy.

"Another month went by. Then one evening, while we were in a Pottery Barn Kids store, crib shopping, your dad's cellphone rang. He answered, turned white as a sheet, and I knew. I could sense what had happened before he even passed me the phone, before the doctor tried to explain. Our surrogate had miscarried. We'd lost the baby."

I can't talk, can't move. I. Am. Literally. Stunned.

"We were devastated," Dad murmurs.

"I don't think anything can ever prepare you for that kind of loss," Pop says, and his voice sounds so flimsy. "I certainly wasn't prepared for the way it affected me. Neither one of us were."

Blinking over at Dad, I watch the muscles in his jaw tick. Finally, he says, "Back then, people didn't really talk about what dads go through in that situation. Nobody said anything, but there was this attitude, like we weren't really allowed to feel the level of grief we did because we weren't the ones carrying the baby. People don't get it. They don't understand how it feels to be expecting your first child and then all you get is a phone call, and suddenly, you're just not anymore."

"We kept going through the motions—work, life—but we were a couple of zombies. We couldn't really eat or sleep. Things didn't seem to matter as much after that. I began to think that maybe we'd never be parents. I became so bitter and angry at the world, at the unfair hand life had dealt us," Pop says. He rubs his eyes and takes a deep breath. "I don't know how she did it, but your grandma Claire eventually talked us into giving adoption a chance."

"Friends of ours had been trying to adopt for years and," Dad says, shrugging, "nothing. That's why we originally went with surrogacy. We didn't want to be in the same boat, waiting for something that may never happen."

"So, the last thing we expected, two months in, was a call from our coordinator telling us about a newborn baby boy whose original adoption plan had fallen through and needed an immediate placement," Pop says, then glances at his open hands with an expression that looks like he's witnessing magic. "Six hours later, the nurse was placing you in my arms."

"He was so cute," Dad says, gesturing to Pop. "He kept grinning down at you and whispering, *How are you real?*"

Pop low-key blushes as he shakes his head, gently laughs, then nods.

"I couldn't believe it. After everything we went through, the dozens of choices we made that could've taken us down a different path, somehow, against all odds, there you were in my hands. *Our son,*" Pop says.

His glassy eyes travel over to mine, and this time when he smiles, it's so big it hurts.

"In that moment, I was convinced it was fate. You

were always meant to be our son. That's when everything changed. The universe made sense again and all the bitterness, all the pain I'd been carrying around was just *gone*. You did that," Pop says. A single tear trickles down to his chin, but he's still smiling. "So, you see, Danny. You weren't a mistake. You were a miracle, a miracle that has filled our lives with so much joy. You're *our son*. We love you, so much, and nothing will ever change that."

I turn away, needing a second to absorb everything, and a photo hanging on the wall practically jumps out at me—the one where my dads are posing with three-day-old me in the hospital nursery.

That picture used to embarrass the hell out of me, but for the first time, I don't even notice my squished-up face or fuzzy little head. What stands out now isn't Pop's messy hair or the cringe puka shell necklace Dad's wearing, it's their lit faces, beaming and bright, obviously feeling the most legit happiness two people can feel on the planet—all because of me.

I don't know why I couldn't see it before. Now that I do, though, I think I realize something else, too. Family isn't really a thing you are, it's more like a special kind of love, and nothing, not even sharing the same DNA guarantees someone will give it to you. But when they do, it's a gift, one I swear I'll never take for granted again.

"I love you guys, too," I say, and fuck, I'm crying again. "I don't say it enough, and I suck for that, but you should know, the reason I kept everything a secret, that I was looking for Ana, I mean, is because I didn't want you to feel like I was choosing her over you."

Pop frowns. "Danny, we never—"

"Wait. And also ... I'm sorry that I ... that I..." There's way more I want to get out, like how I just hate myself for every shitty thing I've ever said to them, and that, after what they told me today, how I see so much so differently. But all the words are getting jammed up in my throat. So, when Dad motions me in for a hug and says, "Come here," I try to tell him and Pop everything by squeezing them both, so tight. This time, though, I don't hug them like I'm a little kid who needs their protection. I hug them like I'm shielding them from every horrible thing the world could ever throw at them, because I would. I will.

"We're sorry too, son. It's hard for parents to accept that there are some things they can't protect their children from. But that's no excuse. We should've told you about that letter a long time ago. There's a lot we should've told you," Pop says.

"It's okay," I say and I mean it, I really do. I think the resentment I had for them about all that began to evaporate the second Ana shut the door in my face. I release them from my bear hug and try to lighten the mood by adding, "And you do know, I'm eighteen, right? I'm not exactly a child anymore."

Dad chuckles and says, "No, I suppose you're not."

"Yes, yes, of course," Pop says in a silly/serious tone with his hands up all like, *whoa there.* "We didn't mean to imply we aren't all *hashtag grown folk* here."

Scrunching up my face at him, I say, "Yeah, maybe don't say that."

"What?" he asks, pretending he's bewildered but I know he's totally teasing. "Hey, I know the lingo. I'm on the TikToks."

"Pop, no, just, immediately no," I say, at the same time Dad says, "That's not a cute look, babe," and I can tell we're both on the verge of cracking up.

"All right, all right. Noted. I'm always down AF

for some honest feedback from the fam," Pop says, and then it happens. We're laughing. All of us, together, and it's big and loud and, damn, it feels so good.

Once we've settled back into ourselves, Pop looks directly at me and says, "But in all seriousness, I want you to know, you can always come to us with anything. We're so sorry if we ever made you feel like you couldn't."

I nod, and we're all quiet for a bit. Then I decide to share something else with them, something I probably would've only told Conner and Sanjay before today.

"So, Ethan ... he, uh," I sniff, "he told me he loved me."

"Oh?" is all Dad says out loud but I can tell he and Pop are having an entire conversation with their eyes.

"Yeah, and uh, I didn't exactly respond in the best way, or at all, actually." I bite my lower lip. Shake my head. "I really screwed things up, and I don't know what to do."

Pop takes a deep breath and says, "Well, before you make any decisions, there's one question you need to ask yourself."

"What's that?"

"Do you feel the same way about him?"

Chapter Twenty-Eight

Ethan

I can't believe I said the L-word to Danny.

Ugh. I've been awake a total of twenty seconds and my brain is already going full OCD. I spent last night sad-texting with Navi and Micaela, bawling my head off for-freaking-ever over this before I finally crashed. I'm not doing this again.

Rubbing the sleep from my eyes, I roll over and feel something poking between my ribs—my phone. I grab it to check the time and the recharge battery icon fills the screen. Then I just sort of laugh because I feel the same way—totally drained with no fucks left to give.

Rising from bed like a zombie, I plug in my phone on the nightstand and make my way downstairs where I find my mom at the kitchen table, slumped over her bowl of cereal like she's praying. It's only when I move closer that I realize she's asleep. The floor creaks under my feet and she jumps, nearly knocking over her bowl.

"You scared me half to death," Mom says with a nervous laugh as she places a hand on her chest.

She's way more dressed up than usual for the office—charcoal pants and blazer with a purple silk blouse and heels. Her long ginger hair is pulled back in a tight ponytail and she's wearing just enough makeup to almost hide the dark circles under her eyes.

Giving her an apologetic grunt, I grab a carton of orange juice out of the refrigerator and pour myself a glass.

"Morning comes way too early these days," Mom says as she walks over to the dishwasher and puts her bowl inside.

I gulp my glass of OJ so fast it burns going down.

"So," Mom continues, with every word that follows sounding like ascending notes on a musical scale. "Two days until WGI. You must be getting so excited."

I shrug.

"Well, listen, I know it's been a bumpy season for you guys, but you—" Her smartwatch chimes. "Oh, that's your dad texting. Hang on."

I pour myself another glass and low-key roll my eyes as she types a response.

"Thank God he went in early this morning," Mom mumbles to herself, then turns back to me. "Anyway. I know it's been a rough season, but I have every faith you guys are gonna rock it."

Without making eye contact, I give her the fakest tight-lip smile before taking a seat at the breakfast bar.

"What was that look for?" she asks, one eyebrow arched.

I shake my head and shrug again, then take a big swig of OJ, knocking my head back like I'm an actor in a movie taking a shot. I'm being overdramatic, but I don't give a shit. Truth is, I want her to know I'm upset. I want her to ask me more.

Mom frowns. "Aww, sweetheart, I know you're disappointed we can't be there to cheer you on in person this year."

Okay, I am, but the fact that she assumes *that's* my number-one worry pisses me off. Like, what, I couldn't possibly have any other problems right now? She'd know if she paid any attention to me anymore.

"I'm not, though," I lie, wanting it to sound every bit as cold as it does.

Mom gives me a suspicious look and says, "If there was any way we could be there, we would." She pauses. "It's just the timing with—"

"Work. Yep. Got it," I say sharply, cutting her off. Then under my breath I add, "If this was Sam's senior year you'd be there."

"What?" she asks.

I say nothing. Instead, I stare at the boxes of cereal lined up on the breakfast bar—Fruity Pebbles and Apple Jacks. Lucky Charms with that damned cartoon leprechaun, mocking me with his cheesy-ass smile. Why should he be so happy, grinning over a bowl of frosted oats and marshmallows, while my senior year keeps finding new ways to suck?

"Ethan," Mom says more insistently, "are you being serious?"

Why did I even bring that up? It's so not what I want to get into with her right now.

"No," I drone in the most unconvincing tone ever. I flick the box of Lucky Charms so it spins a little, turning the leprechaun's stupid face toward the wall. "Forget about it."

"No, I'm not going to just *forget about it*. Is that what you really think? That we'd go if your sister was still on your team?"

Like it's not obvious, but I'm sure she'd never admit it, so why even bother?

"It doesn't matter," I say, then in a smaller voice I add, "We're probably going to lose anyway."

"What in … why…" Mom sputters, sounding confused. "Where is this coming from, Ethan? I have never heard you talk like this before."

"Maybe that's because you barely talk to me about anything anymore," I spit out.

Her jaw falls open and she asks, "How can you say that?"

Every blood cell in my body marches double-time

up my neck, into my face.

"Simple, Mom, because you guys are *never here*!" I shout, flicking the box of Lucky Charms so hard this time the little man on the front faceplants on the counter. "When Sam was still in high school, you guys had all the time in the world for her. Then she graduated, you and Dad started new jobs and, *poof*, I basically became invisible."

"Ethan, you've never been invisible to us. Quite the opposite actually."

"Oh, please, the only time you guys pay any attention to me is when I'm spinning a freakin' flag."

Mom's smartwatch chimes with another text. Her face stiffens, but she keeps her eyes locked on me. "Ethan, that's not true, and we pay a lot more attention than you think we do."

"Really? Okay then, when was the last time you asked me about literally anything else?"

"Because you don't talk to us about anything else," Mom says. "You haven't for a long time."

My body temperature jumps a thousand degrees and I explode.

"How could I? All you do is work, work, work! But whatever, why not? It's just your son's senior year. He only has to live up to everything his whole family has ever done while he multitasks the shit out of the rest of his life. No biggie."

I know I shouldn't say this next part. It's hurtful and immature, but it barrels out of me at full speed.

"And if he fails, he's not the golden child anyway, so, who cares, right?"

Mom narrows her eyes at me. "Ethan, are you done?" she asks so sternly I know it's not a question. "Listen. To. Me. You don't—"

A string of back-to-back texts go off on her Apple

Watch. She glances at the screen, then back to me.

I fold my arms and smirk at her like, *See?* "I'm sure whatever that is, it's more important, so…" I say and stand up.

"Wait. Sit down," Mom commands and I can tell she means business, so I do. She squeezes her eyes shut, takes a deep breath, then pops her lids open. "You know what?"

Here we go. I tense up, preparing for her to go all *House of the Dragon* and roast me to a crisp, but her next words are so surprising I almost fall off my barstool.

"They can wait," Mom says firmly, putting her watch on silent mode. Then in a gentler voice she adds, "I'm talking with my son."

She *what* now?

She walks around the breakfast bar and sits at the stool beside me, then doesn't speak a word for what feels like ages. Finally, she says. "You're right, about a couple of things … and you're way off base about a few others. But right up front, I want to say, just in case the message got lost somewhere, we love you and Samantha equally. There are no favorites in this family."

"I wasn't—"

"I'm not finished," Mom practically sings. Her tone is overly sweet, but I know better than to keep testing her patience at this point. "That being said, however, yes, there are some ways in which we treat you two differently. But it's because you're very different personalities, not because one of you is the *golden child*." She shakes her head, looks up at the ceiling, and chuckles. "I swear, you and your sister are two sides of the same coin."

I push a single burst of laugh-air through my nose.

"You are," Mom insists, then lets out a long, exasperated exhale. "Sam used to accuse us of favoritism, too, you know. But for entirely different reasons. She'd complain, *How come you're always on me about my grades and you never say anything to Ethan?"*

I almost smile at this because Mom's impression of younger Sam is pretty spot-on.

"Of course, it didn't seem to matter that I practically had to tie that girl to a chair to get her to study, while you brought home straight As without us ever having to say a word. Nope, we were simply the most unfair parents in the world and that was that."

I blink at Mom, still unsure of exactly what it is we're doing here.

She sighs again and continues. "The truth is, Sam was a lot like me when I was her age. She needed a ton of handholding and attention, and constant cheerleading. Then she'd turn around and bitch that we weren't giving her enough space. It was always a fine line with that one."

I never thought about it like that before. I mean, were there times I felt like we were all living in *The Sam Show*? Sure. But I hadn't considered it was because they believed she was needier than me.

Okay, I'd totally deny this if anyone ever asked, but hearing that is kind of satisfying. Does that make me a terrible brother?

"For a while there I was worried she'd be too thin-skinned to survive college out of state, but she toughened up quite a bit," Mom continues. "You, on the other hand, I never had those same worries about. You're more independent like your dad—stubborn too."

I tilt my head at her.

"Oh, yes. Even when you were a baby, it was clear you were your father's son," Mom says, smiling. "I remember the first time I realized it, too. You were around fourteen months old and fascinated with this shape-sorter toy we had. Now, your sister at that age, she would get so upset if I didn't help her fast enough with that thing. But you? My goodness, you would throw the biggest fit if I helped you too soon."

Yay, awkward baby stories. My favorite.

"That's when it hit me that you were already this different personality who was going to require me to be a different kind of parent. I had to learn that even if you were trying to force the round-shaped block into the square-shaped hole, you had to try it your way first. So, I'd watch and wait. Eventually you'd hold out the block to me and make your pleading little poopy-pants face…"

"*Mom.*"

"Oh, it was the cutest thing ever, because my baby boy was letting me know he needed his mommy's help." She pouts her lips, exaggeratedly and silly at first, but then a thought seems to form behind her eyes and her weighty expression becomes real. "But you didn't need my help with that—or much of anything really—for long. I used to joke that it seemed like you were growing up on fast-forward. It wasn't a joke, though. Especially once you hit puberty—"

"Oh, my God," I groan and my eyes bolt back to the tipped-over cereal box. Does she have to refer to every stage of my life in the most embarrassing way possible? There are words nobody wants to hear their parents say, like ever. She knows this.

Mom chuckles. "Sorry, sorry. I mean once you became a teenager, everything was, *I got it, Mom. I can do it, Mom. Leave me alone, Mom.*" She shrugs. "It was like, I blinked, and suddenly you didn't need my help with anything anymore, and you became so private— always hell-bent on doing everything on your own."

Mom reaches for the Lucky Charms, but before she can grab the box, some instinct kicks in and I scramble to set it upright first. The knowing smile she gives me makes my face go hot when I realize I've just sort of made her point for her. Fortunately, she doesn't rub it in.

"And, by the way, don't think I didn't catch what you said earlier, about feeling like you have to *live up* to what everyone else has done. Did you really mean that?"

"Um, yeah," I say. "You and Dad were in one of the best winter guards of all time and Sam got to be there at the start of our school's winning streak." I point at Mom, "Family," then back to myself, "shadow—hello!"

"You've become quite the accomplished competitor too, you know. Three gold medals? That's nothing to sneeze at," Mom says.

I drop my chin at her. "It's not like we ever got some world-record score."

She genuinely laughs at this. "Oh, Ethan. You can't compare something we did thirty years ago to what groups like yours are doing out there today. I mean, what's that opening toss you guys throw on rifle this year? A six, turnaround, catch on the knees?"

"It's actually an eight, double-turn, catch in the splits."

"Well, there you go. I would've knocked myself out if I tried that when I was your age," Mom says. "Let me tell you, if we ever had to go up against the likes of you guys, there would've been no competition—and also, that's not the most important thing."

"Maybe not, but it's up there."

She shakes her head slowly.

"Then how come the first year we're not favored to win is the first time you guys aren't going to WGI?" I take a breath and as the air fills my lungs, there's this feeling in my chest, like a door being blown open, and what flows through changes my voice from strong to strained. "Is it because you don't think we're good enough?"

All of Mom's features sag and she goes still. "Oh, honey, no."

I thought I was all cried out, but fresh tears are flowing again.

"That's how I feel, Mom, and not just about color guard. I mean, in lots of ways." I consider telling her about Danny and what a colossal fuck-up of a boyfriend I've been—how I don't even know if we are boyfriends anymore. But there's no way I could get through all that right now. So, I simply say, "I had so many plans for my senior year and nothing is going the way I thought. I keep trying to fix it and no matter what I do, it's never good enough. I feel like I'm never good enough."

"Hey," Mom says, placing her hands on my shoulders, turning me to face her. "Nothing could be further from the truth." Her tone is somehow both gentle and intense. "I want you to know this with absolute certainty. Whatever you do. Whatever you accomplish in your life, so long as you've tried your best, it's enough. *You* are so much more than enough. And if you're feeling like you're not, simply because life isn't going according to some grand plan, son, I think you may be missing the most important lesson we can learn from color guard."

"And that is?" I ask, swiping at my eyes.

Mom leans in a little closer and whispers, as if she's sharing one of life's great secrets. "It's all about the recovery."

She smiles and I don't fight back my sudden urge to do the same.

"Think about it. If you drop a toss or have some break in a show, you can't just fall to pieces, give up. No. You pick up and get right back in there. And sometimes, those recoveries become the most impressive parts of a performance," Mom says.

I chew on my lower lip.

"Ethan, anyone can handle anything when it's all going perfectly. But it's what we do when it doesn't, that's when real magic can happen. That's when we grow, surprise ourselves by being more than we ever thought we could," Mom says. "Trust me, lately, it's been all about the recoveries for your dad and me too."

"What do you mean?"

Mom sucks her lips into her mouth, then forcefully blows them out. "We were going to keep this quiet until we knew for sure how it was going to play out but," she sits up straight, "there's a reason we've been spending so many hours in the office. It turns out a very big company is interested in buying our little startup, and if that deal goes through, well, let's just say it would be life-changing for our entire family."

"Life-changing how?"

"As in, your dad and I could seriously consider retiring in a couple of years—or sooner," Mom says.

It never even crossed my mind that my parents might be working on something big of their own. I mean, *duh*, of course they have been, but I've been too wrapped up in my own drama to notice. I can't even remember the last time *I* asked *them* what they're up to or how their day went. What a selfish asshole I've been.

"Whoa," I whisper.

"It could still all go sideways. In fact, I have a big presentation to make this afternoon. But, yeah, we're definitely in *whoa* territory now. And let me tell you, it's taken a lot of recoveries to get here," Mom says, then her upbeat tone turns more serious. "But our biggest accomplishments in life often do. That's why, no matter how challenging life can get, it helps to remember one thing."

"What?"

"It's still our show."

Mom's words ripple through me in phases. I go from nodding, to laughing softly, and finally hugging her, because as corny as it is, what she said also makes the best kind of sense. For the first time in maybe ever, I realize that people, plans, life in general—if you're only focused on the way things *should* be, you're going to miss all the great things they already are, and what they could be.

"I love you, Mom," I say. She tells me she loves me, too, and we give each other a good, long squeeze before we let go.

"Listen, I know it hasn't been easy with us being so busy lately, but please remember, regardless of what we've got going on, your father and I will always make time for you," she says, then she does the most Mom thing ever. She brushes my hair away from my forehead.

As she pulls her hand back, her watch lights up with a notification, and I see the number of messages she's missed.

"Uh, Mom," I say urgently, pointing to her screen.

She looks at her watch and her eyes go wide. "Good God, *sixteen* messages?" She begins scrolling through her texts. "I'm not there for five minutes and ev—" She stops herself, puts a hand over her watch and looks at me. "Sorry."

"Are you kidding me?" I say, waving her off her barstool. "You have a presentation to slay. We can do this later."

"You sure?"

"If you don't start responding to those messages, I will," I say, pushing her out of the kitchen, into the hallway.

"All right, I'm going," Mom says, grabbing her

purse and coat out of the closet. She rushes over to the front door, pauses, and turns back to me. "What do you say I bring home Thai food tonight and help you pack for WGI? We can chat some more, or not chat. Whatever you want."

"That sounds awesome," I say. "Now would you get out of here? You're going to be late."

She gives me a quick peck on the cheek, and says, "See you tonight," on her way out.

As I head upstairs, each step feels—I don't want to say lighter, but definitely surer than it did before. Like, this is me, literally recovering in real time.

I go to check the status of my charging phone and see so many missed calls and texts. There are a couple from Navi and Micaela, but a ton more are from Danny.

Hey.

You up yet?

Pick up your phone.

Can you pick up your phone, please?

Ethan?

????

Okay. Don't pick up your phone. But I really need to talk to you.

Will you meet me after school?

Chapter Twenty-Nine

Danny

When the doorbell rings, my stomach does an impression of a rifle toss, launching into the air, completing four full rotations on the way back down.

"He's here," I say out loud to no one. The house is mercifully empty. There's no way I could do what I'm about to do if my dads were home.

Quickly, I adjust the edge of my already-made bed, then nearly break the sound barrier speeding from my room to the front door. I open it and my heart does this little squeeze, the same one that happens every time I see him.

"Oh, hey," I say, instantly hating how it came out, like I'm so surprised he stopped by.

"Hi," Ethan replies with an upward inflection that sounds closer to a question than a greeting.

After that, it's like we both run out of words. It's probably not even for that long, really, but it's enough for my biggest worry to cut to the front of the line.

What if, after the way I acted, he doesn't see me the same way anymore?

One day. Nearly twenty-four hours. That's all it's been. But I know better than anyone how a single interaction with a person can change how you feel—change everything—in seconds.

He's here, though. That's got to count for something, right?

"Do you, uh, want to come in?" I ask. My body tenses.

No. He drove all this way to stand on your front porch and stare at your dumb ass.

Embarrassment creeps through me. "I mean, come on in, please."

"Thanks," he says.

As I lead him into the living room, I can't stop myself from asking even more brilliant questions. "How was the drive? Was traffic bad?"

Ethan answers with a low and quiet, "Nope. All good," then nothing but the most uncomfortable silence ever. No, not even uncomfortable; it's more … unnerving, like that *shink* noise that happens when a fork taps your teeth.

Here's a little advice I wish someone would've given me—when you're planning to do a thing, maybe spend some time thinking about how you'll begin instead of putting all your energy into your endgame.

I stop short. He bumps into me and just that millisecond of body-to-body contact is all it takes to light up my nervous system.

Enough.

I whirl around to face him. He mumbles, "Sorry," right before I blurt out, "I can't do this."

An exhale, short and heavy, blows past Ethan's lips. I don't so much hear it as feel the air shift around me. He takes a step back, nodding over and over, bobble-head style.

Shit.

My mind is a maze with words racing in all different directions. None of them can find their way out, though. I'm just opening and closing my mouth.

Ethan's eyes fall. His shoulders fall. Then he shrugs, like *whatever*. "Okay. I get it. You don't need to say anything. I kind of guessed that's what you wanted to tell me."

"Uh, w-wai … w-wha?" I sputter, vocal cords kicking in but the sounds they're making? It's like I've encountered a speech bug and need to download an update.

"So," Ethan says, grimacing, jabbing a thumb over his shoulder in the direction of the front door behind him, "I'm just gonna go."

You know those scenes in old movies, where a computer or TV is on the fritz and someone whacks it to get it working again? That's what happens, in my head, when the panic hits.

"No! I wasn't saying—God, sorry. Fuck." I take a deep breath. "I mean, I can't do this whole small talk thing, that's all. Not when I've got, you know, bigger talk to do."

In the space of what I just said, Ethan's eyebrows change from two surprised-looking arches into a single squiggly line. "Bigger talk?"

For the—*seriously*?

"Wait, that," I begin, shaking my head, "didn't come out right either." Swallowing hard, I decide to break up my next sentence into smaller bits, so I won't screw it up. "What I meant to say is, I've got something, to say, to you, and if I don't get it off my chest, I think, I might, literally die."

"Okay, then," Ethan says, cautiously. His expression goes serious, and I have to remind my lungs that they're supposed to be working now.

"All right. Good. So, uh … so …" Now all I have to do is actually put it out there. "So, you know how, sometimes in life, you're like, heading down a road, and your GPS is giving you the right directions, but you somehow miss a turn anyway, and you get all pissed off, but it's not the app's fault, it's yours. Because you're the one who went the … wrong … way…"

Ethan's eyes are totally glazing over. I sound ridiculous.

"No?" I ask, checking to see if any of this is making sense when I know damn well it isn't.

Ethan gives me a pained half-smile and suddenly it's as if we're existing at two different tempos. He's shaking his head, half-time, while my pulse is pounding out triplets.

"Right. No. Okay." I clear my throat and wish talking in real life was more like texting. I could delete and rewrite all the stupid shit before I hit send. "It's like this. Have you ever taken a selfie and you thought it looked fine, so you posted it, but then someone points out all this stuff in the background that you—wait. No. That's terrible."

Reaching up, I pinch my jaw between my thumb and forefinger, slowly open my mouth as I slide my fingertips down my face, literally trying to pull better words out.

"Let me, uh, let me try that one more time," I say, flexing a grin that probably looks more like a face I'd make in a proof-of-life photo, which makes total sense because I feel like my brain is holding my tongue hostage. I can't seem to untie it. I'm rambling, can't get my words right. "There are times when people—argh. I mean, there are two types of—mm. It's not that … we don't…" What starts as a frustrated growl in the back of my throat travels up my windpipe, becoming an almost hysterical laugh when it hits the air. "How do I keep getting worse at this?" What is *wrong* with me?

He takes both my hands in his. Electricity shoots up my arms, into my chest, activating that magnetic field between us again. Our eyes lock, not that it's a choice. It's a force of nature, this thing between us. There's no fighting it.

"Hey, it's okay," he says, smiling—a perfect Ethan smile—and I'm all buzzy inside. "Whatever it is, you can tell me, or not tell me. Either way, it's cool."

His smile grows bigger, brighter, and the way he's looking at me, with that shine in his eyes and the cutest little crinkle under the bridge of his nose, it's sending this surge of power that's charging me like nothing else can. I've felt it so many times with him before, beginning at a low level on our first date at the top of Twin Peaks, and when we were holding hands on my couch all through Best Worst Movie Night. The voltage increased when he surprised me at my school with all that equipment, and it cranked up to eleven that night when he came to watch us perform. That same current moved through me when he had my back as I made the biggest mistake of my life, and it struck like lightning when he told me how he really felt.

I couldn't have named what that power was before, but I know what it is now, and words alone won't do it justice. What I'm trying to get out is something better said with action. I'm taking my boy Conner's advice and just "skipping to the good part."

"Actually, come with me," I say, grabbing his wrist. Ethan doesn't resist when I pull him down the hall toward my room. "This will go way better if I just show you."

I open the door and the look on his face when he sees what my friends helped me set up in here—it's everything.

Chapter Thirty

Ethan

At first, I'm not quite sure what I'm seeing as I step into Danny's room. Every single inch of his walls, seriously, floor to ceiling, has been covered in what looks like white wrapping paper. On this huge canvas he's drawn a city skyline in black Sharpie that goes around the whole space.

I'm about to ask him what all this is for when I notice he's labeled different spots on the mural. There's a bridge he's marked "Golden Gate," a tall building with "Salesforce Tower" scribbled next to it, and a big, oddly shaped dot on the horizon with the word "Alcatraz" floating above it. My breathing catches as I realize this isn't just any city he's drawn, it's San Francisco.

I turn to him. The nervous, fidgety guy who pulled me in here a few seconds ago is radiating pride. And that lopsided grin on his face? It's the same one he flashed when he offered me his hand and said, "Trust me," right before we ditched that restaurant on our first date.

This is one of my favorite things about him, the way he changes from awkward Peter Parker to confident Spider-Man when he knows he's about to put on a show.

"Shit," Danny says with a start. "I almost forgot." He hits a switch on the wall. The room goes pitch black, and the next thing I know, we're in another world.

Row upon row of soft white Christmas lights come to life, twinkling overhead, like an entire galaxy has been strung across his ceiling. All I can think is *wow*, all I know how to say is *wow*, all I feel is *wow, wow, wow*. This has got to be the sweetest thing ever. He recreated the view from the top of Twin Peaks, right here in his room, complete with shining stars above.

"I was hoping we could, maybe, try another reboot?" he asks, then makes a face. "Or, well, I guess a requel would make more sense at this point, right?"

"A requel?"

"Yeah, you know, like when a movie is both a reboot and a sequel. When they continue the story, but kind of restart with a new direction, retconning all the dumb shit that happened earlier in the franchise. That's—*oh*, wait," Danny says, then pulls out his phone, unlocks it. "One more detail ..." His thumbs dance across the screen. "Ugh! I thought I had this all queued up. Hang on."

Every muscle in my body tenses. I feel like that instant between *5,6,7,8* and the downbeat of a new measure, the pause between *ready, set,* and *go.*

"Got it," Danny announces, smiling wide.

Music blows in from the Bluetooth speaker on his desk. It only takes two notes for me to recognize the song. "Lay Me Down" by Sam Smith.

A sound that's part laugh, part exhale, flies out of me and I press my fist against my mouth before it can become something else. I'm tightening my core and face, trying to keep from tearing up, but it's like a feelings bomb has gone off inside. I can't contain it.

"I'm so sorry, Danny, for what I said yesterday," I blurt, hand still pressed against my lips. "Your family business is your family business. I never should've—"

"No. Hey, no, no, no," Danny says, interrupting, then places his palms on my shoulders. "Don't be upset, please. I asked you to come with me yesterday, and I know that was probably so weird, and you didn't have to, but you did it anyway. That meant so much. I don't think I could've even gone through with it if you hadn't been there. So, for the record, I'm the one who fucked up here."

"That sucks for you, though. That I said all that when you were already feeling like meeting your mom was a mistake."

"I'm not talking about meeting Ana. I'm talking about *you*. I mean, you were the only person in all that mess who was being fully real with me and I freakin' hate that I acted like a complete dick." Danny looks me directly in the eye, draws in a deep breath. "What I'm trying to say is, I needed you there and through good, bad, or *whatever*, I'm always going to need you … because I love you."

"You—" is all I can get out before becoming one big full-body sigh.

Danny slides his hands down to my elbows, leans in closer. "I didn't say it when I should've. I'll never be that stupid again. So, I hope you never get tired of hearing it, because I'm going to tell you all the time, starting now. I love you. *I love you.* I love you."

Suddenly, I'm laughing and crying all at once, burying my face in his t-shirt.

"Uh, is this a good thing or a not-so-good thing?" he asks.

"It's the best thing," I reply, sounding so lame with my nose smushed against his chest, fabric and muscle muffling my voice. But I don't care. I tilt my head up so he can hear me clearly. "The best thing ever."

Danny holds my face with both hands, wipes at my wet cheeks with his thumbs, and then smiles so sweetly I almost can't handle it. He kisses me. I kiss him back. Then I can't tell where my tongue ends and his begins, whose lips are over or under, and when I pull back to catch my breath, the words just tumble out of me.

"I love you too," I say, not even stressing that the

giant smile on my face is probably making me look like a crazy person. Cocking my head, I teasingly add, "Did I tell you that yet?"

Danny pushes his lips out and squints. "Not sure. Maybe you should say it again?"

"Fine," I say, laughing. "I. Love. You."

"Ah, yes, it's coming back to me, but I think at this point I've said it more, so…"

"We're keeping score now, are we?" I ask, playing along. "In that case, I believe I said it first. That should count double."

"Sounds fair," Danny says, and I can tell what he's about to do. The mischievous look on his face is a huge spoiler.

"I love you!" I rush to blurt out again at the exact same time he does. Even our tones match. We crack up.

"I guess it's a tie, then," Danny says. "I can live with that. We good?"

"We're good."

"Cool," Danny says, then in a softer voice he tells me to "come here, you." Coiling his arms around my back, he pulls me in closer and it's perfect, the way my head fits into the crook of his neck, like we're two puzzle pieces snapping together.

Then we're moving, swaying to the music in sync, and I already know when I'm alone in my bed later tonight, I'll be wishing I was still here, slow dancing with him to this song, in this room, beneath these blinking shiny lights/stars.

There's been so much I've been wrong about lately. But me and Danny is the one thing I know is 100% right. I'm confident of that. And what's wild is that I don't think I would be if this two-man show of ours had gone according to plan every step of the way.

My mom was right. Sometimes the best parts

really are the recoveries we make—we're living in one now.

"So, how'd I do, with the apology?" Danny asks.

I smirk at him. "Um, I think you know this is amazing." Seriously, Navi and Micaela are going to freak when I tell them about this.

"Hey, I'm just trying to keep up," Danny says. "You set the apology bar pretty high, you know. Bringing all that equipment for us to borrow a few weeks ago? That was boss. I gotta step it up if I'm going to be a contender for Best Boyfriend."

"Yeah, well, I think it's safe to say you definitely won today," I tell him, but it's not true. He isn't the winner here. I am. Danny Wheeler-Hall said he loves me, and that's the biggest prize in the world.

"Just today?" Danny asks, scrunching up his face. "This should be worth at least a week, minimum."

"Don't push it," I tease, trying to hold back my happiness and failing spectacularly.

"You're right, you're right. The competition is pretty fierce."

"Ugh, competition. Don't remind me. T minus two days until WGI prelims," I groan, exhaling dramatically as I rest my head on his shoulder. Touching so much of him with so much of me is like *ahh*, instant stress relief. "I wish we could both win world championships this year."

Danny kisses my temple. "Maybe we will."

"We could also both lose, you know," I say.

"So what if we do? Would that be the end of the world?"

Abso-fucking-lutely. That totally would've been my answer, even a few days ago. But something I never imagined myself saying comes out instead. "No. It really wouldn't."

I raise my head again, and as I stare at his face, a realization shocks me. I'm not going to pretend like I won't be kind of, sort of, crushed if my group doesn't end up in first place, let's be real. What's crazy, though, is how certain I am that I'll also be thrilled for Danny if he does.

That's gotta be the biggest sign that you're undeniably, all the way, head-over-heels in love with someone, right? When their happiness means more to you than your own. And I'm going to guess by the way he's beaming back at me, he might just feel the same way.

"How about we do what we do, and just let the judges sort out the rest?" Danny asks.

I nod in agreement, even though I know it's not going to be that simple.

"Well," he teases, "if I'm being honest, there is *one thing* that would be pretty cool to get at the awards ceremony."

"A medal?" I ask, half joking.

"No, this."

Danny kisses me again, slower, gentler than ever before, and I'm so into it.

"Um, wow…" I begin, and I need a second because that kiss honestly left me feeling a little light-headed. "Really? Right there in front of an arena full of people?"

Danny waggles his eyebrows.

"Oh, my God," I say, laughing. "Are we going to be one of those really cringe couples?"

"I hope so," Danny says. "I mean, we're probably going to have to practice, like, *a lot*, before we get good at it, but I have faith in us."

Us. I love the way that word sounds on Danny's lips—the electric zing it sends through my body leaves no doubt that *us* is the team I want to be on most of all.

"I don't know. That seems like a pretty big challenge," I say, playing cute. "There's likely going to be a lot of drops and fumbles in a performance like that."

"Then we'll reset. Reboot. Try again."

"Or we could just recover, keep right on going."

"Even better," Danny says, grinning. He gestures with a quick chin-nod at his bed and I understand exactly what he's asking.

"Yeah," I say, "let's practice," and as we lie down together, no matter how far we take this right now, nothing can compare to the feeling I got when he said I love you. So, between kisses, I say it again, and he says it back. Then he pulls me on top of him, chest to chest, and I can feel the rhythm of his heart moving with mine, not beating against one another, but twirling—together.

The End

ACKNOWLEDGEMENTS

In many ways, writing a novel is like creating a Winter Guard program—it takes a team to bring the vision to life, and *TWIRL* was no exception. I couldn't have done it alone, so some well-deserved thank-yous are in order.

To my brilliant editor, dear friend, and real-life fairy godmother, Benee Knauer—without you, this book simply wouldn't exist. From your keen editorial eye to your steadfast belief in this story, you have worked pure magic. I am endlessly thankful for the way you've shaped both this book and my journey as a writer. Bibbidi-bobbidi-thank you for helping make this dream a reality.

For Josh Sabarra, to whom I owe more gratitude than words can express. You didn't just help me realize that writing this book was something I *could* do—you showed me it was something *had* to do. Thank you for being an inspiration, a guiding light, and an incredible friend.

Huge thanks to Lee Ann Sontheimer Murphy and the entire team at Evernight Teen for taking a chance on a "debut" author and embracing this story with open arms. Getting your "yes" on my birthday? Talk about a plot twist I never saw coming! Best. Present. Ever.

To my agent, Des Salazar—for believing in this project (and in me). Your enthusiasm, confidence, and tireless support have meant everything. I'm so lucky to have you in my corner.

To Jay Murphy, Scott Chandler, T.J. Doucette, Stanley Knaub, and every member of the Concord Blue Devils color guard staff—your impact on my life is immeasurable. Thank you for pushing me past my limits and showing me that I'm capable of more than I ever imagined. The work ethic you instilled in me has carried over into every part of my life—including the perseverance it took to write this book. I am forever in your debt.

To the members of the 1995, '96, and '97 Blue Devils World Class Winter Guards—it was an absolute privilege to perform alongside you every season. ("Summertimez" was an experience like no other!) Your friendship, love, and support shaped me in ways I'll always cherish and provided the heart and soul of this story. I can't thank you enough.

To Robert Goman and Nicolle Carrasco, who taught me more than how to spin flags, rifles, and sabers—you taught me confidence, resilience, and the power of showing up for myself. I am endlessly grateful that, from you, I learned how to let my light shine brightly and twirl through life with pride. Thank you!

To every colleague I worked alongside and the marching members of every color guard I've ever directed—especially the performers of Orion Independent, Homestead, Leigh, Los Gatos, and Turlock. Teaching you was a privilege, but learning from you was an even greater gift. So much of who you are lives within the characters in this book, and my experiences with you shaped every part of this story. Because of you, *"I will not fear..."*

To Yan Schober and James J. Siegel, who read early drafts of this book and were the first to get to know (and love) Ethan and Danny. Your excitement for their journey—and your belief in mine—gave me the courage to send this book out into the world.

To Joe Cherubini, the best "best man" a guy could ask for. Thank you for celebrating every win—no matter how small—and for the countless late-night talks that kept me going.

For my fellow podlings, John Lake, Chris Lalli, Matt Townsend, and Edton Mock—thank you for helping me survive lockdown and *thrive* beyond it.

To Matthew Clark Davison—for being the highlight of my SFSU experience and for all the nights spent workshopping in *The Lab*, which helped lay the foundation for this novel—and more to come.

To Adam Sandel, my own personal Obi-Wan Kenobi, thank you for your friendship, guidance, and for reminding me to use *The Force* throughout my life and career.

A zillion thanks to my husband, John Gawrych, for being my rock through the many early mornings, late nights, and caffeine-fueled writing marathons that brought this book to life. You've been my manager, therapist, cheerleader, and so much more—sometimes all in the same day. I wouldn't be the writer (or the person) I am today without you. I love you!

I'm not sure how many kids get to grow up with a

librarian for a parent, but I know I'll always be grateful to count myself among them. Thank you, Mom, for nurturing my love of reading, for summer *Storytime* singalongs, and for listening to my endless grade-school epics about Ewoks, G.I. Joe, and Transformers. I think it's safe to say all that encouragement had a lasting effect.

If I had another hundred pages, I'd fill them with the names of the friends and family who have shaped my life and this book. (*You know who you are.*) Instead, I'll simply say: thank you. Your love, encouragement, and belief in me are woven into every word. I am forever grateful.

Evernight Teen

www.evernightteen.com